PUBLISHING

Love You Like Christmas

**Based on the Hallmark Channel Original Movie
Written By Karen Berger**

Keri F. Sweet

Chapter One

It was going to be a very good Christmas.

The crisp wintery air, the bustle of the crowd, and the magic of the upcoming holidays surrounded Maddie Duncan. As she moved with the throng of New Yorkers on her way to work, she couldn't help but notice the people around her peeking at the spectacular displays adorning the storefronts. She made mental notes about what items were turning heads and which things caused the crowds to smile. The marketing-exec brain never really shut off.

That was perfectly fine with her. With a big meeting this morning, she'd take all the last-minute insight she could soak in.

She approached her office building and glanced up. Giddiness sparkled within her, brighter than the light reflecting off the windows of her brand-new corner office. She could hardly believe it, but here she was, standing on her namesake—Madison

Avenue—and looking up at her new place in the world. Hard work and dedication had taken Maddie to the next level in her career.

Dad, I've done it.

Up next—maybe her name added to the company stationery? She powered through the building and rode up the elevators. Before she could even think of new logos at the office, first she had to show why she'd deserved this promotion. Her busy-bee coworkers staying on task through the holiday season lifted her spirits even more as she passed through the cubicles. She offered good mornings on her way by. The holiday season was their biggest, most important time of year, but not even the stress of Christmas being three weeks away was enough to diminish the holly-jolly tidings of her coworkers. Bits of garland were strung over cubicles, and mini gold bells dangled from the green strands between large red bows.

She swung around the final row of desks as anticipation danced along her skin like the hooves of eight tiny reindeer. She peeked in at her new digs, tightly gripping her briefcase with a deep, happy inhale. What a gorgeous view! A corner office bathed in cheerful morning light, space to walk around in—and it was hers. She could put bookcases to one side with an area left for a small sitting section on the other.

And then in the middle would be her beautiful oak desk. She walked forward and touched the temporary one that had been set up until her things could be moved in. This promotion had been coming for months, and she'd been shuffled from one temporary place to another while her office was being prepared. She paused at the windows and smiled as she looked at the crowded street below. A few minutes ago, she had stood on that sidewalk and peered up.

The light pouring through the windows bathed her room in the morning sun. The rays warmed the white walls and the boxes stacked to the side. Her golden ficus tree shimmered. Soon she would have all her belongings placed just so.

She settled in behind the desk to start her to-do list and to put the final touches on this morning's presentation to a new high-level client, a new feather in her cap that showed she'd more than earned her brand-new corner office. First, she'd landed Irene's new clothing line—a line that Maddie had taken from an idea to a high-demand brand. Now almost in the palm of her hand was Hadley's apparel line, one that needed some marketing updates to grab today's shoppers. The company was using a playbook from five years ago and ignoring today's digital footprint. If Maddie managed to win Hadley's account, her name would be whispered through the marketing world and lift the profile of her company, helping it become one of the most sought-after and respected marketing agencies in the city—maybe even the country.

But to do that, she had to impress Hadley. The click of her assistant's heels pulled Maddie's attention to the open office door a moment before Roz appeared. The brilliant yellow of Roz's shirt brightened the room. Her broad, genuine smile was the bow on top. They'd been friends for years. Maddie had entered the marketing world at the bottom while Roz had been assistant to a group of managers. They'd laughed and grown a friendship over pots of coffee and late nights stuck working together. When Maddie made manager and was offered a personal assistant of her own, she had pleaded with Roz to come with her. It hadn't taken much begging, and Maddie was lucky to have Roz. Without a doubt, she wouldn't be here without the solid help she'd received from the woman.

"Twenty-three more days until Christmas. We need to step up our game." Maddie clicked her pen, prepared for any messages Roz may have collected.

Roz glanced out a bright, large window with a wistful sparkle lighting her gaze. "It looks like it might snow."

Maddie studied pages of figures and charts. A new line hit her that she needed to add to her pitch. She jotted it down in the margins and crossed her fingers against any potential seasonal inconveniences. "As long as it stays within picturesque limits. I don't want the weather to slow down sales."

Roz gave her that familiar look—a sharp, raised eyebrow and a glance down at Maddie. "Christmas isn't all about numbers."

Maddie barely resisted scoffing. "It's the biggest selling season of the year."

"It's also a holiday. Can we throw in some merriment?"

Sure. In the stores. The garland and decorations were cute in the outer offices. And she loved all the gorgeous touches decorating the city, but she didn't have time for all those things here in her working space. "I market Christmas. I don't have time to celebrate it. The last time I got a tree was my first year out of college, and it withered from neglect."

Seriously, how merry had it been to walk into her apartment and find her tree dead when there was still another week to go until Christmas? The cheery decorations, the bright green plants, and the rosy cheeks of Santas all around were simply distractions from her work. They took precious time away from what needed her focus the most. She'd end up knocking some cute figurine to the floor, and it would shatter, which would steal more of her time while she cleaned it up. The traditions people claimed they had and the nostalgia—all of that was just a bunch of talk. People didn't actually sit down and roast chestnuts over a fire. Maddie had given up trying to make it happen long ago, because it simply wasn't realistic.

Roz stared her down with a hand on her hip and a challenge in her eyes that only a best friend could pull off and still put love behind it. "You are not that cynical. I know for a fact that you're down-right nice."

True. Look at Maddie, sounding like Ebenezer

Scrooge. Honestly, that couldn't be further from the truth. She loved Christmas. But she loved making the magic happen for other people more: the brightness on their faces; the pleased, excited gasps on finding the perfect gifts; the giving—the presentation of it all. That was her holiday spirit. Hence, the poinsettias she'd advised to be positioned in the stores—but not in the way of her computer. She couldn't do her job so that Christmas reached everyone if she was too busy drinking eggnog under mistletoe.

She'd learned long ago there were two types of people: those who sat on Santa's lap and ate cutout cookies for three meals a day, and those who kept the cookies rolling out of the bakery.

Maddie was the latter.

Mistletoe, however, didn't necessarily sound so bad. That would mean another date, though, and she shuddered. Maybe she'd skip getting caught under the mistletoe this year. She recalled her last holiday date. He'd sat down and immediately provided all the details of his still-pending divorce. Ugh. Pass. It was going to take a while to forget that guy. Maybe she could try again after New Year's when the Christmas rush was over.

Roz continued staring at her in the way friends do, knowing Maddie could share more. Maddie sighed. "Christmas wasn't real big in our house. After my mom died, the holidays lost their meaning. I got presents, but none of the sentiment." She stacked her sheets to get back to work and shook off the woolgathering. "A happy client means a happy account executive. That's the joy I hope to get from the holidays."

There went that look passing over Roz's face, the softness of her deep, dark eyes, the almost pity. Something lingered in her gaze, and her mouth opened to no doubt inform Maddie of exactly what she thought, but Maddie's boss, Roger Warren, walked in and saved the day.

"Good morning, Maddie." With his perfectly coiffed hair and his square, masculine chin, he exuded confidence. His hands came together with a clap, and he rubbed his palms.

Maddie was ready to make him proud and pleased with his decision to promote her. "I'm loving my new office."

Roger nodded. "You earned it, every square inch." He glanced at the space and her lovely windows. "Now, are you ready to dazzle Hadley?"

The smile that danced at her lips felt worthy of Christmas morning. "Absolutely."

She followed Roger through the offices to a larger, more elegant space. Cozy, modern leather chairs were oriented around a glass table. Sleek cabinets were tucked against one wall, and windows on the opposite side allowed natural light to pour in so the atmosphere was comfortable. The polished space offered a friendly intimacy to match the level of care for their clients. This was no cold, disconnected, punch-some-numbers working partnership. Oh, no. When clients booked Maddie Duncan, they got first-rate service, twenty-four-hour access to her via her cell phone for ideas or a moment of her time to help calm nerves. Whatever the clients needed from her, Maddie was there. She *lived* for it, even those three-in-the-morning calls where she'd practiced answering the phone to sound like she'd been awake working and not sleeping.

One day this sleek, small conference room could be a space she'd be in charge of. But she'd need to continue winning over more clients to earn it.

David Hadley lounged in a chair, his suit impeccable. The top button of his crisp linen shirt was open, and he thumbed through the sales information they'd gathered on his company. Nerves tickled Maddie's spine as she took her place to pitch her heart out.

Roger gestured to her as he sat next to Hadley. "Christmas is Maddie's specialty. She's the best we've got."

She smiled and swallowed back her insecurities. Back straight, she launched into her presentation. Hadley was focused, flipping through spreadsheets and graphs that coincided with her pitch. He wasn't missing a single detail she'd applied. He put off a straight-to-the-point vibe. She didn't waste her observation, and she dug into the heart of his business's issues. "Your numbers are falling short, but I believe we can turn that around."

Hadley nodded. "Which is why I'm here."

A man who knew his business inside out and had come to the right place to get it back on the winning path. "The pre-Christmas sales are as crucial to the bottom line as the after-Christmas sales. Your ads need to appeal to the shoppers on three levels." She ticked them off with her fingers. "The holidays, the prices, and the clothes." She gestured at her smart black suit and the soft white shirt she'd paired it with. "Which I love, by the way. When you can turn your marketing exec into a customer, you're doing something really right."

Hadley gave her an approving look. "You wear our merchandise well."

Darn right, she did. She slipped into a chair across from him. "I can sell it even better. Let me get the marketing on par with the clothing."

Hadley gave her another, longer look and then glanced at the plans she'd given him. Her nerves increased as she treaded that precarious line between being too pushy and being the right amount of convincing to show she cared. Sounding like a used-car salesman was never the way to go, so instead she focused on maintaining a serene, confident smile and friendly expression, ready for any questions.

Finally, he nodded. "Okay."

Yes! Merry Christmas to her, indeed. Who needed garland and whatever else? Success was the best gift Maddie could ever want. "We'll roll out the new campaign at the end of the week."

Roger rubbed his hands together. "Great!"

After handshakes and business cards were exchanged, she slid behind her desk and pushed piles of paperwork around until she'd made organized stacks to study through the afternoon. She kicked off her Jimmy Choos and worked through lunch with the aid of healthy snack bars stashed in her purse. She jotted notes to make sure they didn't forget all their options to explore for Hadley. Maddie intended to reach every possible customer, not a sole demographic. Her plan was long-term rather than a push for one holiday.

Customers were programmed to think holiday colors meant Christmastime only. Hadley needed them to think warmth and comfort instead. Give customers pieces to nudge them into seeing the appeal of the bold colors through winter. Maddie typed up all her notes, sent them to an ad designer she favored, and opened the next client's portfolio to reassess all of their numbers and to make sure they were exceeding her expectations.

Normally, Maddie's heels echoed against the polished floors of the hallway leading to her apartment, but tonight nothing could be heard over the laughter, conversations, and Christmas songs pouring out of a neighbor's open doorway.

Maddie hurried past his door before they caught her walking by and invited her in. She only vaguely knew her neighbors. One of the guys had dark hair, was tall, and preferred jeans from one of her first clients. The other was shorter, blond, and had an affection for partnering sweater vests with frumpy-front khaki pants. He didn't have quite the style panache as his roommate. While they were probably great people, she had work to do.

Based on the noise, the entire building had turned out. Mistletoe hung from the frame and garland had been strung around the entrance. A plastic Christmas scene of a waving Santa had been stuck to the front of their door and hinted that the décor within was as over the top as it came.

One of Maddie's clients had created an ugly Christmas sweater line this year because of their recent popularity. Based on the rambunctious noise, their ideal customers filled the inside. She was tempted to slow down and drop a few hints about where the best sweaters could be found in the city, but she didn't know any of those people and work waited. Getting an ugly sweater ad on the front page of the Wednesday sale papers would do the trick just as well. She slid her key in her lock and made a mental note to email that idea to Roz.

She closed herself inside the blessedly thick walls of her apartment. A rousing round of "Jingle Bell Rock" was cut off.

Maddie pulled leftover Chinese takeout from the refrigerator. She'd no more gotten her shoes off than her phone was calling her name. She swiftly pulled it from her purse. That would be Sam, one of the designers she'd tapped to bring a fresh mix to an old label she was revising. The brand was dying because the company refused to reach a new demographic. Instead of moving with the times, they had practically locked themselves into a marketing mindset from a decade ago.

Sam rattled off cuts and curves and highlights of different styles, and it was one thought after another. This was the energy that line needed, but Maddie had to rein him in a bit. "It's fine to include a younger demographic, but we can't ignore the Gen Xers."

That generation was their key market. Once they rehit the streets, the Gen Xers would check the line out for nostalgia purposes, but they wouldn't buy if all the styles were reaching toward their children's ages. Teenagers weren't wearing anything their parents picked out and fawned over, making them a secondary target. "Go easy on the red and green. Christmas can't overwhelm the clothes."

Sam laughed. "So no obnoxious North Pole–themed outfits to remind the Gen Xers of what their parents would have forced them into?"

She poured a glass of wine and chuckled. "Exactly. Thanks for your hard work and have it to me in the morning."

"You got it."

She'd barely put her phone down and opened her food when a chime signaled an email. She clicked open the evening sales reports numbers that tracked all her clients and sent the files to her printer.

With a long night ahead, she ate while reading other emails. A commotion in the hallway caught her attention. The thick walls of her high-rise weren't impenetrable, and she looked out her peephole as people left the party.

She put on pajamas, grabbed her printouts, and crawled in bed. The numbers were improving for one account and dipping with another. She marked notes and suggestions to tweak placement adjustments. She wasn't even through that when her phone dinged again.

She leaned over, reaching for her device charging on the nightstand, when the lamplight caught on the only Christmas decoration Maddie cared to have.

It couldn't even be counted as a decoration, really. Maddie had kept the picture nearby since it had been taken when she was seven. It was a photograph with her mom, snapped during the holidays.

Classic Christmas danced in the background of the photograph: a beautiful tree trimmed perfectly with golden beads and red ornaments. White bows were attached to the branches, and presents lay scattered beneath as she and her mom were captured mid-laugh. Maddie brushed the frame and fondly touched a corner.

They were happy, cheerful. Looking at the photograph, she recalled the smells of peppermint, spice, and pine. Maddie missed decorations and celebrations at times, but without her mom in the middle of it, the appeal wasn't there. She'd tried for the first few years, but that emptiness had gone unfilled until she'd finally given up trying. The magic of traditions couldn't be repeated without her mom.

Still, the memories warmed her from within, like hot cocoa. That was Mom's standard drink after a day outside in the cold. Maddie could nearly taste the rich chocolate and lightly sweet marshmallows.

Her phone dinged again, and she lifted it to see what needed her attention now.

Maddie worked furiously at her desk. She'd come in an hour earlier to catch up on her existing clients, so that she could focus on Hadley at lunch when everyone else could coordinate. Once Hadley's new campaign was set and running, she could slow down to normal Christmas speed, which was still a seven-day-a-week job but with a little less pressure.

Midmorning, Roz came through with the mail, and Maddie braced for news. She pulled out an envelope. "There's a wedding invitation."

Well, that wasn't what she'd expected. "Who's it from?"

Roz let out a light, surprised gasp. "Irene Parker."

Maddie bolted upright in her chair. Irene had sent her an invitation to her wedding? Seriously? That was, wow, huge. Sure, Maddie had launched her new line, but Maddie didn't know she ranked so well. This was awesome. The networking opportunity alone was a once-in-a lifetime chance.

"Irene is my biggest client." She collected the envelope and mentally flipped through her calendar. Would it be a spring wedding? That would be a bit tight around the final launch for summer lines, but if she prepared ahead, it would be fine. "This woman runs the largest clothing chain in the country, and she invited me to her wedding?"

Maddie tore open the envelope and tipped her head toward the window. "I just can't believe she would think to invite me. She's the whole reason for this promotion." She pulled the elegant, thick cardstock out, and Maddie's heart sank. Not a spring wedding. A December wedding. As in this month. "It says the wedding is December eleventh. And I'm just getting this now?"

Roz winced. "The mailroom must have sent it to your old office."

It was already December third. The wedding was in a week. Going would be a great opportunity. Snubbing the invite? Not an option. "I can't afford to offend her."

Roz nodded. "What do we do?"

Maddie had to get home, pack, and sort her notes so she could work on the road. "Email her assistant and say I'll be attending and explain the delay in my response."

Roz didn't make a move to start on that email. "You sure about this? The wedding is next week, and it's in Denver." Roz cocked a brow. "And you're afraid to fly."

A cold shudder made tracks over Maddie's back. "I can't let that stop me. I have to go to that wedding. I can take the train. I'll get there in plenty of time."

Her desk phone trilled. She'd get there if she could catch a moment to breathe and reconfigure for a road trip. Roz picked up the line. "Maddie Duncan's office."

Maddie steadily worked to gather her things so that as soon as that lunch meeting was completed, she could head out.

Roz covered the phone with her hand. "It's your cousin, Teddy."

The stress found a pause button, and Maddie collected the phone. She didn't get near enough time with the few family members she had. Being as in demand to her clients as Maddie was didn't leave a lot of time for much of anyone or anything else. "Hey, Teddy, how are you?"

"Great." His lovable voice was music through the line. "I got a new job. I'm moving to London."

Maddie nearly dropped the phone. "Congratulations. That sounds exciting."

"It is, and I'm trying to get everything in order to make the move. Do you remember my mother's classic Mustang Fastback?"

Aunt Vivian was a flamboyant and wonderful substitute mom. She used to pick Maddie up in her jazzy vintage Mustang and take Maddie on great adventures, the two of them cruising along the highway and singing to the radio. They were some of the happiest memories of Maddie's childhood. The necklace didn't hang there, but she absent-mindedly found herself fiddling at her neck for the chain. The little charm at the end was a Mustang, and the words engraved across it were *Adventure Together*. It had been a gift from Aunt Viv during one of their last trips. Not quite an accessory that screamed professional appearance, so it hung safely in Maddie's jewelry box. "Of course I do. I loved that car."

"I've been keeping it stored it in my garage, but now I'm selling the house. I'd like to keep the car in the family. Are you interested?"

Her heart skipped a beat. "You bet I am. Does it run okay?"

"It's in mint condition. I take it for a spin every now and again."

Perfect. "What a happy coincidence. It just so happens I'm in need of a car right now for a trip to Denver for a wedding."

"That's ambitious in winter. I think there's some pretty serious weather due to pass through the Midwest this weekend."

"Better than flying. You know how I am about that." She didn't even like to say the word. "Besides, next weekend? I'll be there before the weather passes through. I appreciate this."

"Mom would want you to have it."

"Thank you, Teddy."

"Merry Christmas."

Roz smiled at her. "Sounds like I shouldn't schedule the train ticket."

"Definitely not." Maddie sank back in her chair, not believing the latest turn of events. "I have the most amazing memories from my time in that car. My aunt took me on all sorts of adventures in it." Oh, gosh. Black-cherry red, beautiful classic leather interior. She could remember every last detail. Even the rumble of the engine that made the whole car purr cast a familiar vibration across her skin.

Roz straightened the paperwork in her hands. "Now you'll get to make a new adventure."

Maddie grabbed her things, stuffed her briefcase full, and was ready to go as soon as their lunch meeting concluded. "But not if I don't get on the road. I'll take off right after lunch. I should have Hadley mentally put together by the time I'm packed and can call you with a plan. We'll coordinate and make this work."

Chapter Two

*H*onking cars, yelling, and screaming... what kind of Christmas spirit was that? Kevin Tyler shook his head at the commotion. If people were in that big of a hurry, they could help him reload his trailer. It's not like he wanted his trees scattered all over the highway. This was his life spilled across the pavement. Generations of passion went into making picture-perfect Christmas trees.

And these were ruined.

Dumping them all over a busy highway had never been part of their growth-and-selling plan. They should have been handled with care and delivered with love. They were meant to stand in homes and be strung with lights. It was a promise his grandmother had established, and Kevin's chest pinched. Nothing had seemed to go right since he'd taken over the farm.

This disaster had added more snow to the avalanche tumbling down on his struggling business.

Most of these trees had suffered so much damage when they'd fallen off the trailer that he wouldn't be able to salvage them. Not even Charlie Brown would want one of these sad trees.

Limbs were broken, needles were sheared off, and branches were scraped like road rash. He'd had forty trees bound and ready for an already tight market, and he'd lost over half of them. Maybe more.

A particularly grumpy man shifted his stance as Kevin worked. He'd been standing there several minutes, staring. As if his cantankerous presence would somehow make Kevin work faster.

"I'm a time-management expert." The man sneered. Kevin thought he was more suited to audition for the role of the Grinch in a play. "I'm going to be late."

At this rate, Kevin was going to lose his home. *But by all means, complain some more.*

This never should have happened. It had never happened before. A reindeer had sprung from the bushes and landed in the road in front of him. Kevin had hit the brakes, his trailer tires had lost purchase, and next thing Kevin had known, he'd jackknifed across the highway, blocking all lanes of traffic. Reindeer weren't even native to Ohio. Someone must be missing one from a petting zoo somewhere, and he'd look into that when he got home.

The reindeer had pranced off like he'd won some

sort of game. He'd even given a triumphant snort as he'd taken his exit.

Kevin clutched another tree and hefted it back to the trailer with a huff.

"Yeah." A woman's voice echoed the Grinch's. "I'm afraid we're all going to be late."

Wonderful. The Grinch's complaining had drawn others to point out their misery.

Kevin understood that this was wrecking all of their schedules, and he was sorry for that, but how could the smell of the iced air, in combination with the trees' earthy richness, not instantly calm them? Anytime Kevin was stressed, he took a stroll through his farm—thick green needles; the lush scent of fir, spruce, and pine; the shuffle of the breezes; and the snow crunching under his boots, with the trees growing all around him. But his favorite part was the chatter of his beautiful daughter, Jo, skipping alongside him. There was nothing more soothing than that.

With the way his banker was breathing down his neck, Kevin had found himself taking a lot of walks lately, for the stress relief, and also because, potentially, any of those could be one of the last times he'd be able to walk among them. If this season didn't leave the farm in the black, he was finished. He looked at the mess before him. The outlook was not good.

Kevin stacked a tree on the trailer and then turned for another. Only as he reached down for a particularly beautiful Douglas, a bit of bright color caught his attention. A brilliant pink scarf shined in the dreary day. Lips were painted to match. Blond hair tossed lightly with the breeze. Kevin was trapped in his steps, frozen, as he met the gaze of the woman in the snow.

She was a welcome sight in an unfortunate situation, and he was mesmerized by her sudden appearance. All at once his arms and legs seemed numb. "Hi."

"Hi." A light, breathy, almost airy sound uttered past her lips as she stared at him.

There should have been more words coming from his mouth, but he found himself completely inarticulate. The honking and yelling on the highway receded as she absorbed all of his attention. She didn't dress like anyone fit for the backwoods of Ohio in her heeled boots and loose hair that wasn't warmly contained under a knit cap. She stood out against the typical nasty, gray winter day with a refreshing flush in her cheeks.

She broke their gazes first, glancing around, and the spell dissipated. "I wonder how long we'll be here?"

"I... uh... yeah." Right. He was interrupting her day. From what, he desperately wanted to know, for reasons he couldn't quite explain. But the image of them sitting down for a meal and talking about it formed in his head. Ridiculous idea, but the thought stubbornly refused to let go. "I just called the highway patrol."

She smiled. And there he went again, trancing

out and spiraling into her enchantment. If he could move all these trees in an instant to allow her to pass, he would. But at the same time, he'd like to be in this moment for the rest of the afternoon. The building urge to be nearer, to touch her, was foreign, because he hadn't had this sudden attraction in ages. It was impractical, illogical, yet the stirrings continuing to circle within said, *Walk closer now.*

As he stepped over a downed tree, he ripped his glove away and shook her hand. "I'm Kevin, by the way."

Her lack of gloves left her fingers icy cold. He wanted to surround her hands with his to warm them, build a fire for her to lean near, or pass her an oversized mug of hot chocolate to heat her inside out. Actually, he found all of those options appealing.

She held and then released his hand. She maintained the smile, though. "Maddie."

"Nice to meet you." He tried pinning down what he was supposed to be doing. Nothing came to mind. The only recurring thought was how much he wanted to know more about this woman. She was far more interesting than anything else that had happened all day. "Funny place to meet, huh?"

Her smile broadened, and the smallest laugh tumbled out of her as she looked around. The sound trickled over his spine, for a moment easing the burdens that his business was dying, he was letting generations of his family down, and the day of telling his daughter they had to move was flying toward him faster than he could ever be ready for.

A sparkle lit her gaze. Was that a scent of sweet sugar coming from her? She was as pretty as a frosted cookie put in a bakery for display—look but don't touch. It made sense that she would smell like a sugar cookie too.

Her gaze skated past him. "It's like a horizontal forest."

He blinked and followed her line of sight behind him to the road. Right. Forest. In the middle of the road because of him. He should be cleaning his mess because as off-kilter as she made him, she had places to be, and he couldn't block the road forever.

The Grinch businessman groaned again, as if that was the only thing capable of coming out of him. "This is just awful, delaying everyone like this."

Yes, delaying everyone. It was completely intentional on Kevin's part. Kevin maintained a friendly smile as best he could while he grabbed another tree. If there was one bright spot of the day, it was that he'd gotten to meet Maddie, even if only for a moment, a passing in time they weren't supposed to have, but here it was.

"How does something like this happen?" Frustration was evident in her eyes. The smile and the intriguing, spellbinding woman retreated with her raised brows. "I have a really long drive ahead. I can't sit here all day."

It was too much to hope that she could have been enraptured by the scent of his trees, the magic of the holidays, and not at all bothered by the predicament. He hefted a bound six-footer onto his trailer, determined to get them on their way sooner rather than later. He could have the smaller ones moved and, with help from the highway patrol, the larger ones loaded quickly. "I can assure both of you it wasn't intentional."

Maddie's head dipped to the side. "What are you doing?"

The Grinch gestured at him. "It's his truck—he's the one who dropped his trees."

The frustration that had pinched Maddie's face cracked, and the angel he'd been drawn to reappeared. "I'm sorry. I didn't realize they were yours."

The Grinch huffed. "Not as sorry as me."

If that man was so determined to get away, he could pitch in and help. On second thought, Kevin didn't want him touching his trees. These were bound for homes to create smiles, spread cheer, and serve as a centerpiece for families to gather around. Kevin didn't want the negativity spread to his trees. They were in bad enough shape as it was. Maybe Jo could scrap them for wreaths to hang off the lights downtown, potentially one last parting gift from the Tyler family.

Then again, maybe the Grinch needed some of that happiness. In Kevin's biased opinion, a Christmas tree was a dependable source of joy in life.

Maddie pushed her hands in her pockets and eased away from the Grinch. "It was an accident."

Kevin found himself looking to her again. She was the tree-topper focal point in the middle of all this. "Nice of you to take my side."

More color filled her cheeks.

Another grunt came from the Grinch. "If you two are done getting acquainted, I have somewhere to be."

Kevin also had places to be. He hadn't seen his daughter since yesterday. He was working out the words to placate the man, but Maddie, while wearing a smile, beat him to the punch. "There's no need to be rude."

"I'm stuck here for who knows how long. I'm cold. I'm hungry."

Maddie rocked on her heels and pinned him with a look. "I haven't eaten since Pittsburgh, but you don't see me complaining." And to top it off, she fluttered her lashes and gave the Grinch a bright, charming grin that said she wasn't about to allow his sorry attitude to make this situation worse.

What a woman.

She stood in the frigid cold, no gloves, a jacket far too light for this weather, late for where she needed to be, and she was defending him against this thorn in his side? Jo would like her, and Kevin might be in love.

Horns blasted from the backed-up cars. They picked up in numbers until they were all blowing at him and shouting their frustrations. In all his years in Ohio, he couldn't recall people blowing their horns so aggressively. Kevin wasn't an elf who could wiggle bell-topped shoes for magic to clean up this mess. He was doing his best here.

Cold coated his lungs in a harsh scrape with this heavy work. Sure, he'd moved most of these around alone at the farm, but he'd taken his time about it. Putting an eight-foot tree on a trailer was no quick and easy toss. Some of these were ten-footers. Since he didn't have his tractor to do most of the heavy lifting, he had no choice but to wait for the highway patrol. And with the way traffic was backed up, who knew how long it would take them to get there?

The Grinch rediscovered his cookie-stealing grin. "It looks like you're outnumbered."

As much as Kevin wanted to get to know Maddie, to discover more about this woman, he had to go. He gave her a final smile as he began the backbreaking work of hefting another tree closer to the trailer. "It's nice to meet you, Maddie."

"You too." Despite the delay and everything he'd caused, she appeared to have meant it. There was such sincerity in her gaze.

Kevin had to put effort into walking away from her. Each step screamed that this was the wrong choice. He should go back. He should offer to buy her dinner to thank her for her support against the Grinch. Or maybe offer dinner because he wanted to know more. Actually, he wanted to know every-thing—where she came from, where she was going, and mostly, could she stay? A strong breeze hit him, almost as if fate was pushing him back to her. He looked over his shoulder, but she was walking away.

Maybe that wind had been for her to leave, not for him to call her back. That would make far more sense. Kevin didn't meet women on the side of the highway. The whole situation, the intense pull to be nearer, was insane. He'd overworked himself, and the effects of exhaustion had made him delirious. He didn't fall for women like that. Or at least—a long sigh slipped out of him—he hadn't since JoAnne.

The Grinch hung around a bit longer. "These interstate relationships never work out."

Kevin took the high road to avoid the Grinch. Now that Maddie was gone, he wanted his trees picked up immediately so he could leave. He gave the Grinch a thumbs-up. "Appreciate the advice, pal."

He reached for more trees. With Maddie gone, the respite from the situation was gone, and the frustration crept back in. An engine cranked to life, and he looked up as the Grinch drove off the shoulder, through the snow, and headed up an embankment around the horizontal forest.

The fool was likely to get stuck, and somehow, Kevin figured that would be his fault too. He shook his head. He had spare rope in the truck to pull the man out if he did. He grabbed another tree when another engine started. This was heavier, deeper.

The rumbling carried across the packed snow, demanding attention.

A holly-berry-colored Mustang pulled alongside the highway. Kevin recognized the hot pink of her scarf in an instant. Hope vanished that she would stay of her own accord or track him down after the highway was cleared. He didn't even know he'd been harboring that Christmas wish.

He watched as her taillights disappeared in the direction of the Grinch. She was gone.

Chapter Three

Maddie got behind the steering wheel and shook off the ice crystals that had frozen her mind. What was she doing, standing on the side of a highway, flirting with a stranger? She didn't have time for that.

So he was cute. He had her thinking about mistletoe again. And that smile. Handsome too. A dreamy lift to improve her spirits through the delay.

Gosh, what *was* she doing?

She blinked and cranked the engine. The vibrations that hummed through the seats snapped her focus back to the present. She had to get to Denver for Irene's wedding. She could not afford to sit around daydreaming about the delectably charming Kevin.

Being stranded here was a bit of a problem. She warmed her fingers against the heat blasting from her vents. Maybe she should go back and help Kevin? If the road was cleared, then she could continue. Like she could do much to help him. Some of those trees were bigger than she was. A memory surfaced of him picking them up all by himself, and she found herself fanning her face. Maybe she couldn't move trees, but they could talk more. She couldn't deny a spark of attraction. If she hadn't had the wedding and work obligations, she'd still be on the side of that road.

Right. She shook her head. When did a time exist that she didn't have pressing work obligations? Heck, this was crazy. She'd been on the road for too long without anything to eat. A few hours to take a break and stretch her legs didn't seem so bad.

An SUV ahead pulled off to the shoulder and disappeared over an embankment. The packed snow left tire marks, beckoning her to follow if she wanted to stay on schedule. A bridge on the other side of Kevin's truck blocked her from being able to simply drive around him.

To the woods or stay put?

She bit at her lip, still inexplicably pulled to Kevin, but her responsibilities called louder. Maybe if she were someone else, she could take time to flirt with handsome lumberjacks. Was he a lumberjack? Or was he a delivery guy? If she stuck around, she could discover more about him, but she had a career that required her attention.

The SUV didn't return, so there must be a road over that small hill. She checked her phone to glance at a map, but an empty service bar stared back at her. Of course it did. She hadn't checked alternate paths. She was supposed to be on this road until at least Colorado. She tapped on the steering wheel, and it was almost as though Aunt Vivian whispered for her to go for it. Take an adventure. Be spontaneous. *You gotta grab life by the horns, dearie!*

The SUV still hadn't returned, and nobody had walked back looking for help, either. Maddie couldn't resist the possibilities. *Always listen to your gut* had been another favorite phrase of her aunt's. So full of life and love. Her aunt's advice had pushed Maddie through college and up the career ladder. She hoped Aunt Viv would be proud of all she'd accomplished, and was on the way to earning too.

Maddie hit the gas pedal and followed the tracks of the other vehicle. Driving somewhere had to be better than sitting there. So long as she kept heading west, she would get to Denver. She hit the gas pedal to follow the SUV's tracks.

Across the embankment, a thin rural road met her path. A shout of joy burst from her as her tires met the pavement and continued forth. With luck, this would take her alongside the highway, and shortly she would have the option of returning to the main road.

The pavement was long and winding. The trees were highlighted with snow, and white blanketed the ground. She'd been cruising at a comfortable pace on the highway for so long that she hadn't noticed the beautiful scenery around her. With the slower drive to navigate the frequent twists and turns of this little service road, she smiled at the winter scenes outside her windows. If she'd had her snow gear, what would it be like to walk through those woods? Take time to sit around a fire? Gosh, she could imagine the stunning pictures she could grab for a promo spread. It'd been so long since she'd slowed down for anything resembling a vacation. But she didn't regret her hard work over the last few years. She had a lot to show for it, especially that beautiful new office.

She took another curve and came to a T in the road that caused her smile to fade. She hung a right. More T's forced her into taking several more turns. Was she even going in the right direction anymore? It was white everywhere. She hadn't so much as seen another vehicle or a gas station.

Oh, she loved this car, but she wouldn't mind a compass on the dash, a common feature in newer vehicles. She drove farther, searching for anything to help her out. She rolled around a hill and came to a stop sign and yet another split in the road.

Well, darn.

Beyond the forked road was a snow-blanketed field. Either direction looked the same—more road with trees and snow that was starting to lose that breathtaking appeal. She was kind of growing tired of the picturesque view because she'd rather see a highway. The sign in front of her marked this Highway 6 and Highway 322, no east or west notation.

Her gut said go right. She took the path and hoped for the best.

Maybe she should have stayed with Kevin on the main highway. Surely she could have been able to do something, even if it was just keep him company. She could have served as a buffer to that grouchy man giving him a hard time. By now the road would have been cleared. She'd wasted more time driving around lost than if she'd taken advantage of the moment to slow down and stretch her legs. At least she'd be going in the right direction now and only slightly off schedule, instead of driving to wherever on some stupid wild-goose chase for the highway that seemed to have disappeared. So much for following her gut feeling. And now her gut was rumbling, reminding her again that she still hadn't eaten. As if she could eat. As her car ate empty miles, Maddie grew sicker as she watched time disappear.

Well, there had to be a small town around here somewhere, and once she found one, she'd be straightened back out. She'd be able to fill her tank with gas, grab something to eat while she was at it, and then be ready for a long stretch of road to make up time. She'd make Denver before morning. It was fine.

She topped another hill, and a large red sign stood in the distance. There, that was what she needed: a town. She narrowed her eyes, trying to catch the name as early as possible. Maybe she would recognize it and already know where to go.

Letters on the sign sharpened, and Maddie blinked at it. This couldn't be right. "Christmas Valley? Are you kidding me?"

She didn't think the sign was telling jokes. A sprig of holly was painted at the top, and a notation that it was established in 1917 ran across the bottom in a gold-scripted font, no less. At least it wasn't in Comic Sans. That had to signal something promising about this place.

She'd soon find out where she was and how far off her path she'd gone.

Comforted by that and determined to continue, she pressed her foot to the pedal, and her car let out an unhealthy chug.

Uh. She patted the dash. "What was that?"

The Mustang rattled. The noises rising from under the hood sounded the same way her favorite wet-resistant winter coat with large zippers sounded as it spun in the dryer. It was very un-carlike. It was also getting louder.

"Oh no." She gripped the wheel and pleaded with the car. "No, not here, not now."

Panic scaled her spine, and she rocked in her seat to encourage her car along.

The Mustang answered with a clunk.

"Please."

More knocking and rocking, and why did it sound like someone was hammering in the engine?

"No, no, no."

The more she pleaded, the worse her car shuddered. "Not here, not now. No, no, *please.*"

She climbed up a hill and slapped the dash. *Come on, baby.* With a heavy, *I think we can, I think we can,* she crested the hill, and a gas station came into sight. Oh, thank goodness. She wasn't stranded on the side of the road in the middle of nowhere. Only her car wasn't about to give her a moment of relief. It sputtered and rocked. A final hard jerk thrust her into the lot of an old-timey-looking store. The Mustang gave out a few final clacks as it rolled to a stop by a gas pump.

A young boy lounged in a chair with a guitar across his lap. He couldn't be a day older than seventeen, but as she got out, he put his guitar aside and looked to be in charge as he walked her way. A double garage bay was connected to the store, so that looked like good news. Hopefully it meant a mechanic. There was some bit of luck.

He rounded the front of her supposed mint-condition car. "What seems to be the problem?"

"I don't know. It started making this thumping sound. Then it started driving funny. Then it just died." So helpful. She was sure he could determine her exact issue by that description.

He tossed a rag over his shoulder, and his easy demeanor assured her that her nonspecific description wasn't a problem at all. He gestured at the hood. "Mind if I take a look?"

Maybe it wasn't a big deal. He didn't appear to be overly worried by her description. What was the car version of needing a Band-Aid? Could all that sputtering and jerking be a minor hiccup? Pour some oil in there, and she'd be on her way. "Yes, please."

He lifted the hood and peered in. His brows furrowed as he scanned over engine parts in the way she would analyze pie charts and pages of numbers. He also had the same expression that she got when the numbers didn't add up.

Oh no. "What do you think it is?"

"It's hard to say what's wrong. Could be your distributor, or maybe the alternator. I'd have to run some tests to say for sure."

That sounded like a lot and, worse, not a quick-fix sort of thing. She slapped the side of the car. "I thought this thing was in mint condition."

"Oh it is. You know, except for the broken parts." He shook his head. "It's an old car. I may have to order some of the parts online."

Order online? To the middle of Nowhere, Ohio? Did they get same-day shipping out here? "How long will that take?"

He tossed his rag between his hands. "Shouldn't be more than a day or two."

"A day or two." Breathe, Maddie girl. Breathe. Her throat was closing up. "No, no. I have to get to Denver. It's extremely important. I don't even know where I am. Or how I got here."

"You're in Christmas Valley."

Maddie inhaled and let it go. Okay. She could handle this. She'd been on the road for a long while. She probably had a ton of emails backed up and work to do, that was, if she could get cell signal in this town. A short delay wasn't going to make her late for the wedding. She still had six more days to get there. She could use the time to catch up on the details of the Hadley account. Then when she got to Irene, she could be one hundred percent focused and aid Irene if she needed it. Maddie needed a desk and a pot of coffee. Or a train ticket sounded even better.

Stupid nostalgia. *Aunt Viv's car. Jump in for adventure!* Great idea. If Maddie had taken the train, she could be in a private room with her feet up as the train competently rocked her across the country.

Now she was here, middle of nowhere with a curvy road, stranded at some gas station. Panic had her pulse threading, and she blew out a hard breath to get hold of herself. "Is there a motel around here?"

He winced. Why would he wince? But he did, and he said reluctantly, "Um, about sixty miles away. But there's a boarding house right down the road."

"A boarding house?" That was a—what again?

He lifted a shoulder. He was so darn adorable, it softened the blow. "Yeah. I can take you over there now."

It was cold, and what other options did she have? Warmth sounded amazing. "Thank you. That would be great. My name is Maddie."

"Cory. Let me get the truck, and I'll move your bags for you. Pam runs the house, and she's wonderful. She'll be delighted to have a guest, and her food is delicious."

Maddie's stomach fisted, reminding her she hadn't eaten in hours. Maybe by the time she arrived at Pam's house, the stress knot of this delay would have unwound so that she could eat. "Thank you."

Bags moved over to his truck, she climbed in for the ride across town. The place was interesting, you could say. She couldn't imagine living here, but she supposed that in a place called Christmas Valley, it was probably standard for all the houses and businesses to be dressed top to bottom in holiday wear. Old, classic Victorian homes looked like gingerbread houses. Large snowmen decorated the corners. Festive flags of alternating prints hung from all the street lights. Santas, holly, and Rudolphs were plastered down every street and across every building. Maddie's neighbors, with their North Pole scene on their front door, would have loved this place.

All through the neighborhood, it continued. Maybe the town had some sort of Christmas-decorating competition going on. The theme was definitely not "Subtle Holiday Charm." It was not a boring ride, to say the least, but probably one of the most visually stimulating parts of her trip so far.

Cory parked at a beautiful brick home. "This is it."

Green garland wrapped the porch with golden, glowing lights woven in. Wreaths and large bows hung against the home, and a statue family of gold deer with angels stood in the yard. The lawn was covered in snow, but a walking path had been neatly cleared away. Maddie got out of the truck, awestruck by how well everything came together now that she had a sidewalk to study it all. It seemed the boarding house was a bed and break-fast. "Wow. This town really lives up to its name."

Cory chuckled. "I'm guessing you're from the city."

"New York."

"You're a long way from home."

A family stood on the porch, hanging even more decorations. They were picture-perfect. They laughed together, and the man tapped the little girl on the nose. It caused her giggles to echo down the walk. This seemed like a production for a TV show, not real life. Not Maddie's life, anyway. An ache that hadn't bothered her in years pulled at her heartstrings. "A million miles."

Barking pulled her gaze from the family, and she turned to find a lovable, jumping ball of fluff.

Cory lifted her bags out of the truck. "His name is Rowdy."

Rowdy did a hop-spin dance in circles as he barked, and Maddie found some of the stress of the last hour swept away by the swish of his tail. "That name seems appropriate."

Cory walked ahead of her. "Pam, you've got a new boarder."

The woman came around the corner with a

smile as warm as the Christmas lights in her hand. "I like to think of them as friends I haven't met yet."

Okay. Maddie liked this woman. "That's very nice of you."

The little girl popped around a thick post. Now that Maddie was closer, she could tell this girl was older than Maddie originally thought. Maybe ten or eleven. She had that youthful enthusiasm with a twinkle in her eyes. "I'm Jo!"

The man turned. He had gray-topped hair, flushed cheeks, and a broad smile. "Bob Harding."

She shook his hand. "Maddie."

He kept shaking hers. "What brings you to Christmas Valley?"

"A broken car." Still he continued their handshake. She'd loosened her grip, but his held tight. "That's quite a handshake you have there."

His gaze dropped to their still-joined fingers, and a sheepish wince climbed over him as he released her. "I am so sorry. Force of habit. I'm a traveling salesman."

Oh, he was basically a fellow coworker. It was always nice to meet her *own kind* as people would say. "What do you sell?"

"Not enough."

She was a sucker for anyone who could make her laugh. Especially when these people embraced her on one of the most trying days of her life. Maddie loved all of this. If her car had to break down, it couldn't have selected a better place to do so. Pam's red hair was similar to Aunt Viv's. Jo, with that bounce in her step, made Maddie remember her younger, more adventurous days. Bob favored her dad, whom she didn't get to see near enough. In fact, he reminded her of the cheerful man he'd been before her mom died.

Bob pushed his hands in his pockets as his gaze lingered over Pam. "Luckily, Pam here takes in strays until people can get back on their feet."

Jo's brows pulled together, and she looked up at Pam. "Am I a stray?"

Pam's smile seemed to deepen. "Oh no, sweetheart." Pam lifted her gaze to Maddie as she brought the girl against her side. "She stays with me while her dad is away working."

Rowdy barked and leaped onto the porch. He took position in the middle of them all and plopped his furry behind down for attention. Bob bent and rubbed on the pup. "Rowdy and I are strays. He wandered in last Christmas and never left."

Not her. She had to get to Denver. "I'm only here for a day or two."

Pam patted her arm and brought her inside. "Let's get you settled in."

The festive decorations outside carried on inside the home—mini trees, poinsettias, snowmen. Lighted garland framed all the doorways. It was stuck in every nook and cranny. Cereal glued to paper to represent snowflakes; footprints that made snowmen. If Maddie saw this as a marketing plan for a place in New York, she would say no way. It even came complete with a framed picture of an older man with a long white beard. Instead of a chipper red outfit, he wore a brown suit.

Maddie smiled at the photograph. "Santa Claus?"

Pam laughed. "That'd be too corny, even for me. That's Jeremy Christmas. He founded the town a hundred years ago."

This place could not be for real. "The resemblance to Santa is accidental?"

Pam winked. "I think he played it up. He was actually sort of short and skinny. But from the chin up he fit the bill."

Maddie's nerves had been stretched thin, but she found herself oddly comforted and drawn to know more. Did everyone in town hang this man's picture on the wall? Or just the Christmas decorating fanatics? Maddie recalled the town on her way in. So, everyone then? Surely not. "Are you related?"

"His wife was my grandfather's cousin. When I got the place, I felt an obligation to keep up the Christmas theme."

"You certainly managed to do that." Every inch was dripping holiday as if someone had taken a Christmas water hose and doused the place.

"In an over-the-top, wall-to-wall kind of way."

It was every bit of all of that. As Maddie walked around the space and continually spotted new things, she was kind of digging it. Pam seemed to like the holiday in a way Maddie had never been able to. "But it works. I just got stranded, but you managed to distract me."

"Why don't I get you something to eat? It's almost dinnertime."

Now that the shock of the afternoon had worn off, Maddie wasn't hungry so much as worn and tired. She was ready to trade her heeled boots and stylish pants for socks and pajamas. "Thank you, but frankly, I'm exhausted. It's been a really difficult day."

Jo met them at the base of the stairs. Her winter gear had been stripped away, and somehow she'd gotten even prettier, with large brown eyes and a sweet smile. Maddie had an impulse to sit with Jo and ask her all kinds of questions. The girl gave off this friendly vibe of taking it easy, and surely she spread joy wherever she went. Maddie was in desperate need of some of that, but she was also in need of rest. "I'll see you in the morning."

"Okay." Likely it was simply the exhaustion that kept Maddie from poking into this little girl's life. She looked ready to paint toenails and braid hair the night away. Pam said she stayed with her while her dad worked, so where was Mom? It was a mystery that wasn't any of Maddie's business.

She followed Pam upstairs and found her breath a bit taken away as she walked in the bedroom. She expected her room to be decorated, but this was more of that wall-to-wall thing. She had her own tree. The red-and-white quilt on the bed was cozy. A string of flags read out *Falalalala* over the headboard. It was akin to a vacation at the North Pole.

She couldn't remember the last time she'd taken off and gone somewhere on an actual vacation where work wasn't involved. She dug her computer out and powered it up. She wouldn't be taking time off now either, but sometime after New Year's, though, something to squeeze in before the Valentine rush. Maybe take a for-fun-only road trip in her Mustang. Down a certain Ohio highway where she might find a certain man who delivered Christmas trees.

Chapter Four

Maddie lay in bed with her sleep mask still covering her eyes. Maybe it was all a dream, a weird hallucination that wasn't technically bad, but terrible on her schedule. All she had to do was peel back the sleeping eye mask, and she'd see a hotel room in Denver. It would be lovely, with sensible furniture and a little table in the corner. Her computer would be set up and plugged in over there. A cup of coffee from last night would be left abandoned. Or maybe a glass of wine to wind down after the long drive.

"Good morning, Maddie!" a chipper voice called from the hallway outside.

Maddie groaned and lifted a corner of her mask. The moose print of her quilt still covered her, a tree glowed from the corner, and the heels of her host's shoes clicked as Pam descended the stairs. Not a dream, at least not the happy kind.

Maddie sat up and pushed her mask away. "Welcome to Christmas Valley."

She collapsed back in the red sheets that matched the pillow with *Noel* stitched across the front. How could there be so many different holiday items in one place? Clearly her thoughts about the décor yesterday were affected by her exhaustion. Last night everything had grown on her and was charming and delightful. Today, she rolled her head to the side and found lighted garland trimming her bedroom windows. Ornaments were fixed along its length.

She laughed.

She was losing it. That was the only excuse. Stress was clearly getting to her. She tossed the covers back to get out of bed, and a jar of tiny candy canes on her nightstand snagged her attention. Because, of course. She fingered through the sweet mints. Pam left no stone unturned. Well, when in Christmas Valley, right? Maddie tore open a mini candy cane and popped it in her mouth for a pick-me-up.

The refreshing peppermint pushed her on with her day. Dress, then breakfast, and then work to obtain some normalcy during her delay. Her stomach rumbled in agreement with the food idea, and she was aching for some yogurt and oatmeal. She pushed open the bedroom door and scents wafted from below. *Oooh, or maybe...* She'd give anything for some breakfast from Sarabeth's. The restaurant was a few blocks from her office and created the most amazing coconut waffles with chopped mango and organic maple syrup. Her stomach rumbled loudly at the thought. Typically, Maddie ordered the vegetable frittata, but after skipping meals yesterday, and now with delicious pastry scents filling the house, it would be a day she'd take the time to splurge. She headed down for sustenance to power her through the day.

Jo's melody-sweet voice echoed up the stairs. "Maddie and me have the same color hair."

Maddie paused on the steps as a smile hit her.

"Yes, you do," Pam told her.

"She has the prettiest eyes."

Maddie touched her hand to her heart. This kid was going to melt her.

"Yes, she does," Pam echoed.

They were quiet, and Maddie waited a moment longer so they wouldn't think she'd been eavesdropping.

"Maddie's going to love this."

"Depends on if she likes Christmas cuisine."

Maddie was stopped short on her journey downstairs again for an altogether different reason. What exactly was considered Christmas cuisine? Sugar cookies? Surely not. But all the decorations caught her gaze again and, well, maybe so. Sugar cookies and hot chocolate were probably likely. There was that strong sugary scent pulling on her sweet tooth.

"Who wouldn't like green eggs?" Jo asked in her upbeat voice.

Green eggs? Maddie was afraid to know what was next.

"Let's hold off on the sprinkles. She's pretty sophisticated," Pam's words of warning sounded in the morning.

"Who wouldn't like sprinkles?"

"A stranded New Yorker."

Maddie straightened. She could do sprinkles. Maybe not on her eggs, but she wasn't some stuffy, pinched-faced stereotype who lifelessly walked the streets of Manhattan every day, drinking her meals via a smoothie. Okay, so she did do that most days, and maybe it had been a long time since she'd eaten sprinkles, but she did eat them.

Pam's *hmm* chased Jo's giggles. "Just a couple. But not the eggs."

Oh, gosh, they would have put sprinkles on eggs? A few more moments passed as they worked in the kitchen.

"Whoops." Jo laughed again. "I got some on the eggs."

Well, Maddie could pick those out. Water ran, and Maddie figured enough time had gone by they wouldn't think she'd overheard anything.

"I wonder if she's up yet?"

"Should I go and see?" Jo answered.

That was Maddie's cue. She hustled down the last of the steps. "It's okay. I'm up."

She rounded the corner, and, wow, she found herself stopping again at the spread of food before her. Carbs. It was all carbs. Festive carbs, but so many—donuts frosted and drizzled with green swirls and red dots, croissants the size of her hands. It was a table that promised a carb-coma nap. Based on what Maddie had overheard, none of this was made with almond flour and soy milk. This was not food for someone who had to concentrate on work.

Pam walked over and set down a plate of, sure enough, green eggs.

"Green eggs," Maddie found herself saying.

Pam chuckled. "In honor of the season."

Maddie had a sneaky suspicion that whenever Jo was here, they always had green eggs. A pot decorated with snowmen occupied the middle of the spread. *Please let that be coffee.* She sat with them and desperately searched for protein that wasn't altered with colors that would stain her mouth red and green. Yogurt? Steel-cut oats? None. Not even regular oats. Even the boiled eggs had suffered through a Christmas-color dunking. Well, there was fruit. "It all looks great."

Bob lowered a plate of more carbs in front of her. "Wait until you try the pancakes."

Or not, but she didn't want to be rude. They had obviously worked very hard. The pancakes had been made into stars, and it all looked amazing. It was just that she couldn't eat this. If she ate this, she'd have to buy new clothes to wear at Irene's wedding because of puffiness—not to mention the zits—from the sudden diet change. She could not show up in Denver with a swollen pimple at the end of her nose and mimicking a certain reindeer.

They all stared at her. Crap. She overloaded her plate with fruit and looked at Bob to get all the attention off her. "So, a traveling salesman?"

"I'm a real anachronism." He loaded his own plate with a tall stack and then did Jo's as well.

"What's that?" Jo piped up, turning her gaze away from Maddie's plate and focusing on Bob.

"A person or thing that belongs in an earlier era."

Jo nodded and glanced over at Maddie. "Bob knows about everything that starts with the letter *A*."

Bob smiled a little sheepishly at the compliment. "I sold encyclopedias, and the first volume was my sample. When I got bored on the road, I'd crack open the book and memorize another *A*. Go ahead, try me."

Games over breakfast? Maddie could go for some mental stimulation along with her plate of fruit to wake up. "Aardvark."

"A burrowing, nocturnal mammal native to Africa."

Hm. Interesting. "Alaska."

"The forty-ninth state, largest in the Union, and the capital is Juneau."

"Angel," Jo proposed.

Bob leaned toward her and tapped his knuckle under her chin. "That's easy. You look up 'angel,' and there's a picture of you."

Jo's smile was shy, and her cheeks colored. Maddie was not immune to the endearing effect.

Bob caught her gaze. "What do you do, Maddie?"

Work, lots of it, and while this was fun, she needed to make the most of her time during her delay. Which meant she didn't have time to sit around playing breakfast games. CEOs of million-dollar companies waited for no one. "I'm in marketing, and I actually have a lot of work I need to do. If you'll excuse me." This was perfect. She climbed out of her chair, grabbed her coffee and plate of fruit, and ran from all the bread. "Thanks."

Maddie rounded the corner, and Jo's whispered voice followed behind. "She's so pretty."

Aw. Maybe she should have stayed? Sure, she had a lot to do, but she could have spared a few more minutes.

"A fashionable fish out of water," Bob replied.

Bob was completely correct on that matter. Maddie blinked out of the weird, slow-it-down spell this place kept attempting to cast on her. This fish out of water had a lot of work to do. She continued to her room and set up a workstation best she could.

A vase of twigs and holly and platters of stuff that came out of a forest took up most of the area on a small table that was placed in a sitting section of her room. She moved all that to a corner on the floor and set her laptop down. She tossed the pillows crowding the chair to the side and got comfy with her coffee. All powered up, she crossed her fingers. *Please have enough service.* She clicked on her mobile hotspot and WiFi bars appeared. She silently cheered. It wasn't full-service, but by gosh, it was enough to run her email. Finally, something was going right for once. She was in business. She turned for her bag and jumped.

Rowdy sat there, eyeing her fruit.

"Oh no, you don't, bud."

She moved the plate to a higher dresser. He answered with a whimper, but her email loaded, and she hunkered down to power through the morning. She clicked through her messages for the latest file to set their market path for Hadley. All it needed was her approval. She opened and read through. Her heart sank. Her notes must have gotten crossed or something. She dialed Roz.

Rowdy picked then to stick his wet nose in her face. She pushed him off. "Silly thing. I have to work now."

Roz answered on the second ring. "And how was your night?"

Maddie closed her eyes, opened them, and she was still in her rented bedroom. "It was, well, I slept well."

"That bad?"

Was it really? Her gut said yes, but it was more out of her routine, her plans, and her expectations for what she should be accomplishing at the moment. Nowhere in her schedule was there a penciled-in note tasking her to take a trip to Christmas Valley. Another time, when she didn't have so much work, then she could write this off as a trip Aunt Viv would have loved. She was stressed, and if she could get some work in and feel as though she had some control, all of this would improve tenfold. "No, it's lovely. I've got breakfast, and I'm settling in to work for a few hours. That's why I'm calling. I'm looking through emails, and the copy for Hadley is wrong. It's got the everyday shopper. For the Hadley line, we need to appeal to the upscale shopper."

"Okay. How do we do that?"

Rowdy whined, protesting her continued work ethic. She turned back and found him stretched across her bed. Great. Fine. He could stay there, so long as he quit with the whimpering. "*Shhh*, you."

"Did you just shush me?" Roz answered through the line.

Maddie remembered the phone in her hand. "Sorry, no. Not you, Roz."

Roz chuckled. "What is that?"

"A dog." She focused on her computer to try to get back to work. "He came with the room."

"I can't picture you in a boarding house."

Maddie could practically see Roz's amused grin. Rowdy must have sensed the cheerfulness coming through the phone, for he rolled to his back and whined some more. He probably wished Roz were here instead of Maddie. His big brown eyes called to her and, oh, fine. But just this once. She moved to the bed and petted him, and he quieted down. There. She had this. Pet a dog with one hand, and then it would be quiet so she could work with the other.

A soft laugh came from the doorway, and she looked up to see Bob.

He leaned slightly in. "Looks like you made a new friend."

Yes, and he was keeping her from her work, and now this.

"Who was that?" Roz came back through the line.

Bob thankfully moved on, and Maddie stared at her screen to try to remember where she was in this conversation. "That was Bob. He's a traveling salesman."

"This gets better and better."

"Yeah." Maddie resituated her work area. "Enjoy yourself. About the copy—"

Jo skipped through. "Pam says not to feed Rowdy."

Roz, ever amused by all of this, asked, "Who was that?"

"Jo."

"She sounds like a kid."

Maddie glanced back, and Jo had curled herself on the bed with the dog. "She is."

Roz's laughter was louder than Jo's behind her. "A kid and a dog. This is fantastic."

"And all the Christmas I can take." She rubbed her head. She couldn't do this right now, not with all of this commotion. "Email me the latest sales reports. I'll call you back this afternoon."

Good grief, this place was busier than her New York office. But now Bob was gone. The dog was quiet. Maddie sat at the computer and typed up her notes to fix the copy. Roz would know what to do once she got the email.

Jo jumped off the bed. "Wanna take Rowdy for a walk?"

Like now? Gosh, no way she could swing that. She was actively typing here. Maddie would speak a little more frankly, and then hopefully Jo and Rowdy would play downstairs. "Maybe later. Right now I have to work."

"Or we could watch a movie on TV?"

Hint totally not taken. She had to learn to work through it. It was the same as college when her roommate had wanted to gossip about boyfriends while Maddie aimed to get her degree a year early. "Maybe."

"You know that kid in *Home Alone*?"

"Mm-hm."

"This boy in my class looks exactly like him." Jo left the dog and came closer. She sprawled in the other chair and propped her elbow on the arm. "How can you tell if a boy likes you?"

Oh, sweet roasting chestnuts. Maddie froze. "Maybe that's something you should ask your mom."

"I can't ask her. That's how come I'm asking you."

Maddie's fingers were poised over the keyboard, and she realized she'd stumbled into something by mistake. Right. Pam had mentioned Jo's father being away from work and never brought up the mother. Maddie gave her full attention to Jo then, not knowing what to expect.

"She passed away when I was six."

Maddie's gut clenched with familiarity. "I'm so sorry, Jo. You must really miss her."

"Yeah." Jo nodded, but her spirits were up. "Especially at Christmas."

Gosh, this kid. It was so much like her own life. Had she instinctively known and that's what had locked Maddie in on this girl last night? "I know how you feel."

Jo gave her a puzzled expression, but then quickly brightened. "My dad is coming home today. I'll be going back to the farm this afternoon."

"Well, I'm glad we got to meet."

"Do you want to take Rowdy for a walk before I go?"

Maddie couldn't tell her no. The pressure of work, the stress of the situation, it all went away at the bright brown eyes of Jo. Maddie knew too well the loneliness, the aching for new company. The emotions flooded back to her and left her dizzy. The way it had been before she'd been driven into work to find satisfaction and a purpose in life. Maddie didn't have much advice she could give the kid, but she could offer a few hours. There was a time when Maddie would've given anything to have a few hours of real attention from someone. Mom had been their glue, and without her, Dad had floated away. Maddie would've given anything for her dad to have eaten dinner with her, or gosh, spent time with her on most weekends. Maddie had endured a void of existence until Aunt Viv blessedly picked her up for adventures.

Maddie didn't have quite the spunk of Aunt Viv, but she would try. "Okay."

The girl's cheer of excitement was worth how late Maddie would be up working tonight, but she needed to get these emails to Roz first. "If you can keep Rowdy entertained for three hours to let me work really fast, then we'll take that walk. Deal?"

"Deal."

Jo took Rowdy out, closing the door behind her. "Everyone, Maddie is working for the morning!"

Maddie found a bit of unexpected cheer bubbling up in her throat, and she tackled the tasks that needed her immediate attention. She worked steadily, sending off emails about the Hadley account and messaging concerns over a few other ideas they were finalizing for other clients for shortly after New Year's.

Her back had grown stiff, her eyes itched, and her stomach grumbled at the meager snack bar she'd fished from her bag to go along with her fruit. She was going for another vegan treat when the patter of footsteps pounded up the stairs. Three hours already?

Her door burst open with a wide-eyed Jo, and Rowdy already on the leash. "It's been three hours!"

"It sure has." She grabbed her coat, pulled on her shoes, and followed Jo outside.

After the bundling, cozy warmth of the boarding house, the Ohio cold pierced her cheeks with a shocking hit. Smoke puffed from her in the air as she breathed, and, well, this would perk her up for more work after their walk. "I'm following you."

At the end of the driveway, Jo steered them to the right and down the short sidewalk. She strolled with the girl as they talked about school, books, and fashion. Jo was easy to chat with, for a kid. Or maybe it was this whole situation had everything different. Maddie didn't randomly talk with kids. Sure, she smiled at babies and waved at toddlers, but hold conversations with them? Never.

Maddie should feel so out of her depth she ought to be drowning, but instead, it was easy. "So tell me about this boy."

Jo's cheeks were pinked already, but a new sparkle lit her eyes. "He's got blond hair, and he's taller than me. Which is crazy because I'm taller than everyone."

"Height isn't a bad thing, kid."

"Yeah. But I'm still taller than everyone." That joy dimmed on her cheeks, and her shoulders slouched.

Ouch, right on the nose with Jo's insecurities. Maddie didn't know a lot about kids, but she remembered growing up. She'd been the tall one for a bit, but she had been quickly passed up by classmates. Then she'd become that kid with a book.

"And one day they'll catch up to you, just you wait. Besides, all the best clothing styles will have your number."

Jo peered up at her. "Yeah?"

"Oh, yeah. Skinny jeans, maxi dresses, it'll all be perfect for you. Not to mention you'll get to rock a pantsuit like nobody's business."

"I've never been *shopping* before."

"What?" Maddie somehow managed not to fall over at the very idea.

"I mean, I've been to the store and gotten clothes, but actual shopping, like they do on TV? I've never done that." Jo met her gaze with a puzzled brow. "Do you think you could take me?"

This kid was killing her. "Well, I have to leave soon, but I could send you a few things? Fresh off the line. Sometimes I even get dibs on stuff before it goes to the store."

"Really?"

Maddie was already seeing the line of clothing she was at liberty to pick through. As the marketing executive, she had to have access to the product she was selling, and designers loved giving out samples. Off the top of her head, she could think of at least seven outfits that would fit Jo's willowy frame. "Yes."

"I would like that."

Crazy enough, Maddie liked that thought too. She could box up surprises and toss in a few other fun things. Hats and gloves. Scarves as well. *Ohhh*, and, of course, shoes. They walked in silence for a moment, and Maddie tried recalling the last time she'd spent a joyful day full of nothing but shopping. All her items of late had been picked up while she'd run through stores, checking displays. She should ask Roz about a Saturday afternoon shopping excursion. They could pencil something in for around March and hit up the new spring offers.

Maddie had walked with Jo farther than she'd realized. The sidewalks of a quaint neighborhood had eased away as they continued down a quiet lane. A beautiful, snow-topped forest surrounded them. There were sections of trees that were different heights. A set of low growing ones that were no taller than Maddie's waist showed off a sweeping, vast landscape. To the other side of the road were towering trees.

It was so idyllic, walking with Jo, and Rowdy trotting alongside them, happily panting in the frosty air. It was freezing cold out, but it was invigorating too. An energizing rush swam through Maddie's limbs. She wanted to run back to her computer and apply these elements to some of their winter advertising plans coming up in February—huge snowflakes against crystal blue skies, lush, green fonts, and a backdrop of a frozen lake.

"Okay, we're here." Jo's voice interrupted Maddie's spinning mind.

She looked around and saw a lot more trees and snow. "Where?"

"Home."

"You live here?" Maddie saw nothing more than

breathtaking views. No doubt, it was an amazing place to live, but where?

Rowdy barked and took off. Jo, holding the leash, laughed and chased him around a bend.

"Jo!" Maddie called and ran after the pair. She caught them at the corner and gasped. A log farmhouse sat nestled among the trees. Garland and red ribbon wound the posts on the porch. Large candy canes stood tall on either side of the base of the steps. A rustic barn and a field of snow completed the picture. This subtle but striking holiday magic was décor that only existed in promotional layouts. *This*, this was what Maddie called Christmas scenery. It had all the decorations anyone could dream of, without the overpowering impact of places closer to town. "Wow. This is absolutely beautiful. It's like a portrait of Christmas."

Maddie turned in the driveway, catching sight of their footprints in the snow where they'd walked up and could barely catch her breath from the picturesque scenery. Stunning. She was speechless, an impressive feat for her. She'd give anything for her good camera to capture all this. It was packed near her computer when she traveled. Opportunities for inspiration were always waiting to happen.

Snapshots on her phone would never do the details justice. The way the snow clung to the bark and hugged each individual green needle would be lost on her phone. A light dusting of Roz's beloved snow tickled the afternoon air as it fell. According to Maddie's mother, that's why light snowflakes fell so fluttery—the air was giggling. Seeing the light trickle of snow falling, it was hard not to see her mother's imagery.

Maddie turned and came face-to-face with a man. Kevin? Spilled-trees-on-the-highway Kevin? No.

But he blinked at her. "Maddie?"

"It's you." Again in a matter of moments, she was rendered speechless, and that sudden flutter returned to her insides. Had it even left when she'd walked away from him on the highway?

Jo walked up to him and leaned against him. "You know my dad?"

Dad? Kevin? The trees? Maddie blinked, still scrambling. "Yes… no… not exactly."

Kevin rubbed one of Jo's arms. "We met on the road, honey."

"Yeah." In a freaky, crazy, unexpected way. Was this really happening right now? "And then I got off and got lost. And I ended up in Christmas Valley." Back here. With Kevin.

Jo looked between them both as a bigger grin spread across her face. "Well, isn't that lucky?"

Kevin seemed as surprised as she was, but he still managed to give her that heart-seeking look from the highway. "What are the odds?"

A billion to one, she'd have said. Even more, what were the odds she'd still feel this pull, this breathless longing, this desperate desire to know more? "Yeah."

Chapter Five

*K*evin scrambled for words. On the road with his trees thrown everywhere, he'd seemed to be brimming with questions that he hadn't been able to force out of his mouth. But staring at her now, when there were no honking travelers, no Grinches standing over his shoulder, Kevin was at a loss for something to say. Just mentally paralyzed in her presence and confused how she'd gotten here. And how did she end up with his daughter and Rowdy?

Jo tugged his hand. "Dad, it's cold. Let's go inside."

"Right." He snapped out of it. "Why don't you come in, Maddie? You can warm up for a bit."

She rubbed her arms. "That sounds great."

Jo skipped ahead of him and across the porch. He lingered, waiting for Maddie. He wanted to walk with her. Moving seemed to have unlocked his brain because he'd found his thoughts.

He hadn't realized how tense she'd been on the

highway. Now, she inhaled deeply and turned her face up to the sky. If he didn't know any better, he'd think it was her first time outside in months.

Her scarf was loose around her neck, and happiness bloomed in her gaze, sucking him right in. There was that attraction flaring within him again. An inner voice steadfastly and determinedly saying *want* as he looked at her. He pushed the thought away. As much as he might crave to know everything about her right that instant, it was lunacy to think she'd sit down for a cup of coffee and unload all her secrets to a man she'd just met. "Are you out seeing the town?"

"Jo asked me for a walk with Rowdy, and I couldn't resist her charming face."

He eyed his daughter skipping ahead and jumping over the porch steps. He sighed. "Yeah, I have that problem too."

"She's a sweet girl. I ran into some car trouble, and I'm staying at the boarding house while my engine is being repaired. I didn't realize Jo was yours." She tucked a few stray hairs behind her ear. "Pam mentioned Jo stayed with her while her father worked, but she never said more than that, and I didn't pry."

"Pam's a godsend for us." After they'd lost JoAnne five years ago, he'd been a wreck, trying to manage the farm, Jo, school starting, and getting through it all. Pam had stepped in and established a routine. She'd said Jo was to come to her after school and stay over while he made routes to sell trees. No exceptions had been made, attempts to disagree had been swiftly knocked away, and Pam had saved him. The whole town had. Holly had kept food coming from the diner. Roy, a fellow farmer, had assisted so Kevin could stay on top of the farm's needs that first season. Christmas Valley was the town that continually gave year-round and was always there when its residents needed it most. He'd succeeded at finding people who loved and cared about his daughter.

Unfortunately, he wasn't sure he could save and protect the farm any longer. They were precariously close to losing it.

Maddie adjusted her pink scarf. "I find that easy to believe about Pam."

"Everyone in town deserves some credit for keeping us put together."

"Just one big family?"

"We are." He stomped snow off his boots on the porch and pushed opened the front door to let her in ahead of him. He toed his shoes off and glanced at hers. They were pointed heels and zipper things. He wasn't sure how she'd managed the walk from the boarding house in this weather. Really, in any weather, he wasn't sure how she walked in those. JoAnne had liked tennis shoes, snow boots, and during the summer, slip-ons. It was lucky Maddie hadn't fallen and broken something. Where was the traction, thick soles, and layers of warmth? Did she even have room for wool socks in those shoes?

She opened the zippered boots and left hers at

the door. His large winter black ones, her stylish heel things, and then Jo's pink snow boots. He blinked at the sight of the three of them lined up. For years, it had only been two pairs comfortably taking up that spot. Even with Maddie's impractical shoes, the set of them fit against the wall as though they belonged there.

A deep longing for something *more* assailed him.

"Dad, are you starting the fire?"

Leave it to his daughter to keep his mind together. "Yeah."

He crossed the living room and got to work warming the place up.

Maddie walked through with her phone in her hand. She seemed to be absentmindedly tapping it against her palm as she turned in a circle. His home wasn't a luxurious five-star hotel, but in his opinion it was pretty perfect. He'd grown up here always thinking the house was small. He'd always been able to hear Dad's Westerns blaring from the living room TV over the radio in his bedroom upstairs.

When Kevin had moved back, he'd fully intended on expanding the cabin. Step number one was moving Jo's bedroom to a different place, so she'd have the privacy growing up that he'd always wanted. JoAnne had walked in and fallen in love. She said the cozy size would keep them close and he wasn't knocking down one wall, adding an expansion, or so much as changing a single detail with the footprint. Amazing how with a little perspective he'd seen his old home in a new light. He couldn't imagine Jo being on the other end of the house from him, as he'd originally planned in renovations.

Maddie touched one of the posts that separated the living space from the kitchen. "This place is so nice."

A wall of pride expanded in his chest. It was quaint and rustic, but it was their place. "Not what you expected?"

"It's my first farmhouse." A fondness filled her smile as she continued to move through the room. She touched the log walls and ran her finger along a thick row of chinking that sealed the house together. "I only have *Little House on the Prairie* as a reference."

He chuckled. "We even have indoor plumbing."

She walked to the rows of bookshelves. "You must be quite the reader."

"Like me," Jo announced.

Kevin tossed wood on the fire and built it up until it was roaring so high, it would be too hot to sit near. "I am. I enjoy the downtime and read a little bit of everything. Do you?"

"I wish I had the time. I mostly read reports and information for work."

He was starting to get the picture of her life, and it sounded miserable. That moment on the highway of itching to be on her way, the risk she'd taken by going off-road to get where she was going, even the steady tapping of her phone in her hand. Was it a mindless movement or a comforting habit to have her phone in her hand? All work and no play. "So where are you from?"

"New York." She sank into an oversized chair.

"Yeah?" He had an irrational negative reaction to her response. That was a long way away. He knew she had to be from somewhere in a city. There was a fine edge to her. A put-togetherness in her clothing. On seeing her again, part of him had hoped she'd hailed from Cincinnati. Maybe as near as Indianapolis. But New York? That was another world. "And where were you headed before I derailed you?"

"To a wedding in Denver."

He found himself sunk again. It would have been nice if she worked in a nearby city and passed through often. But Denver? That was far away too. He was nothing but an accidental blip in the middle of her long drive. A drive that she would likely never be making again. Except, maybe? "Friends or family?"

"A client. It's a business thing."

From New York to Denver to a wedding of people she wasn't friends with or related to. Heck of a business there, and crushingly, no reason for her to be making this drive through his hometown again. Was there no reason at all he could fathom to bring her back to his part of the world? There was an aching emptiness inside that wanted more answers. He didn't know how long she was in town, but whatever the length, he already knew it wouldn't be enough.

He blinked away the frustrating thoughts. What was he thinking with Maddie? It was coming at him too fast. Exactly the same speed as he'd fallen for JoAnne, and that couldn't be right. JoAnne wasn't replaceable. He didn't like that there seemed to be a fight taking place within him. He was torn between what was right and what he was feeling, between believing that Maddie couldn't—*shouldn't*—be stirring up the same feelings JoAnne had, and the fact that, despite everything, Maddie was indeed making him feel things he hadn't experienced since JoAnne. He cleared his throat and searched for a neutral topic. "What line of work are you in?"

"I'm in marketing. Mostly women's clothing."

Jo perked up. "Is that how come you dress up?"

Maddie smiled at his daughter. "Kind of. It's part of the job."

He put his arm around Jo and tucked her in to his side. "She's going to be a standout here in Christmas Valley."

Maddie's lips parted, and she seemed about to speak when her phone dinged. Whatever thought was going to come out shuffled away immediately as she instantly responded to the call of her phone. Her brows puzzled together, and her fingers swiftly keyed across the screen. He had no idea clothing was such an intense job, but looking at her then with that intent focus and the serious set of her mouth, she could just as well be a doctor delivering life-or-death instructions.

"Sorry." She dropped the phone down in her lap and glanced around. In the blink of an eye, she shifted seamlessly from the concentration on her phone to a return to their conversation. It was almost like—to her—she'd never had the interruption. "How long have you had this place?"

"It's a family farm. I took it over after my dad retired."

Jo had curled her feet under her, and Rowdy hopped on the couch to cuddle. "Daddy, can she stay for dinner?"

"Ah..." He looked at Maddie to gauge her thoughts, and he didn't see any excitement reflected in her features. He swallowed a lump that had formed in his throat at the loss of time with her. "Well, uh, Jo, I'm sure—"

Maddie softly smiled, and her gaze shifted from her phone back to him. "I should get back to Pam's. I have a lot of calls to make."

"Right." Whatever work situation she had must need her attention, though what kind of an emergency someone could have in women's clothing, he didn't know. He pushed hair away from Jo's face. "It's beginning to get dark outside too."

But while he was disappointed Maddie didn't stay, the crushing look on Jo's face as her shoulders dropped was the hardest thing to take. "But, hey, why don't we give her a lift?"

Jo stirred, set the pillow aside, and jumped up. "Okay."

He sent Maddie a smile and hoped she wouldn't disagree. Relief flooded him as she grinned back.

They bundled up and got in the truck. Maddie sat in front, and Kevin's fingers itched to reach across the console and hold her hand during the evening drive now that the sun had set. He kept his hands to himself. He had no business touching Maddie in that kind of intimate way. It was liable to send her jumping out the door of a moving vehicle. She hadn't even wanted to stay for dinner. Holding hands was certainly off the table.

Christmas Valley was never a disappointment when it came to holiday lights, and he drove slower, took a scenic route, and enjoyed the ride while looking at the sights.

Jo pointed out her favorite things on the houses, the Santa falling off the roof of the Smith house and the elves juggling gifts in the yard of the Johnsons, while Rowdy put nose prints all over the truck's back windows. Kevin was always fond of downtown. The courthouse looked like the North Pole, and the bakery that ran out of an old Victorian home had been transformed into a gingerbread house.

Stan's diner was the only place that went skimpy on the Christmas cheer, a paltry string of lights hanging around the outdoor windows. And Stan hadn't even been the one who put those up. They always appeared in the middle of the night by someone else's hand that Stan could never catch.

Though Stan had recently moved away, so no telling what sort of transformation his niece may make, if any at all.

With all of Kevin's favorite decorations outside, not even the sleigh and reindeer taking off in mid-flight on the hardware's roof pulled his attention as much as the woman sitting next to him.

Maddie's eyes were bright as she looked at the displays surrounding them. "Is this a tourist town, or is it just crazy about Christmas?"

He laughed. They were a little nutty, but it was all with love. "Just your average small town. The name tends to make us go a little overboard. Jeremy Christmas certainly left his mark."

Jo perked up in the backseat. "What if his name was Jeremy Easter?"

"Then we'd be knee-deep in rabbits every spring."

Maddie leaned toward him, resting against the console separating them. "Have you always lived here?"

"I did a stint in Boston when I was in college." He'd met JoAnne freshman year, started asking her to marry him by sophomore year. By senior year, she'd agreed, and they'd come home.

"But you prefer Christmas Valley?"

"I do." It was kooky and crazy sometimes, but this was his home. "I've never seen a prettier place or met nicer people."

"I'm strictly Manhattan, born and raised." She

pulled on the edge of her gloves the way a woman on TV would.

"Good to know." He definitely kept his hand to his side of the truck, no matter how strong the scent of vanilla coming from her called to him. It was foolish, anyway, for his thoughts to continue wandering in that direction. It could never work out. They had too many cards stacked against them. She wasn't moving here any sooner than he was moving there. Their geography was too great for anything to happen besides a lot of disappointment.

He knew that, and still, he wanted. His hand still itched to cross that slender space and touch her. He gripped the steering wheel tighter to prevent it from happening.

It was a little crazy, anyway. Once he got to know her, he might find he didn't even like her.

He told himself that, but he didn't believe it.

Jo leaned between them. "I'm strictly Christmas Valley."

Bless his daughter for having the natural grace and social skills to break up awkward silences. "Born and raised, right?"

"Uh-huh." She agreed with a firm nod.

He'd taken the longest way possible to keep Maddie at his side, but the short drive could only last for so long, and he pulled up at Pam's. Maddie unbuckled and climbed out as soon as he got the truck in park. His mind raced with a need to find reasons to hold her near. "Jo, do you have anything in Pam's to get?"

"No."

"Are you sure?" Normally, Jo would have something she needed to grab, and it would delay their trip back home at least another fifteen minutes.

Maddie was already out of the truck.

Jo gasped then. "Oh, wait, I can get my headphones."

A tight breath unwound from him, and he climbed out. He met Maddie at the front of his truck as Jo ran ahead with Rowdy hot on her heels. "Do you know how long you'll be in town?"

She winced. "I don't. Cory said he may have to order parts. I hope not long. I need to get to Denver."

Right. While he hoped for days, she still pleaded for hours to be out of here. "I'm sure Cory will have you fixed up as soon as possible."

"I hear he's the best."

"He is. There's no one else I'd rather trust my equipment to."

"He surprised me when I pulled up. He's so young."

"He graduated high school last May. We had a big party for him at Pam's. But don't worry about him with your car. He learned from the best—his dad and grandma. They taught that kid everything they know. He's been fixing my tractor since he was sixteen."

"Tomorrow I plan to check—"

She slipped.

Her arms went wide as she yelped. He reached out and caught her by the elbow, his other arm reaching around her slender waist. He stood that way a long moment with her half-caught in his arms. Surprise passed over her face. Her lips parted, a quick inhale, and her eyes widened. He could kiss her. He wasn't entirely sure she would push him away, either.

It wouldn't be wise. He didn't know her nearly well enough, and he wasn't too sure about the way she made him feel, but everything in him said to take that chance. Her grip on his arm tightened, and time seemed to float away, leaving them suspended. His pulse thundered in his ears and ticked off a countdown of him leaning in and making that move.

She licked her lips, and her gaze fell away. The scenery around them whirled back into focus. Right. Walking to Pam's porch. His daughter about to come back outside. The moment passed, and he held her another beat longer than necessary before reluctantly releasing her, but he maintained a hand at her back in case. "Careful."

She pushed her hair back and stared hard at the sidewalk. "That slick spot came from nowhere."

"We need to get you some different shoes while you're here. Can't have you falling down all over the place." Though as long as she continued to fall against him, he wouldn't complain. He cleared his throat. "You'll twist something."

She walked up the steps, and he had little choice but to let go of her. "If I was staying longer, I'd look into that."

"Right, right. You're leaving soon." There weren't enough reminders in the world to drill that thought into his head.

She looked at him, then away. "Yeah."

The front door opened, stealing their time, and Pam stood there. She opened the door wider for them both to pass through. "Hey, you two."

"Hi, Pam. Thanks for looking after Jo."

Pam smiled. "Always a pleasure."

Jo trotted down the stairs and stood at his side. "I'm ready."

He was all out of excuses, and everyone stared at him. "I guess we should get going."

"Well, thanks for the ride." Maddie pushed her hands in her back pockets and eased away, leaving him with this notion that she was slipping through his fingers again.

"It's a small town. I'll see you around." Lame, but what else could he do?

Jo hooked her hand around his arm. "Me too."

Maddie smiled. "I'd like that."

Maddie's grin lingered, renewing his hope, and there was nothing he could do to extinguish the want that warmed him all the way through. He turned to say his goodnight to Pam and Bob. Bob wistfully stared at Pam, while an unknowing Pam fiddled with the cord to Jo's headphones. The two weren't dating, but Bob sure did look at Pam a lot in ways that Kevin used to look at JoAnne.

Maybe even in ways that Kevin now glanced at Maddie, foolish as that thought was.

A trill slashed through the tranquil moment, stealing Maddie's attention and pulling her away as she brought a phone to her ear. "Hey, Roz, hold on a minute."

Then she was gone as she headed up the stairs. Another day, another moment of her walking away. She sure was attached to her phone.

Chapter Six

Maddie headed downstairs to face another day. The scents weren't quite the same as yesterday morning, but there was a definite smell of bread in the air. Bob and Pam were around the table. Green eggs sat center stage, a plate of biscuits nearby. The low-key meal was likely due to the fact that Jo had gone home. As Maddie stood back and took in her options of things around the table, it wasn't the carbs pushing her away this time.

Pam and Bob sat across from each other. Bob complimented the food, but Pam's blush? Now that was interesting. It was as intriguing as the quick glance Pam shot at Bob while he looked down to spoon jelly on his plate.

Pam glanced up and Maddie was caught. She stepped forward into the dining room. "Good morning."

Bob smiled her way. "Hey, Maddie."

Pam arranged a napkin setting next to her. "Did you sleep okay?"

"Actually, I did." After she'd gotten the reports she'd needed from Roz, Maddie finally had a moment where she felt as if she had a handle on everything. Warren was even impressed with her competence from the road. He'd agreed she should go to Irene's wedding, but the pending Hadley account had given him pause. Consider all those worries of his effectively put to rest. Maddie had gone to bed satisfied.

Rowdy trotted by and licked her hand on his path to the couch. The goofball had whimpered at her door last night until she'd let him in to curl up with her. Maddie Duncan, not even a goldfish in her apartment, had slept with a dog all night long. "And so did Rowdy, once I let him in."

Pam winced. "I hope that's okay."

Maddie gave him an affectionate glance. "He's hard to resist."

"Can I get you something?"

While Maddie was almost feeling good enough to eat a meal of carbs to nap off later, she wouldn't dare interrupt this romance brewing before her. She didn't think they were an item, but she wasn't going to stand between them if something was on the verge of happening.

A silly thought struck her that she'd like to have breakfast with Kevin, but how ridiculous was that? She didn't have his number, for starters. It also served no purpose. She was leaving soon. "No, thanks. I think I'll head into town."

She bundled up, zipped on her shoes, and started down the sidewalk. The sky was a bright, brilliant blue. The air smelled of nature and snow. It reminded her of the ski trip she'd taken three years ago when she'd picked up the new women's sporting goods lines by Snow Day Outdoors. It was her work navigating that men's-only company into the women's market that had caught Irene's attention.

While Maddie loved the city and would never leave it, the great outdoors was invigorating to check out once every few years.

Pam's boarding house was two short blocks from town, but the walk was nothing compared to what she hiked every morning in New York. Try twice this length with a crowd and traffic. While she continually passed people on the sidewalks of Christmas Valley, it struck her as empty. If this was New York, she'd be shoulder-to-shoulder with a crowd. Instead she passed one person at a time. Traffic was light. The drivers eased by at a leisurely pace. No cranky horns or grouchy people yelling out their windows. They also stared at her and offered good mornings as she went by. Where she was used to being lost in her own thoughts on her way to work or observing the people around her, a friendly smile had been on her face since she'd left Pam's driveway as she nodded at strangers.

Last night she'd enjoyed the scenery of the

downtown shops in the dark with lovely lights, but this morning she was able to check out the window displays. Nothing like Macy's would put on, but a cute, homey feel filled the air. Teddy bears were propped against jack-in-the-boxes. Giant red bows were tied all over the place, and wherever a pole existed, it was wrapped in green garland. It was so classic Christmas—that old-school, back-to-Grandma's-house feel.

She shook her head and tried ignoring the unexpected craving for Aunt Viv's fruitcake. So weird. She hadn't thought of the stuff in ages. Aunt Viv always baked two, and one was rum – soaked. She'd occasionally—on the sly—give Maddie a very tiny piece that was just big enough for one bite before bed, calling the rum version "the good stuff."

On a deep inhale, Maddie picked up that alluring scent of bacon. Where there was bacon, there was usually—hopefully not green—eggs.

Another Christmas Valley resident walked toward Maddie. The woman's smile was as brilliant as the sunshine. "Good morning."

"Morning." Maddie tried absorbing some of her cheeriness in the absence of coffee. "Where's a good place to get something to eat?"

"Stan's. It's right over there."

"Thank you."

On the corner ahead was a store with huge front windows and thick red curtains covering most of them. A simple blue sign labeled the place as Stan's, and there wasn't a lot else. In one window hung a little neon coffee cup with black cords curling beneath it. One single strand of large red bulbs dangled from the awning. The place looked plucked from the fifties from a different small town and placed on the street. It lacked the overachiever decorations, and Maddie was instantly intrigued.

The door dinged on her opening, and somewhere within a man shouted. "Club sandwich! Pick it up!"

The inside continued that fifties vibe with a long counter bar to eat at and faded red booths against a window. A glass display boasted homemade pies, and faded signs nailed on the walls advertised the diner food.

A waitress was behind the counter. Maddie moved toward her and sat at the bar. "Hi."

The waitress eased over. She had brown hair as big as her friendly grin. "Hi, I'm Holly. You must be the girl with the red Mustang." She shrugged. "Small town. Word gets around."

Can't stay a stranger in a place like this. "Is it too late to get breakfast?"

She shook her head. "Luke can make you some breakfast." She turned to the side. "Luke!"

"Yeah?" a voice answered from the back, and then a husky man appeared at the serving pass. He wore a cap reminiscent of another time and an apron to match. There was practically a twinkle in his dark eyes. Apparently there was not a single person in this entire town who didn't have some sort of jolly-go-lucky glow.

It was beginning to sucker her into the spirit.

"Egg whites only. And some whole wheat toast, please."

"Coming right up." He winked at her.

Holly came around the end of the counter and let out a large, dramatic sigh. She then slid onto the stool right next to Maddie. Whole counter available and she sat right there. The woman even leaned in toward Maddie, arms out wide as she gestured at the room. "I'm the owner, and I just gave myself a coffee break."

Well, all right then. Maddie eyed the restaurant's name on the woman's shirt. "What happened to Stan?"

"He's my uncle. He got married and moved to Cleveland a couple of weeks ago." She huffed. There was a summer freshness about her even though it was December. She turned on her stool until she faced Maddie and flipped the hemline of her uniform. "I never thought I'd end up in an apron." She tossed hair off her shoulders and sat up impeccably straight. "You are talking to the former Miss Ohio. Runner-up, but... you know." She shrugged.

Oh, okay. They were doing the bestie thing. Maddie could do this. She did it genuinely with Roz on occasion. Not a lot of time for girls' nights on her schedule, but she certainly knew the routine. She'd played this role often enough to hook a client. "Oh, well, now that Stan is gone, maybe you should think about renaming the place."

Maddie found herself not faking at all. Holly was so vibrant, and she was easy to talk to. It's not as though Maddie had anywhere else she could get to at the moment, so sure, why not mingle with the locals and be charmed by their exuberance?

"Hmm." Holly nodded. "Yeah, I guess. But what to?"

"How about Holly's?"

"*Hmm.*" Her brows pulled with thought.

Movement from behind Holly caught Maddie's eye. Her mouth went dry as her gaze focused on the man casually sitting in a corner booth.

Kevin lounged with an arm over the seat; his fingers that had curled around her waist last night were hooked on a coffee mug. "How about Reluctant Holly's?"

Maddie found her gaze lingering over him. How could it not? He was casual, and a cheeky grin played at his mouth. Where had he even come from? How had she missed him on walking in? Had he snuck in after her? Except he had a coffee mug in his hand, and Holly hadn't served him since she arrived. So weird since Maddie had been thinking of seeing him over breakfast, then he appeared.

"Hey," Holly announced and interrupted the tension. "I didn't know this would be my thing."

Luke tapped the food pass and pointed at her. "You could make it your thing."

"Yeah, I know. I guess we should redecorate." She tossed hair from her forehead and faced Maddie again. "You got any ideas?"

Maddie glanced the room over, and its obvious lack of camaraderie with the rest of Christmas Valley couldn't be missed. On one hand, it could serve as an escape for the people, but Maddie didn't think that would be the case with this town. Rather, the diner stuck out like a sore thumb. Kevin lounged against his booth in the corner, and she was mentally swept away to his home, the subtle décor and classic feel of the place. She'd walked in, and it had whispered *home*. Not a house, but a loved home. Maddie wasn't about to start humming Christmas songs while she listened for a clatter atop the roof once she got back to her apartment, but she could see the people of this town doing it. That's what Holly's needed. That heart of the holidays to take you back when Christmas was more than flying wrapping paper, but the memories of what it could be like. That nonexistent fairy-tale idea of the holidays. "Given the town's affection for Christmas, I'd go with that."

Holly nodded. "That is a good idea. I grew up here." She swiveled in her chair and announced to the room at large. "My affection for Christmas is off the hook."

Luke cocked an eyebrow at her. "Stan wouldn't even let us put up a tree."

Holly wagged a finger. "It's my place now."

Maddie sank into the familiarity of her work, her business. She was in this charmingly strange town, but this was her element, her playground. Forget the Christmas Valley spirit, *this* was Maddie's domain of Santa's workshop. "You could do a whole holiday theme—the colors, the ambiance, the menu."

Holly mulled it over with an interested twist of her lips.

Luke eyed Maddie. "Young lady, are you in the restaurant business?"

"I'm in marketing."

Holly nodded. "Lucky for me you wandered in here. I'll take all the advice I can get."

All the lights turned on and flashed in Maddie's head. It was completely insane for any other place, but it worked for this town, and that's what Stan's place needed—no, not Stan's anymore, *Holly's*—down-home Christmas decorations absolutely dripping from the walls thicker than the syrup they poured over the pancakes, but minus all the consumer gimmicks. This should be old-school.

Thinking over the town again, her gaze impulsively pulled to Kevin, and she reevaluated everything she'd assumed about Christmas Valley with her first impression. His home was subtle, with little touches like those really old large, colorful bulbs. The neighborhoods were spiked with cheer. Pam's home was loaded in items that Maddie doubted were random purchases. None of it matched each other, but Maddie would bet the townspeople carried one thing in common with each other—*joyful memories*. In the short time since she'd been here, she'd had several thoughts she hadn't in a long while about forgotten vacations, Aunt Viv, and food.

That was something to work with. "Don't target kids directly, but evoke the child in all of us. Christmas is about memories. That's what makes it a great marketing tool." She turned in her chair to glance over this fifties-style diner, but she was drawn to Kevin again. He was intent and focused on her. His attention added a bundle of nerves, but Maddie was too keyed up and into the redesign of Holly's place. She returned her gaze to Holly. "Maybe get a jukebox that only plays Christmas songs."

Kevin's stare affected her more, and she pulled back toward him again. The smile on his face had tightened, and the amusement that had been at his eyes was now strained. Instead of hitting her with that breathtaking gaze of blue eyes that often left her knees wobbling, he barely looked at her. He gave her another quick glance and then dropped his gaze almost awkwardly.

She didn't. "What?"

Kevin rubbed his chin. "That's a pretty calculated take on Christmas."

Calculated? She leaned away. Was he calling her a hack? "That 'calculated take' makes me a pretty good living."

Kevin cleared his throat. "I just don't think the holidays should be about dollars and cents."

Seriously. Was he kidding her right now with this? "This from a man who sells Christmas trees."

He gestured his hand with a so-so wobble and gave a shrug. "I fulfill a need for a fair price. I love what I do. Working the land is a day well spent."

What part of anything she'd said gave the impression she didn't absolutely love her job? "I fulfill a need for a discounted price, depending on the sale. The client is happy, and so is the customer."

He leaned forward against the table. "And how about you?"

What was this, a therapy session? Did Roz give him this message? He was starting to sound like her. Well, Maddie meant it as much then as she did now. "I'm tickled pink."

His brows twitched, and he dropped her gaze. He reminded her a lot of an unimpressed client. What part of this conversation about giving Holly's a makeover involved his criticism of her character? Her behavior and where she took value in life? How dare he? "Shouldn't you be on the farm, tilling the soil?"

"Christmas trees don't require much tilling." He stood then and gave her a half-hearted wave as if he was brushing her off. "I'll see you around, Maddie."

Why? For more of his evaluations on her person that he knew nothing about? Hard pass. "You need a new exit line."

"Okay." He caught her in his look, and this was the Kevin she was more familiar with. The judgment was washed away—open interest swam on his face. "You look really pretty when you talk marketing."

She straightened as heat settled in her cheeks. Well, it wasn't an apology, but as far as exit lines went, solid ten. She brushed the tops of her thighs and found she flushed too hard to look up.

An older gentleman who'd been sitting between them tapped a pencil on his newspaper. "That was kind of fun to watch."

Holly hopped off her barstool and caught the man on his shoulders. "Behave, Roy."

Maddie was served her plate and left alone to eat. Maybe they didn't know what to say after Kevin's exit. That man. One moment he had her riled up and the next melting.

After breakfast, she headed back to Pam's. Her head was still lost in clouds they didn't belong in, so she reached for what would ground her—work. She sat in the living room of Pam's house with reports from the Hadley account. She read it all, but none of it was sticking in her head. She closed her eyes for five seconds, opened them, and attempted the pages again.

Pam sat across from her, hand sewing a square to a quilt. She had a stack already completed on the floor by her chair. On the opposite side of her, a basket of cut triangles was ready to go. "What are you reading?"

"A client's sales report."

"Looks like a real page-turner."

Usually, it would be. Instead she gestured at the piece in Pam's lap. "That's very pretty."

Pam held up the square, a white background with a sort of star pattern of red and green was stitched in the center. "It puts me in a Christmas mood."

Maddie had a hard time believing Pam needed to do something to be put in a Christmas mood.

The front door opened, and Bob walked in with Rowdy. "Took Rowdy for a walk, and it is a beautiful day."

Right behind Bob, Jo came skipping around the corner.

Maddie might as well throw her reports to the floor. No way she would be digging into dry reading when she had Jo to talk to. The girl must have gotten her spirit from her mother, because her judgmental dad lacked all this positive pep in his step. Unless he was being nice and handing out compliments. Then, well, he wasn't so bad. A moment of panic struck her. Oh gosh, was he about to walk in the door behind Jo? Maddie wasn't sure she wanted to see him again this soon. She did, but then didn't. Ugh, maddening man. "Did your dad go away again?"

Jo plunked herself down on the couch next to Maddie. "He's around."

But evidently not around outside. Maybe he'd be tied up for the rest of the day, doing whatever maintenance trees needed.

Jo curled her legs under her. "I came over to see you."

Maddie's afternoon was looking up. This was the sweetest girl Maddie had ever met. She'd never had people in her life who came to visit her just because. Maybe once upon a time people had offered, but Maddie was constantly in the swim of work and never had time for socializing that didn't involve a business advantage.

"So whatcha up to?" Jo leaned over and looked at the papers in her lap. "Is that your homework?"

Maddie laughed. "Kind of. I need to see if my marketing is working."

Jo's mouth twisted with a puzzled thought. "What is marketing exactly?"

Maddie twirled her pen between her fingers. "You know when you buy a bag of chips? Something made you pick that one brand over the other. I help companies sell their brand."

Bob pulled up a chair and sat with them. "She's a salesman, just like me. She gets a title and more money. But I get to wear comfortable shoes." He showed off his brown loafers.

Maddie laughed. "Not a bad line of work if you're into shoes."

"Ask him another *A*."

Maddie studied him and wondered how she could stump him. "Alexander the Great."

Bob thought for a moment. "A Greek king who conquered the world wearing no shoes at all."

Maddie found herself chuckling again. No doubt, he was a very good salesman. "You could've been a copywriter."

He gestured around the space. "And give up my rented room in Christmas Valley?"

Jo leaned in toward Maddie. "It's a really special place. That's what my dad says."

While Maddie didn't think Bob was sticking

around for the town by itself, she was coming to see the appeal of the location. Not only the town, but the people. Especially this sweet girl. She reached out and curled the ends of Jo's hair around her finger. "Almost as special as you."

Chapter Seven

*K*evin walked into Stan's for his midmorning coffee the next day and halted in his tracks at the doorway. Was he at the right place?

Holly passed him with a carafe of coffee and patted his shoulder. "Don't just stand there gawking. What do you think?"

A wreath hung on the inside of the door. Ribbon trimmed the counter. Even paper snowflakes decorated the sides of the napkin holders. They weren't fancy or perfect. They looked hand cut with glitter glued to them. A string of lights dangled haphazardly around the frame of the serving pass. It was everything Maddie had described, and he was taken back to his childhood. Back to when he was old enough to help his mom decorate but not old enough for his attempts to be perfect.

Holly had nailed every last detail, down to the way the green garland hung loosely on one side. It looked similar to something a nine-year-old version of himself would have put up and asked his mom to fix, but instead she'd have smiled and said, *It looks perfect the way you did it.* He cleared his throat and chewed on a few of the critical words he'd said to Maddie. She may have had a calculated take on Christmas when describing the presentation, but the effect was heartfelt. "Festive."

"All thanks to your girlfriend."

Heat filled Kevin's face. "Not my girlfriend."

"Well, not if you keep talking to her the way you did yesterday." Holly passed on by him and filled Roy's cup. She tapped Roy on the shoulder. "What do you think, Roy? Would we call yesterday an adventure in flirting or a display of judgment?"

Roy leaned back in his chair. "You've got to back off on the judgment."

Kevin eased on in the small diner and headed for the counter. "I was not judging. I made an observation."

Holly cocked a brow at him. "What am I going to do with you?"

Luke rang the bell for an order up. "My money is on Kevin!"

Kevin pointed at his favorite short-order cook and found a seat at the bar. "Thank you, Luke."

Holly flipped him a coffee mug right-side up and filled it. "Still, you should ask her on a date to make it up to her."

He laughed. "Right. That'll happen the day she puts down her phone. Which is never."

"Maybe she hasn't had a good enough reason to put away her phone."

He wanted to laugh at that to dismiss the idea. It would give the immediate socially acceptable response to such a suggestion, but Kevin couldn't quite manage a chuckle. Could Holly be on to something with that? "Think so?"

She arched a brow at him. "Based on what I saw yesterday, trust me. I know these things. Ask her out. She won't say no."

"If I see her again, I'll think about it."

Holly's smile slowly widened. "You keep that in mind."

The dinger over the door announced a new arrival, and Kevin turned to see who.

Maddie walked in, and for a moment, his breath stopped in his lungs. She was strikingly, jaw-dropping gorgeous. He knew this, and still she continually took him by surprise. "We have to stop meeting like this."

Maddie eyed him for a moment and then faced the kitchen. "Egg white omelet, please."

Was she sore at him about yesterday? He didn't think so. She was smiling and coming his way. He knew enough about women to know if he'd crossed a line, she wouldn't look happy to see him.

He swallowed. She was happy to see him, right? That was the only thing that smile on her lips could mean, right?

She sat next to him.

It had to mean something good. Holly must have

been confused. He hadn't judged Maddie yester-day—he'd challenged her. Not the same thing. She was a strong woman. Consider how she efficiently handled the Grinch on the highway. If she'd been bothered by something he'd said, she'd make no bones about directly saying so.

Still, she didn't say a word to him, and he couldn't resist poking and trying again. "All these chance encounters. Are you following me?"

Maddie tossed hair off her shoulder. "You're the one who dropped his trees."

"Then you showed up in my hometown." At his house, with his daughter. Continued popping up in his life as if she were supposed to be there, not temporarily delayed. It seemed like a meant-to-be situation that continued to circle in his thoughts. In all his years of delivering trees, he'd never dropped them like that. And from that location on the road where they'd met, she'd ended up in Christmas Valley. There were multiple other small towns in the area she should have stumbled on first, but somehow she hadn't. Could it be fate or Christmas magic?

He discarded the idea for the umpteenth time, because it was ridiculous, and he was a fool for even entertaining it. There was no way this would ever work out. She was leaving.

Maddie turned a coffee cup over. "How's Jo?"

Then, just when he was beginning to discount anything between them going anywhere, she reeled him back in. He loved that she'd asked about his daughter. She didn't ask about Jo as often as Jo asked about Maddie, but it was nice that Maddie thought of his little girl. Jo asked a lot of stuff about Maddie he wasn't entirely sure how to answer.

Don't you think she's pretty?

Can we go to Pam's to see her?

You should show her around the farm. I bet she'd love it.

Maddie is going to send me clothes from New York! She thinks it's great that I'm taller than everyone, and I think she's right.

How was it that after a few days this woman, this virtual stranger, had such a turnaround on his little girl? Jo wasn't a troubled child, but he couldn't remember the last time she'd been this excited by something or someone. Losing JoAnne had been hard, and Jo was resilient, but her mother was still gone, and Kevin knew it had left a hole in Jo. It seemed, for the moment, that hole was being filled by Maddie. All Kevin could hope for out of this world was that Jo was happy. Ever since Maddie had walked into their lives, Jo had become an ecstatic girl who was thrilled with the idea of stealing more time with Maddie. He didn't exactly disagree with the idea of that either. "She's okay."

"She's a great kid, by the way."

Roy chuckled behind him. "How do you feel about her dad?"

Oh no. There was meddling. Ribbing him without her around was one thing. Putting them both on the spot was—well? While the spotlight shined on them, he faced Maddie, admittedly anxious for a response while also braced for anything. If she would even answer at all.

She fidgeted with her lips and gave him an assessing look over. He knew then she'd answer. She wasn't afraid. She'd been all but dared by Roy, and she wasn't going to back down. Her bottom lip was caught in her teeth as she sized Kevin up and then clicked her tongue. "I haven't decided."

With that, she turned away from him and left him conflicted. *What do you think of Maddie, Dad?* That was one of the ones he'd struggled to answer. He thought a lot of Maddie and wasn't real sure how to say any of it. Because while he'd love to tell his daughter he was fond of Maddie and that he hoped they'd get to know each other more, logistically, it wasn't going to happen. This flirtation was nothing more than a one-time deal.

Maddie touched a set of snowmen salt-and-pepper shakers as Holly brought her a glass of water. "I like all the holiday touches."

"I'll drink to that." Kevin finished his coffee, left money and a tip, and then got up before Holly picked up where Roy left off. This whole idea of wanting to see her more and know more about her was ridiculous and getting away from him. It didn't matter if she liked him. It didn't matter if he liked her. She'd said it as plainly as possible the other night. She was a New York woman, and she wasn't doing anything to change it. Kevin was setting himself up for disappointment by dreaming of anything else.

Luke hit the bell. "You're leaving already?"

Before he said something stupid or was blocked into a corner by a well-meaning neighbor? Yes, yes, he was leaving. "I have to go plant some trees."

Holly moved closer to the door, where she unloaded gingerbread cookies on a tray. She cleared her throat and gave him a hard stare that said he wasn't about to walk out this fast. Her grin was encouraging, with a side of downright demanding him to do something. He figured he had about two seconds to do this on his own.

He turned back and faced Maddie. How could this feel like such a big mistake and the right thing all at once? "Speaking of trees, you want to join me?"

Maddie blinked at him and straightened. There was that look—the shifty, evasive eyes, the need for a quick exit that was so familiar from when Jo asked her to stay for dinner. "I wish I could, but I have to edit some copy."

And there it was. What he'd suspected. Truly, the right thing to happen anyway. He passed Holly a look. So much for her knowing things, but maybe now Holly would give it up. "Maybe next time."

Holly grinned and continued with her cookie task. "There won't be any next time. She lives in New York."

He returned a glance to Maddie. Was she sitting on the edge of her seat? Her hand gripped her bag. Wouldn't she be putting that down and getting comfortable if she wanted to stay? Perhaps Holly was on to something. And maybe he'd hit his head. Despite knowing better, despite knowing it was going to kick him when she left, he still felt that pull. "Then maybe she needs to seize the day."

Maddie looked to be fighting a smile. "I guess I could carve out a little time."

He didn't want to define the emotion that clamored inside of him as she stood. She walked toward him—in her fancy clothes. "You might want to change. You're a little overdressed for farming."

She shrugged. "This is as farm-worthy as it gets. I was packing for Denver and a client who owns a chain of clothing stores. I needed to impress her with my impeccable taste."

Holly nodded at her. "It's so impeccable."

"Thank you."

No. No work talk. No phones buzzing and stress of whatever thing that called her attention. Kevin opened the door for her. "Let's see if we can get your mind off Denver for a little while."

Maddie walked out with him. "Good luck. It's only my career at stake."

He had a feeling her career was fine. He had a lot of questions about other parts of her. What did she love? What did she hate? What did she do in her downtime? What about Sunday afternoons? Big dinners with family? Or maybe she played paintball on the weekend? Options were endless. All he knew about her was that she worked.

Surely there was more to Maddie Duncan than selling women's clothing.

He aimed to find out, and he took her to the farm to introduce her to his first love and happy place. His home and all the quirks and beautiful parts of it. With her in that fancy white coat, boots, and bright pink scarf, she looked more like a model than a farmhand as he took her into the forest. He struggled to keep his eyes off her and on the baby trees he'd loaded on the sled.

Jo was normally his savior in not sounding ridiculous, but she'd grabbed a handful of trees and skipped about thirty yards away to plant. He dropped to his knees and realized he should have brought something for Maddie to kneel on, but she crouched as fast as he did.

Working together, seamlessly at that, he dug a hole and showed her how to place in a tree. Maddie patted straw he scattered around the base. "How long until they're fully grown?"

"About eight years."

"I wonder who's going to get this tree?" She fluffed the straw and adjusted it a bit more with care. "I want you to go to a good home."

Kevin smiled. "The well-dressed farmer, communing with her crop."

She sat back on her heels. "What happened to all those trees on the highway?"

He dropped his gaze and found himself wanting to grab the land. If he gripped the ground and held tight, it couldn't be taken from him. If only it worked that way. "Most of them were too dam-aged to deliver. So I lost another tree lot." Another vendor gone meant another stream of income he couldn't afford to lose. Kevin had known the results of that accident were going to knock him back, but he hadn't anticipated that an entire dealer would close its doors to him.

Maddie's brows pulled together. "One delivery matters that much?"

"We had a flood last Christmas and lost a lot of trees. The tree lots turned to the big suppliers when we couldn't fill orders. They didn't want us back this year and stuck with their new big companies. I can't afford to lose the few lots I have left." He'd put a mortgage on the place to pay their bills after the flood. And now with no one buying, chances of survival were grim. The tree they planted was perfect, but he needed it to be more than perfect, and he adjusted crumbs of dirt to give this little guy the best chance. Kevin lowered his voice so Jo wouldn't hear. "I don't usually plant any trees in December, but I'm not sure how much longer I'll have the farm."

"I'm sorry to hear that." She touched his hand. "Is there anything I can do? Use my calculated take on Christmas to help you out? My going rate these days seems to be in cups of hot chocolate and warm fires."

"We'll be okay." She made him smile, and he liked that about her. It didn't seem as though he'd had enough joy lately to really reach inside him.

"You know, I've been growing these from seed." He pulled off his gloves and rubbed the thin needles of the fir between his fingers. "There's a hundred or so left. It's kind of a sentimental gesture, but I wanted to be the one to plant them while I know the farm is still mine. In case."

She eyed him, and her offer lingered in the air. She couldn't make more lots appear out of thin air. He knew—he'd tried.

She let it go and admired the tree between them. "So this is a special occasion?"

"Yeah, I guess it is." He touched the little tree a bit longer, and pain struck him. All the other trees he'd planted, shaped, and cared for. This one was unlikely to have the same considerate care by him. He sat back on his heels and glanced at the forest around him. Every variety, in different heights, surrounded. They were all as individual as people. They weren't just trees. They were a part of him, of who he was, and his mark on the world. He'd been running this place for twelve years now, never mind the time he'd clocked under the watchful eyes of his parents. It was all slipping away, and Kevin didn't know what he'd do when he lost the place.

If, not when. It wasn't final yet. He still had a few more days to come up with an impossible amount of money.

"I'm really glad I'm here," she said.

He was glad she was here too. This place and being able to share it was what it was always about. That was what his parents and grandparents envisioned. They weren't a money-making industry who counted pennies. They were about family and memories, togetherness and being neighborly. Even those aspects were going by the wayside. "Last year we had two farmhands. Now it's just me. The hardest part is being away from Jo when I make deliveries."

Maddie covered his hand with hers. "The important thing is how much you care." She seemed to hesitate, her fingers combing over the tree. "My father was always working when I was a kid."

"What did he do?"

"He had his own ad agency, hence my name—Madison." She framed her face with a shrug of raised palms. "As in Madison Avenue."

He was at a loss for words. She was named after a street. For money, for advertising. The thing her father associated with her was *selling something*? Kevin had learned enough from yesterday to not say that out loud, but the thought of a father being so detached from his daughter was alien to him.

"So marketing is in your genes."

"I suppose. He remarried and had more kids. We're not close. Just a congratulatory call when I get a promotion."

Rough life. Talk about an absentee father. Kevin called Jo every evening while he was gone. He texted her at stops and kept her informed of how things were going. When he was in town, she was often at his side. "What about your mom?"

"She died when I was a kid."

Keri F. Sweet

That was a kick to the stomach. "I'm sorry."

His gaze strayed toward Jo. She would have it better than Maddie had. He wasn't leaving his daughter or finding a new family. He was both Mom and Dad and all he could be between. And if he stumbled, she had Christmas Valley too. Their family may have dwindled to the two of them, but the town had given them so much to compensate.

Maddie touched him again. "She'll be fine."

He struggled to get air through the sudden lump in his throat. "Nothing matters more to me."

"You know, fatherhood is your best feature."

He found her gaze and was lost in a sea of her blue eyes. Most times he felt like a letdown. He couldn't even work so that Jo was home every night; he had to hand her off to people. For what? He was losing time with her, and he wasn't gaining anything in the long run. He needed something more. He didn't know what that could be, but Maddie's approval and her understanding gaze made the looming future seem less bleak.

Chapter Eight

*M*addie tucked her phone against her ear as she buttoned another notch on her jacket to block out the blistery wind sweeping through the streets of Christmas Valley. Why was it so much colder here than in New York?

She tugged the tails of her jacket straight and continued on to Cory's. She was getting her car back soon. That was all there was to it. And she aimed to find out exactly when that soon was. She had to get to Denver and then get back to New York to stay on top of her new account. It was all floundering in her absence.

At least in Denver she would have tech access to set up video conferences with her team. In Christmas Valley, her only options were phone calls and email. There wasn't enough signal strength to dig in for a time-intensive meeting. All her years of hard work, of climbing to the top, and she was derailed by an alternator and a small town. At least her boss still had faith in her. As far as she knew. She didn't want to know if that had changed.

She rubbed her forehead as she talked to Roz and tried to relay everything she could think of. "Hadley's numbers are up, but we need to boost same-store sales."

The ticking of Roz's nails across a keyboard in her faraway office sounded through the line, and Maddie longed for home. "When will you get to Denver?"

Excellent question. Maddie was two blocks away from the garage and would find out. Cory had called the day before yesterday and said her alternator needed changing. Surely the part was in by now. "On Thursday, Friday at the latest." She hoped. And prayed and crossed everything that she had that it was true.

Roz's typing paused. "The wedding is on Saturday."

Gah, don't remind me. "I know. Don't worry. I'll be there." Maddie wasn't sure if she was talking to Roz or herself. "I better be, after all of this."

"All right. I'll talk to you later."

The line disconnected, and Maddie shoved the phone in her back pocket. What a disaster this trip had turned into. After all the good times she'd had in that Mustang with Aunt Viv, Maddie couldn't believe it had let her down like this. It was her adventure car. Her take-her-across-the-country car.

She worked out some of the frustration with a power walk as the garage came into view. It wasn't

Cory's fault, and she shook her arms to loosen the tension as she crossed the parking lot. Guitar music sounded through the air, and the calming tune worked wonders on her rattled nerves.

It was a country song she didn't recognize that had a fresh edge of soul wrapped around the lyrics. Was it Cory? Gosh, it was good enough it could be coming from a radio, but there was a rich acoustic sound that gave it a feeling of being live. The tune mentally swept her to a place in New York where she'd met a client. Low-key live music and a comfortable vibe perfect for discussing business. She felt all that as she ducked under the low bay door.

Cory's back was to her as he worked the guitar, and, holy cow, that was *him* singing? Color her completely impressed. She was drawn closer, desperate for more when he looked up.

He jumped with a startle, ending the music. "Hey."

"You sound really good."

"Thanks." Red filled his cheeks and to the tips of his ears.

"You should do a YouTube video or something."

"Me and my band are trying to get noticed. There's a lot of competition."

"Yeah. Get some buzz going." Gosh, if he was on YouTube, there might be some way she could use his sound to get him a leg up. Surely there was a campaign on the horizon she could pull his voice in for. He had that smooth, sultry male vibe that would make a nice fit for something during

Valentine's Day. But if he didn't have a track out there, she couldn't pitch him when the opportunity came. "Maybe a Christmas song. It's an easy sell this time of year."

Cory nodded. "I might just do that."

"Making music is only half the battle—the other half is getting it out there." As with everything that was for sale. Maddie turned for her car and touched the fender, noting then that the hood was up. That wasn't a good sign, was it? "Any word on my alternator?"

"They shipped it. It'll get here tomorrow for sure."

Well, that was something. Tomorrow sounded good. Did that mean he could also install it tomorrow, possibly by lunch so she could be on her way? "I really need to get on the road."

"I'll let you know as soon as it's here."

She couldn't ask for more than that. Nagging him wasn't going to make the delivery truck drive any faster. "Okay. Great, thanks. And great song."

"Thank you."

As he nodded, she eased away, desperate to move and do something. She needed to keep her hands busy, and she had nothing besides her email. It wasn't enough. What was email going to do for a presence at Irene's wedding?

She ducked out the door and noticed a familiar-looking large black truck at the gas pumps. That was a distraction, though one she didn't need. What was she even doing with Kevin?

It was a mess, and she should skirt around the side of the building to safely avoid him, but instead she walked straight ahead. "Hey."

He gave her that easy, make-her-wanna-fall-into-his-arms grin. Seriously? Oh, but it was so true. He was competent, caring, and a great dad. An undeniably attractive combination.

"Hey, Maddie. Can I give you a lift?"

Tempting. So very tempting, but she had enough wits about her to resist. Plus, she couldn't sit still. She had to get out of this town, and asking him to take her to Denver was bit over the line. Besides, it was mostly fine. She could drive into Denver at the last minute and be fine. Have the wedding, immediately make the long drive home, and work through to Monday morning. See, all of it, *fine*. She could sleep when she was dead, as her dad would say. "Too much adrenaline. I need to walk it off."

He winced and pointed at the garage, where her car was broken. "Was it because I dropped my trees?"

Look at him. So thoughtful and considerate. He carried the weight of the world on his shoulders with his business worries, and he stood there with his brows gathered in fear that her wrecked situation was his fault. Did they grow men like him in New York and she'd missed them over her spreadsheets? She refused the thought as soon as it arose. No, she had a feeling Kevin Tyler was one of a kind. His snow-and-soil-dusted boots would be running for the hills as soon as he stepped in the city. Too much concrete and not enough community, she would suspect. Oddly, her heart stirred. She was going to miss this place and him once she was gone. "No. My car would've broken down anyway. Better here than somewhere else."

"Oh, okay."

His shoulders eased in visible relief. She should get to walking, but walking would mean she would have to leave him, and she didn't want to do that either. "The thing is, I'm afraid to fly." Whew, there it was. Now she was talking, and she didn't want to stop. "It's the turbulence. One little bump and I practically pass out."

Concern marred his features. "But you've tried it?"

"Only once, and that was enough." Worst topic ever, but a softening sensation blanketed across her shoulders because she was talking to him. She wasn't quite sure what it was all about. He was attentive, and he looked as if he cared about the words coming out of her mouth. Typically, when she talked to people, it was about *their* businesses and *their* lives. They didn't care about the matters in hers. She found herself drawn in a step closer to him by the ready-to-hear-more expression in his eyes, and his head moved slightly her way. "My mom died on a plane."

He reached out and put a comforting hand on her arm. "I'm sorry."

She found it awkwardly difficult not to close the final space between them so she could put her forehead to his shoulder. So wild, but a steady, pulsing need encouraged her to do so. She had to put serious effort into resisting that kind of intimate contact with Kevin. She didn't touch people like that. She supported others, held hands for others, offered assistance *for others*. Maddie stood with him in that parking lot, and realization dug its claws into her brain. Did she have anyone beyond Roz to talk to? And when was the last time she and Roz had sat down for an actual, real conversation not related to work in some way?

"It was a small private charter plane. She was flying out on business. She and Dad used this company a lot. It was one of Dad's favorite planes too. It was freak accident when the engine failed. So, you know, the turbulence and... yeah, so I mostly travel by internet, but this wedding requires I be there in person." She was rambling a bit, but the thought of flying made her beyond anxious.

"It's that important?"

"The bride is my biggest client, whose business I need to keep. It's actually a really big deal that she even invited me." Irene. Goodness, Irene. She was a force. Maddie had been so lucky to land her. When it came to women's fashion, names didn't get much bigger than hers. Irene expected efficiency, perfection, and on occasion, phone calls at two in the morning to talk sales numbers and product plans. Maddie had been all of those things.

Had been? No, she still was, and as soon as

she got out of this joint, Maddie and her thirst for conquering the marketing world would be back.

"I'll be sorry to see you go."

The raw, honest, and tender care in his voice soothed the hard edge of her determination and woman-on-a-mission mentality. As much as Maddie was anxious to leave, part of her didn't want to go either. Christmas Valley had become a pleasant place, an out-of-nowhere soft spot in her heart. She had friends here who weren't work-related associates. Roz was basically all Maddie had outside of work for those nonexistent occasions when she wasn't working. Maybe that was the appeal here—she got a few hours of not-work. But that didn't seem right either, considering she loved her job. Why in the world would she be drawn to something that was the opposite? If she stayed, she could probably figure out that answer, but as appealing as the idea felt, sticking around longer wasn't an option. "Me too."

"Bye."

"Bye," she echoed and started back for Pam's.

All of a sudden, that adrenaline she had needed to walk off had fizzled. She shoved her hands in her pockets and more or less ambled her way to Pam's. Maybe she'd stop by Stan's and see Holly. It was later in the day than she normally went, but there was that pie in the display case she hadn't taken time to try yet. Plus there were new gingerbread cookies. It wouldn't hurt to do a little product testing to ensure it delivered the full, classic Christmas experience.

It was either that or sit in her room. She could see if Pam needed a hand. Until Maddie had her car or Roz called with updated numbers, Maddie was a sleigh without reindeer. She couldn't move forward.

The sound of barking pulled her from her thoughts. Cheerful laughter she'd know anywhere echoed. Maddie turned, spotting Rowdy running her way and Jo shortly behind him.

Maddie squatted to catch the dog for a quick ear rub and accepted his tongue across her cheek. "Goofball."

Jo caught her breath. "Rowdy saw you and took off."

Maddie rubbed the fluffy ears of her new bedmate. Maybe she should get a dog when she got back home. People did that. They took walks in the park with their pets and looked to be having a good time. She saw it all the time when she jogged around the path to try to sharpen her mind to complete a project. She could pop her earbuds in, run with a dog on a leash. Yeah. And then after, she could dump the dog back home while she spent the next eight to twelve hours at work? Maybe even more, depending on whatever current project. Her heart sank a little. She couldn't care for a dog, not on her schedule. It wouldn't be fair to him. "He's a good boy."

"Yep. What are you out doing?"

"I just checked on my car."

"Oh." The drop of Jo's shoulders almost killed Maddie. Jo put on a stiff upper lip. "I wish you were going to be here for Christmas."

At the moment, Maddie couldn't think of anywhere else in the world she'd rather be than in Christmas Valley for the holidays. She would bet it was a once-in-a-lifetime experience. Probably the whole town came together. Not a glass of wine and a box of brown rice crackers to pass the evening away, as Maddie tended to spend her holiday. "I want to get you a present before I leave."

That brightened Jo's spirits. "I don't want a toy or anything."

Interesting. "What would you like?"

She tapped on her chin for a moment and then grinned. "To hang out with you."

Gosh, this kid.

Jo went on. "Come to the farm, and I'll show you how to make a wreath."

Maddie laughed. "I wouldn't even know how to hang a wreath, but whatever you want."

"I can show you. Can we go now?"

"Right now." She held out her hand, and Jo took it.

Together they walked the blocks around Christmas Valley until heading up the lane Maddie had come to know over the last few days. Their clasped hands swung, and Jo's enthusiastic tone with every life event she talked about warmed Maddie more than anything else possibly could. She pointed out different aspects of the neighbors and the meanings behind some of the decorations. Jo highlighted what she'd helped with over the holidays and through the year, and it was basically a culture shock that Maddie couldn't get enough of. Jo's childhood was comprised of everything Maddie had grown up wanting to experience but ultimately had decided only existed on TV. Maddie couldn't help but wonder what else about life and childhood and family she had wrongfully assumed.

"Dad's here." Jo's voice pulled Maddie out of the depths of her bleak memories.

Maddie glanced around, seeking the man himself but only spotting his truck parked to the side with a backdrop of sweeping snow-topped trees. The scenery stole her breath just as much as the first time, but the smell coating the air wrapped around her. She paused and deeply inhaled to soak it in as much as possible. This was the first time she'd noticed the rich, earthy pine scent of the forest growing all around them. Central Park was, without a doubt, beautiful, but it lacked this scent.

Jo led her to a barn, and Maddie couldn't stop smiling if she'd wanted to as they walked in together. Kevin stood to the side, with a tree across a table, and her heart did a quick flutter thing as their gazes met. He blinked at her.

She returned the blink, not knowing what else to do about this man. They always seemed to be passing and meeting back up. So weird. She shouldn't be seeing him right now, had even walked away from him, but yet there he was.

He chuckled. "I could have given you a ride if you were coming here."

"I didn't know I was. I ran into Jo on the way to Pam's, and she invited me to spend the day with her."

Jo skipped into the room, seemingly oblivious to how her dad made Maddie's thoughts go a bit haywire. "We're going to make wreaths together. Maddie is spending time with me as my Christmas present."

Kevin's gaze lifted to Maddie's, and she found herself trapped in that heart-pounding look. "You two have fun. I'll be binding trees and trying to stay out of your way."

And Maddie would do her best to ignore him, but she seriously doubted her ability to succeed at it. Jo served as a good distraction, though, and quickly had Maddie wrapped up in the task of wreath making. With wire wound in a circle and strips of boughs she was to tie on, Maddie tested her natural talent. It turned out she had none. Jo had mastered this skill and quickly set to the impressive work of a lush, thick, beautiful wreath.

Maddie eyed her skimpy contraption and watched as Jo tied another strip of greenery to hers. Maddie could do this. It should be as simple as adjusting the sweeping drape of a promotional display. She picked up a piece and added it to her wreath. It was the biggest hot mess she'd ever seen in her life. She considered herself to be quite the expert saleswoman, but even this was beyond her skill to pass off on someone else.

Kevin walked by, glanced her way, and lightly chuckled. "I like your wreath."

Liar, but his compliment made him that much harder to ignore too. "This is so out of my wheel-house. And so much fun."

Jo passed her more boughs. "You want some more bows and holly?"

"I need all the filler I can get." If she glued ribbon and berries all over it, no one would even be able to see the terrible wreath under it all.

Kevin passed by her again. "If the marketing thing doesn't work out, you have a fallback."

Maddie held up her lopsided wreath. Goodness, it was like a circle that turned into a square that was trying to turn into something else. It was awful and a disaster, but she loved it and held it to her face like a picture frame. "If only New York could see me now."

Her phone chimed. She flipped it up and spotted Roz's name. Maddie answered right away and couldn't wait to tell her about this adventure. She'd get a huge kick out of it. Roz would think Maddie sharing a bed with a dog in a boarding house was something. When Maddie finished with this wreath, she should make another for Roz. Maddie answered the phone. "Roz, you won't believe it. I'm making a wreath."

Roz's clearing of her throat signaled seriousness. "Mr. Warren is here. He'd like a word with you."

Maddie lowered her wreath and straightened. Oh dear. That wasn't good. When had her boss ever called her? Never. Messages were passed through Roz. Or they scheduled an appointment for a face-to-face. He didn't discuss business over the phone. He liked in-person commentary because no one was better at reading a person than Roger Warren. She swallowed a lump in her throat. "Okay."

No click, no passing, no signal of anything. Suddenly, Roger Warren's voice passed through the line. "Hadley wants a presentation on the after-Christmas sales campaign."

"Yes, sir, absolutely. I'm on it." Or she would be if she had access to all of her work. Her job wasn't designed to be handled on the road long-term with multiple tasks to juggle.

"Roz will send you all the information."

The line clicked dead.

Short of breath, Maddie lowered the phone. Her boss called her. Gave a curt message. Then hung up on her. Oh gosh.

She was on a tree farm in the middle of Nowhere, Ohio, playing at—what was this? Her career was crashing around her, and there was little to nothing Maddie could do about it. She had to get out of this place. Corey said the next hotel was an hour away. That meant a bigger town, right? Great. That was what she needed. How could she get there? Could a train even get her to Denver before the wedding at this point? What about renting a car from there? Drive to Denver, come back, trade it in, back to Christmas Valley, get her car, then home to New York. She was getting dizzy and gripped her phone until the hard edges of the case bit into her palms. It was still fine. Her car was supposed to be ready tomorrow. By the time she made any other arrangements, she wasn't gaining much and would only extend her trip back home by circling through Christmas Valley again.

Jo caught her gaze. "Is everything okay?"

No, it wasn't, but it wasn't Jo's problem to stress over either. Maddie pasted her best sales face on to show everything was fine. Her car would be done. She could still make Denver, then back to New York and have Hadley taken care of. This wasn't her first work emergency. She could do this. She gripped the wire to mask her trembling fingers. "Just a work thing. Where were we?"

Kevin clipped something that caused a loud snap in the room. "Bows and holly."

Right. She needed more filler for her pathetic wreath. She wished it were shaped better. She tied on a bow and fiddled with the edges to try to force it into a circle. All that did was create a bendy point on a different side. She tried reaching for that earlier spunk of the day. She couldn't do any work until Roz sent her information, so panicking would serve no purpose. Tell that to her racing pulse. Maddie needed a clear head to tackle whatever was sent her way and currently, that was Jo's gaze.

Maddie forced a smile and tried to sell some enthusiastic participation. "Who says a wreath has to be round?"

Her phone chimed for a message and canceled the sorry attempt she'd made to regain the light-hearted afternoon as Roz's name passed across the notifications. "I'm sorry. I'll just be a minute."

Jo held up a basket of wreath decorations. "You want some more berries?"

"As soon as I answer this email." Maddie read through the information being tossed around for after Christmas. Her ad team was putting a focus on sales and clearance to get people to buy ahead for next year. *No, no, no.* That wasn't the initial goal. They must have crossed the Hadley details with a different account. For Hadley, they wanted shoppers to buy through the winter season. She fired off a quick response to Roz to get her staff back on target. What were they thinking? She checked her email, but there wasn't an unanswered message she'd missed. The rest marinated in the back of her mind so that when she got Roz's response to why the change, she'd know what was going on.

Jo stared up at her, the whole world in her eyes. Maddie rubbed her hands together. She could do this. It was fine. "Okay, I'm back. Ready to pursue my true calling."

She attached a ribbon to one side and worked on looping the red sash into a large bow. She had intentions for this great classic, country Christmas bow with large swoops and long ties. Instead it looked the same as the laces on her tennis shoes when she was five.

Her phone rang. There was no missing the disappointment in Jo's eyes.

Maddie's heart said to let it go to voicemail. This afternoon was her one promise to Jo, and Maddie didn't enjoy breaking that. Maddie always took care of everything she juggled. She could chalk the missed call off on walking through a low-service area.

Her heart said all that. But her head said get the phone. "It might be my boss."

She answered, but there was a click and then silence. "Hello? Roz? I can't hear you?"

There was nothing. Emptiness. She pulled her phone away and saw a nightmare. Her screen was black. Nothing happened when she tapped any of the buttons—and she tried them all. Dead. Over with. Her battery was gone when she needed it most. Maddie faced Jo as her heart formed a knot. "My battery is dead. I have to go make some calls. I'm so sorry, Jo."

"That's okay." Jo's words belied the hurt in her eyes.

Kevin's normal fall-into-attractive gaze was all sharp and narrowed as he focused on Maddie. Super. That disappointed look he pointed her way was an expression that was all too reminiscent of home as she slunk outside. A chill crossed over her that had nothing to do with her inadequate coat for the climate.

Keri F. Sweet

Did she want to leave? Of course not, but what else was she supposed to do? This was fun, and she loved hanging out with Jo. But as soon as her car was fixed, Maddie had to return to her real life where she needed her job. No job meant no home, no food on the table. She didn't know how to explain that to a little girl, and it wasn't a stress she wanted to introduce into Jo's life, either.

Chapter Nine

It had been a long night, and Maddie was in need of some coffee and eggs before tackling another day devoted to saving her job. She *thought* she'd overcome some challenges in the past. There was that one time she'd run eight blocks in heels at lunchtime on crowded sidewalks to deliver a thumb drive of promotional material to a printing press because their email had gone down. Also that time when she'd worked twenty hours fueled on vending machine junk to finalize, print, and oversee a display that was then built overnight.

But those were nothing compared to trying to work her New York City job in Christmas Valley. This town and its limited cell service was going to be the end of Maddie's career if she didn't hurry up and get out of here. She should have gone to the next town with the hotel. She could be cozy in Denver by now with a rental car in the parking lot. That was in the past, though. Nothing she could do about it now, and more than likely she'd be pulling out of town today. This was fine. It was all fine.

Maybe if she said that enough it would come true.

She shoved on the metal door of Stan's diner and was greeted with the tinkle of "Sleigh Bells" playing through a packed place. Holly was bussing a table that had an old-school cloth across the top, a cream color with a pattern of Christmas leaves down the center. Each table had its own unique covering, a variety of reindeer, snowmen, and Santa patterns. Holly had hit the ball out of the park executing Maddie's design ideas. A tickle at how well it had all pulled together lightened Maddie's stress.

Without a doubt, seeing the realization of her ideas was always the coolest part of her job. Holly had taken the kernel of an idea out of Maddie's head and brought it to life with such perfect detail. It never failed to rock Maddie back in her step that this was her job. Maddie got paid to do this.

She walked in, awestruck as she approached Holly. "This place looks great."

Holly stood and blew the bangs from her eyes. She even had on a red apron with a glittering gold front. How cute. "I ordered a new sign and more tables. Holly's is really becoming my thing."

Maddie didn't know which one had a fresher glow—Holly or the diner. Again, blown away this was her job. Not a paying job this time, but making people happy by helping their dreams be successful; what more could she want from life? "Maybe you should have a grand reopening."

Luke dinged the bell as he delivered a new plate of food to the pass. "On Christmas Eve!"

Holly managed to brighten even more. She was always a cheerful person, but there was no denying that jolly-happy redness in her cheeks now. "What a good idea. I love a party." She spun in the diner and addressed the whole place. "You're all invited to the opening of Holly's! Tell all your friends—and their friends." She faced back to Maddie and gave her a sad smile. "I wish you could be here."

Gosh, a kick right to the feelings. "Me too."

And speaking of kicking, Kevin was at the counter again, his gaze shifting between her and his coffee. So much for that fluttery feeling he tended to create in her. As she eased closer, his disapproval was a heavy weight slamming down on her shoulders. She felt like the Atlas statue in Rockefeller Center, but she knew she really didn't deserve the burden. She had a career and a focus on climbing that corporate ladder, a drive for success that apparently didn't make any sense to the most handsome resident in Christmas Valley. His *I-do-not-approve* side-eye was so obvious that it could have been embroidered on his sweater. He glanced at her again, and the look was still there. The feeling grew heavier. She was sorry she'd had to leave Jo, especially for no more than Roz's phone call had amounted to.

She took one of the remaining seats at the

counter, right next to him. This chair had never felt so hard on her bottom. "Hello."

He responded in kind, so there was that. It was a little flat, definitely didn't come with a grin or that entrancing gaze. He barely gave her a glance, and it was so different from the man she'd come to know and crave over the last few days. This guy with his cold shoulder could fit in any café in New York City. All he needed was a phone in his hand. The idea of it left a nasty taste in her mouth. He didn't belong there, and his current cloak of indifference was something she wanted to grab by the fistfuls and strip from his shoulders. Kevin was warm, energetic, and he wore his large heart on his sleeve—for the community and the people around him. Nothing made this morning worse than knowing she was the source of his stoic demeanor as he rested against the counter.

Luke hollered from the pass. "Egg white omelet coming up. I may go crazy and toss in some bell peppers."

Holly forced a laugh in hopes the mood would ease. "A gourmet short-order cook."

Luke's head quirked, the overhead lights reflecting off his dark bald top. "How do you feel about scallions?"

"Great, thank you," Maddie responded. It probably would taste wonderful, if she could get them down past Kevin's judgment, but the look he shot her way tightened around her throat. She had been having fun yesterday, and she wished she didn't have the interruption in the middle of it, but there wasn't much she could do about that.

Her phone chimed, saving her from further awkwardness as she keyed in her response.

Roy turned a page in his paper. She'd come to know him a bit over the last few days and discovered he was a fellow farmer too, but yeah, his gaze was similar to Kevin's. Wonderful. Did the whole town know?

Roy lifted his mug. "That phone of yours has no manners."

Yep, confirmed. The entire town had pegged Maddie a heel with more concern for her work than these people she would never see again.

"Or sense of timing," Kevin added with a side glance from the corner of his eye.

There it was. But she wasn't about to let him get by with a light insult. If he wanted to say something, she would insist that he say it all and they have this conversation. Preferably somewhere else though. If he wanted to talk, she'd stuff her arms back in her coat, and they could go outside. He wanted to act as though his job wasn't valuable to him when she knew it kept him awake and troubled his thoughts through the day too. They may have different careers, but the caring about them was the same. "What do you mean?"

"Yesterday at the farm, it ended kind of abruptly."

"What did you expect me to do?" Did he think she'd wanted to leave Jo yesterday? She'd have given anything to have been able to stay, but she couldn't. Please, dear man, explain her job to her and how she could effectively do it better because he obviously knew her work better than she did. She so wanted to hear it.

"Stay in the moment."

"Yeah." Oh good grief. Knowing they were being watched by half the town, she bit back what she'd really love to say to that and responded to the series of messages steadily pinging her phone. "I wish I had that luxury."

"Being tethered to your cell phone is making a substitute for a real connection with people."

Super. So insightful. So impressive. What a sage. If he took time to understand her job rather than just think he knew it all, he would know she didn't have an option with her phone. It wasn't an eight-to-five kind of job. It was either *tethered* to her phone—and by extension her clients—or lose her job. It was that simple. If she couldn't do it, someone else would, and Maddie liked to eat. And the plain fact of the matter was she *enjoyed* her work. "I'm connected to my clients."

"It was a really special day we can't reclaim." He glanced away. "I'm just telling you the truth as I see it."

What was that? The smarmy put-down that was supposed to make her feel worse because she'd clearly broken Jo's heart yesterday? News flash, she couldn't feel worse. The look of Jo's crushing disappointment had followed Maddie all the way back to her phone charger. And for what? For Roz to give her the update that the newest copy would be forwarded to her in about an hour, as soon as it was compiled and the figures confirmed. She'd left, hurt Jo, disappointed Kevin, and loaded herself with guilt, all for nothing. But the phone call *could* have been something, and it was clear he'd never even try to see that truth.

"The Christmas Valley truth. I live in the real world where making a wreath doesn't come before doing your job."

And she would bet if a fire had broken out in the middle of his forest, he would have put the wreath-making down to tend to his business. That was the best comparison she could make. Her career was burning, and she'd done—and would continue to do—whatever was in her power to put out the flames, even from the wilds of Christmas Valley. Since her work wasn't his work, it clearly didn't rank on the same scale in his opinion. Her jaws were hurting from holding all this back, but Maddie was not going to have the version of this conversation currently playing in her head in front of everyone.

He lifted an eyebrow as if he knew the secrets of the world. "Where does having fun fall on your list of priorities?"

She couldn't believe it. He hadn't listened to a word she'd said about her career since day one. He didn't get it. Her job was fun for her. Look at what Holly had done to Stan's place to transform it. Holly was glowing now, and three days ago she'd plopped on a chair in a huff of frustration that she'd inherited something she didn't even want. Maddie had changed that unsatisfied-and-dead-end-job Holly into someone practically skipping as she worked. "Okay, you made your point."

His totally off-the-mark point. Things Maddie didn't have time for? Arguments with people who intentionally chose to ignore her viewpoint. No, thank you.

"Look, I'm just saying, Maddie, there's an art to slowing down. Sharing Christmas is worthy of your time."

What if he slowed down and listened to the words coming out of the mouths of the people around him? *Ugh.* Why did this man get under her skin so much? Worse, she knew he could wiggle under there, and she let him. It was maddening. He was frustrating on all fronts. "You don't even know me."

"I'd like to..."

If that were true, then he would listen to her when she talked. She started to tell him that when her phone rang. He hit her with another arched brow, as she'd expected. Oh look, there's her phone again, wreaking havoc during a vacation she didn't ask for. So this was it, her moment of choice to be invested in a conversation with him, to prove she had her job, could make personal connections, and enjoy the holidays too.

He shook his head. "If you could just ignore your phone."

She pointed at him with the phone. "Stop reducing me to a stereotype. I worked really hard to get where I am."

"Oh, okay." Condemnation dripped from his voice. "And where is that exactly?"

"A corner office on Madison Avenue." She glanced at the caller. Thank heavens. Not even Kevin's judgment was enough to put a damper to this call. Something was finally going her way as she lifted her phone.

"Is that your boss?"

She gave him her best smile to counter his patronizing attitude. "No, it's my mechanic." And she answered, "Hi, Cory. I'm on my way."

She hopped off her chair and grabbed her things, but the sudden softness in his eyes stopped her.

"Have a safe trip," he said.

"Thank you," she shot back acidly.

"I mean it."

The irritation that had been wound into a knot eased. How did he do that to her? She clenched her hands and headed out.

"Call me." His voice chased her out the door.

He was so wonderful in so many ways as a person, but he had such a blind spot about her career and its importance to her. Look at the way he spent time with Jo and how he raised her. He was caring and considerate and everything a woman could possibly want in a man. He just wasn't for Maddie's life. She walked around the corner, leaving Kevin and all his complications behind. It was time to go home. Unexpected sadness made her stride falter, and she slowed her walk.

Ridiculous. She shook her head and picked up her pace. Cory had called. That meant her car was ready, which meant it was time to blow out of this Christmas popsicle stand. She crossed the garage parking lot with a nasty taste in her mouth from her thoughts. Fine, she could admit it—she'd come to enjoy this place.

Maybe when she wasn't in the middle of a new ad campaign, late for a wedding, and all of that happening right at the busiest season of her job, she would come back here. What did Christmas Valley look like in the summer? Santa in Bermuda shorts with a chocolate milkshake and a jumbo marshmallow tucked on the side of the cup? His shorts would have to be red with a snowflake pattern, of course.

She laughed, but the thought circled back through. Maybe that sounded like a pretty good plan. She could take some of those never-before-used vacation days, actually be prepared for time off, with a system in place for emergencies, and prove to Kevin she had all this at the same time. She didn't begin to have an idea of what that system would look like, but she had months to figure it out.

She ducked in the garage and found Cory leaning over her engine. Her heart stalled. Why was the hood of her car up? On that same note, why wasn't her car parked outside, keys in it, ready to roll?

Cory glanced her way with a twist of his lips that had Maddie groaning. He grimaced and looked back at the engine. "I have good news and bad news."

Aw, crap. Maddie crossed the rest of the way. She didn't know a lot about engines, but she didn't think parts were supposed to be stacked in there that way. The hood wasn't even capable of closing. "What do you mean?"

"The alternator got here." He rubbed the back of his neck. "But it's the wrong one."

Oh my—She couldn't—Words choked in her throat. She scraped her nails across the top of her head. A shriek was climbing up, and she couldn't stop it as she practically vibrated with frustration. "Now what am I supposed to do?"

"Chill, Maddie. It'll be okay."

She closed her eyes and tilted her head back. She was being chided by a kid who was doing his best. "*Chilling* is not in my nature."

"I already ordered another alternator. It should be here tomorrow. Or the next day."

She was going to be sick. *Tomorrow? Or the next day?* Crap, crap. That wasn't going to work. She couldn't do tomorrow. She sure couldn't do the next day. "Maybe I should walk to Denver!"

She felt sick as she left the garage. The nausea didn't leave even as she arrived back at Pam's and pushed inside the front door. Where she *should* have been packing her things to leave and saying bittersweet goodbyes. Instead she was still stuck here with no idea of what to do. Rent a car? She accessed her phone for some research. If the next hotel was sixty miles away, it could be a big town with options. She'd charter a whole bus to herself at this point. Results loaded, and there it was! Her hotel right off the side of a highway. She zoomed in. Off the highway in the middle of another nowhere. Where was a city around here? The urge to scream ripped through her mind, and she resisted throwing her phone. She paced through the house, walking into the den where Pam worked on her quilt.

Maddie had no choice and delivered the news to Roz as her friend answered the phone. She didn't even wait. She spit it out in one breath while she had the nerve and the nausea under control. "I can't make it to Denver on time."

Roz's hesitation spoke volumes. "This is not good."

"Send Irene all the flowers in Denver with my deepest apologies." Maddie paced the downstairs of Pam's house. Disaster. There was no other word for this. An invitation from Irene was practically a demand for Maddie's presence, and she'd freaking blown it.

"I'm sure she'll understand."

"If she doesn't, my new office may be in the basement." Maddie rubbed her temples and paced back into the sitting room. Irene, while a doll, was high-strung, with even higher expectations, and Maddie had failed her. Maddie's entire reputation was based on doing whatever her clients wanted. Her clients wanted her attention—she gave it. It was so much her cornerstone that it was on her business cards. This time she couldn't fulfill that obligation. She was going to be sick.

"What should I tell Mr. Warren?"

Oh gosh. That churn in her stomach jumped to her throat. "Nothing, not yet. I have to figure out what to say."

Roz's heavy exhale echoed the catastrophic problem of the situation. "What are you going to do now?"

What could she do? She could work, but not from here. Now that the Denver trip was clearly off the table, Maddie had to make her compromises and do whatever necessary to climb back up to that corner office she had earned and would keep. She would pitch in some *pro bono* work for Irene, call in any and all of her best favors, and work the best deal any marketing exec had ever accomplished before. "Get back to New York as fast as I can. Less than two weeks until Christmas, I need to be at my desk."

Maddie clicked off the phone and spun in the room for an answer. Nothing jumped off the walls at her, and she plopped on the chair near Pam.

Pam's quilt had gotten quite a bit larger. Maddie usually found comfort in watching Pam make the careful stitches, but not today. Pam's steadfast work reminded Maddie of what she couldn't do right now.

Pam gave her a small smile. "I'm really sorry about your car."

Maddie nodded at her offer of sympathy, but she couldn't sit down and wallow in her frustration. She couldn't even stand still. She grabbed her scarf. "I think I'll go for a walk to try and figure out my options."

"Bundle up. It's cold out there."

Chapter Ten

*K*evin paid and headed out of Stan's—Holly's, whatever the place was now. He knew he was getting gone before Roy, Holly, Luke, or anyone else with an opinion told him what a gigantic idiot he was. He'd picked a fight with her—in the middle of town. As soon as the words had left his mouth and the fire in her brown eyes had turned on him, he'd realized his mistake.

His phone chimed a message from Jo.

Going to Pam's to see Maddie!

He replied with a quick acknowledgement, and his heart sank. She'd get there in time to watch Maddie pack and leave. Jo had grown so attached to Maddie. When Maddie left town, his daughter was going to be crushed. Jo would never let it show beyond a deep frown and sad eyes, but Kevin would know. He feared that Jo's reaction would mimic far too closely what had happened when JoAnne had died. Jo had managed to form some type of bond with Maddie. He wanted it to, but it couldn't lead to anything good.

Now this disastrous fight had happened between them. He needed to find Maddie and try to make things right before she was gone. He'd been too far into their argument to pedal back—

not that he regretted anything he'd said. She didn't understand the position she'd put him in— what she'd done to Jo, the mess he'd be forced to clean up after Maddie left. Maddie had promised an afternoon with Jo, and then at the first beep from her phone, she'd been gone. He wasn't sorry for telling Maddie that she could do better.

He could have, however, picked a better moment.

It didn't matter anymore. Cory had called. Maddie was surely packed up and on her way out of town now. The last memory she'd take out of Christmas Valley was of his criticism. He winced. That was not Christmas Valley. It definitely wasn't *him*. That wasn't what the town was about or who they were. Trying to force her to see his way of life by attacking hers wasn't going to get them anywhere.

With a lump in his throat, he headed for Cory's. Maybe he could catch her before she left, and they could have a moment to talk. He hadn't been kidding when he'd asked her to call him.

When he looked at Maddie, he wanted a lot of things that he hadn't wanted in a long time. When he saw the way Jo looked at her, he wanted even more—a life, a future. Dare he hope for it, something of the forever kind? It was frustrating to want someone so much—all the while knowing he couldn't have her.

He skidded into the parking lot at the garage, and Cory pushed out the front door, big grin on his face, before Kevin could get out of the car.

Cory hooked an elbow on Kevin's door. "You didn't miss her."

Hope filled Kevin. "She's inside?"

"Nope. They sent the wrong part. She'll be here at least two more days. Maybe even three since we're nearly at the weekend."

Three more days? Kevin almost punched the air and stopped short of letting loose a shout. He cleared his throat and contained himself. "You're kidding."

"Nope." Cory gestured in the direction of Pam's place. "She walked that way. All fired up and ready to march herself to Denver."

Kevin wouldn't put it past Maddie to try either. "Thanks, man."

He pulled away and started for Pam's. He wanted to start this morning over, get them back to the laughing and merriment they'd experienced yesterday before her phone had ruined it all. At the thought of her phone, a cold, dark cloud descended on his mind. That phone. He'd never seen anything like it. Even when he'd been at college, his classmates had put their phones away. A bunch of people who'd lived for their social lives could turn their devices off to talk to each other, but not Maddie.

He drove all the routes around the neighborhood, and he ended up parked in Pam's driveway. Bob was pulling the trash to the curb and shook his head as he walked to Kevin.

Kevin rolled his window down, and Bob's chuckle sounded through the air. "She's not here."

Kevin's arms fell heavy by his side. "Cory thought she was coming here."

"She was. She came in. Pam said she paced all over the house, made some calls, and couldn't sit still. She took Rowdy for a walk. Jo's here. She popped in looking for Maddie but just missed her too. She's working on the quilt with Pam. Maddie hasn't been gone long and probably won't make it far. She needs a good winter coat and boots to stay here."

"She's only here for a few days. I'm not sure she needs a new wardrobe."

Red stained Bob's cheeks as he gave the house a fond glance. "Eh, you never know. I was only supposed to be here a few days, and here I am."

True. Anyone could see why Bob stuck around, but why he and Pam weren't officially dating—that was a mystery that no one could solve. Kevin shouldn't be poking his nose into other people's personal lives. His own life was a wreck enough. He put the truck into reverse and headed out to continue his search. Where would Maddie go? He took a chance and headed in the opposite direction of his house. After their last interaction, he couldn't imagine her going anywhere near where she suspected he would potentially be.

He circled the block, the neighborhood, and spread his path out wider. It was possible he could've missed her. He tried one more loop through the neighborhood—and nothing. He texted Jo and asked her to let him know if Maddie turned up at Pam's.

Disappointed, he turned and headed for home. He had work to do, and driving in circles wasn't going to save the farm. A mile away from home, a familiar sight caused heat to bloom in him.

Maddie was walking along the shoulder with Rowdy. She stumbled and kicked at something. Her arms were banded tightly across her chest, and any residual anger he was holding onto from their fight fizzled off. Distress was clear on her face as she tossed her head back—and had she just yelled at the sky?

He rolled down the passenger side window as he stopped alongside her. "You okay?"

"No, I am not." Frustration echoed in her tone. "These boots were brand new, and I didn't even get them on sale."

At least she didn't sound angry about their argument. "All right. Look, let's get you back to the farm and try to rescue them."

She stomped a foot and tucked her hands under her arms. "This coat works in Manhattan, but it's useless in the wilds of Ohio."

Even fired up, he'd take her. He'd take anything she'd give him, because—for the moment—her ire wasn't directed at him. "I'll build us a fire and maybe throw in a little hot chocolate."

She eyed him a moment, and the tight twist of her frown gave way to a smile. "You had me at the fire."

"Come on, get in."

She opened the back door. Rowdy took his spot, and then she climbed in the front next to him. "My car still isn't ready."

He nodded and looked away so she wouldn't see him smile about that fact. "I heard."

"Yeah, I know. Small town."

He laughed. "Buckle up."

She buckled up and pointed the heater at her face. Her teeth slowly stopped chattering as they drove the last bit to the farm. She rubbed her hands together, puffing her warm breath into her cupped fingers with a final shiver. "Thank you."

"You're welcome."

He parked and guided her inside, unable to do so without putting a hand on the small of her back. Her coat barely felt lined. It probably had some minimal inner layer, but that was definitely not intended for long walks in Ohio snow.

He guided her inside and directly to the chair closest to the fireplace. By the time her boots were off and ready to dry, he'd stoked the embers left from this morning back into flames and pressed a mug of hot chocolate in her hands. Her sock-covered toes were curled and tucked under her, and the fact that she was half-sitting on them was the lone reason he didn't have them in his lap warming them in his hands.

Rowdy was curled up next to her, and no doubt the lucky dog was sharing her body heat. Maddie rubbed his ears and buried her fingers in his fur. "Where's Jo?"

Ah, Kevin probably should have texted his daughter the moment he'd seen Maddie. Then again, he wasn't sure he wanted Jo becoming any more attached than she already was—if it wasn't already too late. He didn't know what to do about that. One moment he wanted to encourage Jo to know Maddie since it made his daughter so happy, the next he was remembering how hard it had been losing JoAnne. It had been even harder trying to convey to a six-year-old little girl why her mom had never come home from the grocery store.

"Jo went over to Pam's looking for you," Kevin said.

"I really want to see her before I go," Maddie replied, uncertainty in her voice.

He nodded. As much as he wanted to protect his daughter's heart, surely saying goodbye was better than a sudden disappearance. He was out of his depth here. Teaching Jo about survival, growing trees—all that was in his element. These other issues creeping up on him were things he didn't know how to handle. There were other things—Jo's height. She'd shot above all of her classmates over summer and had been slumping all through this first semester. Maddie had come along, and in a day Jo had been standing tall and proud like the girl he knew. What was going to happen next year, and how would he fix the new problems that would inevitably arise? What would he do when she got older and had girl-related questions and was in need of someone she trusted to talk things over with? He shuddered in fear of that day's arrival. She had Pam—Holly, of course, too—but there was something special about Maddie that Jo had gravitated to.

"You've, uh, made a very big impression on her," he offered, conflicted about stressing the gravity of that impression.

"I wasn't sure I had a maternal bone in my body, but I'm really going to miss her."

A softness filled her eyes and sadness pulled at her mouth. The way she looked punched him in the gut, and he felt the ripples of that impact slam into the rest of him as well. It *was* going to be hard on Jo when Maddie left. As for himself, he wasn't sure he understood how he would feel.

The fire crackled and sparked. He stared into the melting marshmallows floating atop his chocolatey drink. It offered no advice, no options, no answers.

"So," Maddie said brightly, looking everywhere in the living room except at him. "How are my trees doing?"

"Right. Your trees." He laughed. Thank goodness. This was a discussion where he had footing.

"They're pretty straight stock. I'll make sure to give them some special attention."

A smile teased at her lips, but her eyes were downcast. "And what's happening with the farm?"

Now this was a part of the farm he'd rather not talk about—the failure part, losing generations of investment, all of it circling the drain on his watch.

"You know, the flood took its toll. A lot of the smaller farms are going under."

They were right there on the edge, so close to holding on this year. If the weather behaved through next year and he could hook some buyers back, they would be okay. There were a lot of ifs and hopes—it was difficult to maintain optimism. The banks were knocking, and his wallet was emptying. He wasn't going to discuss the looming doom with Maddie.

"I think we'll be okay so long as we get to the end of the year."

"I hope so. This place is so idyllic. I didn't know places like this actually existed."

"You going a little country?"

She glanced away from him. "I have more facets than my wardrobe suggests."

"I know that." He shook his head, wishing that the action could somehow keep his mouth shut. He prayed that he'd not brought up this disaster of a conversation again. He'd been an utter jerk with his bluntness, and he hoped she knew he didn't think of her as completely cold and unfeeling. "I know."

"Well, I couldn't tell by your coffee shop critique," she said.

He nodded. Now he was the one who found it difficult to make eye contact. Without her attention constantly on her dinging phone, could she not feel the charge in the air, the energy that pulled him near? He wished she could ignore her phone for little bit. It hadn't buzzed since he'd picked her up off the side of the road. Getting uninterrupted time with her did things to him—things that increased the longing in his blood.

"I think it hurt because I know it's true."

Wait, what? He met her gaze, but she seemed lost in her thoughts.

"Christmas, kids, stray dogs." She shook her head. "All that was never for me, but now I'm not so sure."

He wasn't sure what had happened or how things had turned around for her, but he was glad to hear it. "I'm sorry about the wedding. I really am. I'm not sorry you're still here."

She chewed her bottom lip. "I have to go back to New York. You live here. I don't want to start something we can't finish."

"I'm afraid it's already started for me." The moment stretched. Was she holding her breath?

His phone vibrated. He was torn, thankful for the break, and also frustrated. He reached for it. He had to make sure it wasn't an emergency text from Jo. He didn't want to hear the hard truth from Maddie about this thing between them being impossible—how it was never going to work. He didn't want to talk about how she was leaving them all behind.

He wanted to go back to the conversation about her falling for Christmas Valley, for Jo—

and maybe a little bit for him?

For all of Kevin's talk about how Maddie was connected to her phone, his vibrated and what had he done? He'd immediately picked it up and looked at it. She could see that he was a little *do as I say, not as I do.* Now he—Wait. He'd put it back down, and his gaze returned to hers.

Well, consider her schooled in the art of ignoring a phone. She wasn't sure this was a lesson she wanted to learn. "I admire your restraint," she quipped.

He smiled a slow, sexy smile. "You're very compelling company."

"So are you." Darn him. How was she supposed to resist him when he talked to her like that, when he leaned toward her as his eyes softened? Everything about this place was surreal. It was a fantasy—it couldn't amount to anything.

Even as she thought it, the mug of hot chocolate warming her hands said *this is so very real.* But it was all too much—the crackling fire, the room, him. It was as if she were lost in a dream. Maybe not so much a dream as a forgotten fantasy of hers from when she was nothing more than a little girl, sitting alone before a tree with the lights twinkling around her. Was this an attempt to recreate a time she'd lost when her mother died?

This mug of hot cocoa in her hands—Maddie could almost pretend it had been given to her by her mom. She'd closed her eyes and pictured moments like this, moments when she wouldn't be alone. Every detail was exactly as she'd imagined it, right down to the marshmallows melting in her cup. Her eyes were opened now. This was no unattainable dream that she'd come out of to find Kevin gone. He was right there, making his way into her heart.

She blinked. It *was* unattainable. This *was* going to end. It wasn't going to be some perpetual happy moment where Maddie's everyday life was in a home full of laughter and love. She would go back to New York in a matter of days, walk into her crisp and tidy apartment. The joy and love of Christmas Valley would fade, much the same as they had after her mom's death.

The nearer Kevin got, the tighter her throat felt, and her urge to stay here intensified. It was ridiculous to be swept up in this kind of emotion so fast, but how could she possibly pretend that the warmth stirring inside of her was nothing but heat off the fire? She knew for a fact it was all a reaction to him. It was frustrating and complicated, and facts were facts. She was leaving soon.

"Which causes a problem, given my departure," she said, a little breathless.

He wasn't deterred, desire pooling in his eyes. She was all but on the edge of her chair. She itched to wrap her arms around him and feel his hands flat on her back, tugging her against him in return. His breath was across her cheek, his eyelids dropping.

It was all so achingly close. Everything about this was a disaster—but kissing him and touching him would seem so right too. This cabin, this beautiful scenery, and this man who kept taking her by surprise at every turn somehow righted Maddie's world, and made the streets of New York feel like the distant memory or the place that wasn't real. She leaned forward to close that final bit of space left between them... and the front door swung open.

A cold blast of air spun through the room, and Jo walked in, stomping her boots on the mat. She looked up and her gaze met Maddie's. The girl beamed. "What are you doing here?"

"Hi, uh." Maddie readjusted in her seat and refused to look at Kevin. "I was waiting for you."

"Yeah," Kevin echoed. His normally smooth voice was strained.

Jo bounced farther into the room. "Wanna go gather some pinecones?"

"Pinecones?" Maddie rubbed her dry, warm toes. "Outside? In the wet and cold snow?"

Jo's giggles eased the tension in the room. "You can wear my rain boots. And my hat and scarf. It's so much fun."

Kevin's hand lightly grazed Maddie's as he moved. The tingle from the gentle touch spread through her body and drew her back to him. Her mind spun from the intensity of the moment, the thought of what had almost happened. It would've been a kiss that would surely have made her need more.

As he looked at her, a flurry of emotions danced in his eyes, and she wanted him to define all of them. What thoughts ran through his mind as his gaze dipped to her mouth and back up? What did he see as he looked over her face? What caused him to blink and glance away?

"It's like an Easter egg hunt, but with pinecones."

Jo nodded. "It's a game my mom made up."

Another hook, right in Maddie's heart. "Then I'd be honored."

"I usually win, but I'll give you a head start."

She laughed. *Gosh, this kid.* "Okay."

Kevin shifted in his seat. "Why don't you give us five minutes, Jo?"

Jo glanced between them and her grin widened. "Okay!"

With that, Jo went back outside and the tension returned with the closing of the door—awkward, but thick with wanting. The fire popped and Maddie was at a loss. She couldn't be here, doing this, falling for this guy, whose daughter she'd already fallen for. But here she was, stupidly doing that very thing and not wanting to stop either.

She tucked hair back. "She's waiting."

"Yeah." He rubbed his palms across the top of his thighs and stood. "I'll grab Jo's winter gear for you."

He walked away and left her wanting everything she'd never needed. His departure scrambled her thoughts. She had couches and fireplaces and hot chocolate at her house too. *But she didn't have him.* He made all the difference.

That was the crux of what was so difficult about his coffee shop critique. Walking in the snow with Rowdy, it wasn't the loss of her car that'd had her so worked up. It was Kevin's dismissal of her and the facts he'd slammed in her face at the diner. Was her work preventing her from connecting? Was she so *tethered* to her phone that she couldn't meet people?

She hated that word. Tethered. As though it was a ball and chain on her ankle. Was it an inconvenience, though, if it was a *welcome* tether?

The coldhearted truth seeped into her bones as she stared into the flickering flames. Maddie wasn't so sure she wanted that tether anymore. The more she was here, in Christmas Valley, the more her work seemed an inconvenience rather than something she enjoyed. It was difficult to wrap her head around that realization.

What else could she conclude? Every time it chimed, Maddie's phone—and her work—

pulled her attention away from the people around her and the experiences she *wanted* to have. That was what hurt the most: the pain in Jo's eyes that Maddie had put there. The girl had asked her for nothing but time, and Maddie had botched it. She'd never failed to deliver on her promises when it came to her work—ever.

She'd worked thirty-two hours straight before, tolerated the worst bosses, the most horrible of customers, and she had completed every task without fail. That didn't mean she had never known disappointment—she'd had plenty. Maddie could handle disappointment on her end. She knew how to come back from that. With Jo, Maddie had screwed up on an epic level. She'd let her down. Maddie didn't have a clue how to fix it, either.

Maddie put on the winter wear, accepted a pail for the pinecones, and they got started on the game. The disappointment in Jo's eyes had haunted Maddie since yesterday. Running through the snow in search of pinecone after pinecone didn't make up for it in the least bit. This wasn't money on the line. The cost was emotional, and the difference was greater than Maddie could have ever imagined.

Jo ran past, a pinecone clutched in her hand. "I have ten!"

Maddie would never make up for her error, but she could ensure that it didn't happen again. She spotted a pinecone a few feet from Jo that the girl hadn't seen yet. Maddie ran, laughter spilling out of her, and she snatched it up. "I have six!"

Jo giggled and dived for another one. That joyful, enthusiastic sound would echo through Maddie's ears every time she saw a pinecone for the rest of her life. Kevin casually walked with them. He didn't have a pail but followed them through the woods with an amused look on his face. Walking with his trees, being on his land—it was a good look on him. It caused a good feeling in Maddie. She was in this strange place, with a different way of life, but Maddie felt comforted and at home. She was happy with her life in New York, but running in these woods, playing this game, was all-encompassing joy.

"This is as much fun as the wreaths." Maddie spotted another pinecone and reached for it. As she stood, she knocked a branch, and a cascade of snow tumbled on top of her.

Kevin's eyes danced, and a smile tugged at his lips. She dusted fallen snow from her hair. She wore a thick-cabled green cap, red coat, her hot-pink scarf, and purple boots. Nothing matched, and now she was dusted with snow. "I must look ridiculous."

He brushed his fingers across her cheek. "You look beautiful."

Jo ran by in a flash of pink, and snow dusted up in her wake. "I have twelve!"

Maddie returned her gaze to Kevin's. A rush of emotions returned and raced over her. "I'm becoming very fond of Christmas."

"You've got a pretty soft touch."

Soft. She couldn't be soft. She was a New Yorker. They were supposed to be hard-edged people. *And* she was an executive. They were the worst of the worst—serious, business focused, all about the money, according to the stereotype. And for years she had effortlessly projected all of those things in order to do her job. Now she stood in this picturesque, beautiful place with this man and his daughter, running around, and—what corner office on what street? The hard-nosed woman she'd shown the world practically rolled over and asked for a belly rub.

"I'm in danger of losing my edge," she teased him.

"In Ohio, no edge is required," he replied.

That was the problem. She wasn't an Ohioan— Ohioer?—whatever they called themselves. This life wasn't hers. In a matter of days, she'd be back in the real world with her job and career and late nights spent alone reading reports. Her days would return to back-to-back meetings and problem-solving all the sales tactics that had gone awry. Christmas Valley would be nothing more than a lovely dream, and her soft side would need to return to its secure box so she could survive the cutthroat business world.

"I had a really good time today. I'll never look at a pinecone without wanting to lunge for it. But this is nothing more than a sweet time-out. It isn't me."

"You sure about that?" His eyes searched hers.

No? Oh crap. Not the right answer. Not the right mindset. "Yes."

How could her heart exist in two places? It was like she was ripping down the middle and she was powerless to stop it. Each moment here pulled her apart a little more.

She managed to find sixteen total pinecones, and Jo kept up her winning streak at twenty-five. They had overflowing pails of them. With a heavy heart, she shored up the shambles of her work ethic and headed home.

Back to *Pam's*, not *home*. This wasn't home. Good gracious.

She headed inside Pam's, skipped a shower and food, and set herself up in front of her computer for hours of devotion to work. This was home—at the computer with the things that needed her attention. Not Pam's house here in Christmas Valley.

A sigh escaped her as the sun set and the moon rose on her steadily flipping through emails, reports, and feedback from stores. There, this was feeling normal again. Maddie gazed around her festive room and locked on a tray of pinecones decorating a side table. Had those been there the whole time? She sat transfixed by memories of a laughing Jo, the fresh winter air, and Kevin's soft touch on her cheek, where a tingle managed to still linger.

Pam paused in the doorway. "You're working awfully late. Can I get you anything?"

"A new alternator?" Maddie tried keeping her spirits up, but her cheer these days fell short of the *ho-ho-ho* kind. Her holiday spirit was the kind that made her celebrate when the Santa pictures were purposely poised near the women's clothing so moms could pick up a shirt or two on impulse while they waited. Christmas Valley cheer was all boughs of holly and melting marshmallows in snowman-shaped mugs.

"Cory promised me it'll be here tomorrow. Or the next day."

Pam leaned on the doorway. "Christmas Valley runs a little slower than most places."

"I noticed."

"If you're in too big of a hurry, you might miss it."

Maddie caught her lower lip in her teeth, waiting for the rest, but Pam just gave a smile. Pam was too polite to go dropping pearls of wisdom without someone requesting them. Maddie gave in.

"Okay, I'll bite. Miss what?"

"Whatever it is you really want." Pam smiled and eased out of the room. "Don't work too late."

"I won't." Maddie intended to sit at this computer until the world was right again, until it returned to the proper tilt—an angle where her email was one of the most valuable parts of her life. She'd regain her normalcy and reset to a sphere that rotated on her nightly glass of wine, just her and the paperwork spread across her bed. Maddie steadfastly worked until her eyes couldn't stay open. She tried to focus on the screen of text before her, but not a bit of it made sense. She saw pinecones dancing before her eyes.

It was going to be a long night, but Maddie would get there—right after she emailed Roz for an overnight package. One of Maddie's clients had an upscale Mommy and Me collection. There was a dress that would be perfect for Jo to wear to Holly's grand reopening.

Chapter Eleven

Kevin walked into the diner at his usual time and quickly took a seat at the bar. He flipped the mug over for Holly and waited. Not for coffee, but to see if Maddie would appear. Based on her usual arrivals, she should be walking through that door any moment. There wasn't much else he had going for him today.

The bank was taking the farm.

He couldn't stop it. He couldn't save it. His last three attempts to find a buyer had netted him nothing. He'd called every tree lot in the county—and the surrounding counties. All had given the same response—*no*. Not one sale to a lot and he had nothing left to mortgage, no savings to empty. Nothing. There was nothing. The land had been taken for collateral first, and then in cleaning up the damage from the flood, he'd been forced to gamble the house too. There'd been so much sludge and muck coating parts of his land, but he'd never anticipated that the cleanup would eat into all his funds or that the lots would turn him away when he needed them most.

He clenched his hands, aching to grab anything, but then relaxed them. He hadn't done enough to stop this. For the morning, he didn't want to think of anything. Or do anything. He wanted to see Maddie, who seemed to be the only person he could talk to. For a moment, he wanted to be able to forget this nightmare.

He couldn't tell Jo. Not yet. He didn't even know how to tell her. So here he hid, waiting for a woman he could never have. In this moment, he found himself desperately needing comfort. The farm was Jo's home, the place where she had memories of her mother, the only life she knew.

Roy snapped his paper open. "Heard you and the missus made up."

Ah, right to the gossip this morning. Kevin turned on his stool and leaned against the bar, wishing more than anything that was true. "She's not my missus."

"She's not going to be if you don't get more direct with her either."

"You know she's not staying." He said it as much for himself as he did for Roy. Okay, more for himself. If there had been anything he could've done, he would've done it, but Maddie wasn't staying.

"Then why do you keep sitting at the counter?" Roy asked.

Kevin laughed. "What is that supposed to mean?"

Roy lifted a shoulder. "Just an observation."

Luke tapped the dinner bell. "What he means is that you always used to sit in a corner booth, but ever since my omelet special walked in the door and sat at the counter, so have you."

Holly walked by and clamped her hands down on his shoulders for a friendly shake. "Stop denying it and accept it." She patted his arm then continued around the end of the counter and got coffee for him. "We all know this is happening."

And he'd like it to be happening, but how could it? It was hard to convince a woman who was bent on leaving. They had two different lives in two different places in this world. How did a couple overcome that? Even though he was losing the farm, he couldn't move away from it all. Leave Christmas Valley—his home, his neighbors who were family? *Jo's family?*

The door dinged as it opened, and there she was—his new daily dose of warm air on a cold winter morning, a warmth that unwound some of the aches echoing through him. How could he not want her, not want to figure some way to make this work?

She turned as she walked in and looked the room over. She glanced toward the added Christmas lights, the additional ribbon, the little touches here and there that Holly had created at Maddie's suggestion. It was a vision, Kevin had to admit.

Holly spun as she walked by. "Welcome to the North Pole of the Midwest."

Maddie nodded. "It certainly is."

Pretty was far too tame of a word to describe Maddie when she talked about marketing. As she looked around, when she saw the fruits of her imagination come to life, there were not enough listings in the dictionary to define the warm glow on Maddie's cheeks.

Luke leaned out the kitchen window. "Egg white omelet, coming up."

"Add anything you like." She sat next to Kevin.

Luke rang the dinner bell. "The Maddie Special."

She faced Kevin then. "Who's following whom? I can't tell anymore."

He'd follow her just about anywhere. Maybe he should. He could follow her right to New York. *And what—move Jo away from everything?* Instantly, the idea of chasing Maddie anywhere was gone. What would he do in New York? There wasn't exactly a thriving agriculture market in the big city. What would Jo do there? It would all be different, and he was about to upset her life enough. He was taking her from the farm. He couldn't take her away from everything else too.

Maddie stared at him, waiting. Her eyes were a delight that he wanted to fall into and forget the last hour he'd spent at the bank. "Oh, come on, I was here first."

Roy chuckled. "Maybe she's here for me."

"*Oooh.*" Maddie's grin broadened and she twisted around. "My secret is out."

Kevin loved that about her—how she'd fit into the town, and her openness with everyone in it. Everywhere he went people commented about her—one positive thing or another, as if he didn't already know. It was nice that everyone else saw those things too.

Roy stood up. "You'll have to settle for him." He tossed money on his table. "I have some grain to take to market, provided I can find a buyer."

Kevin smiled at his old friend. "I believe in you, Roy. Take care." Kevin got as comfortable as he could on his barstool while he tried to ignore the unquenchable want crawling all over him. How could he steal her away for another day, for a few more hours—maybe an evening ride looking at more lights? This time he would reach across that console and take her hand.

Today the cards were not in his favor. Her day was probably already spoken for. On this occasion, he didn't mind her slipping through his fingers because if all went well, Maddie would be spending time with Jo. Kevin didn't have much left to give his daughter, but he'd love to see her happy and smiling one last time before he ruined her life.

"So, Maddie, you have an invitation today from my daughter. I think it involves baking."

Maddie winced and the brightness on her face dimmed with her frown. "I have a conference call with a client."

"Right." He would have to explain to Jo, and they would have to be reminded again that Maddie couldn't be there at their beck and call. Even though she was only here for maybe one more day. Now there were two disappointments he'd have to lay on Jo.

Maddie eyed him, stress evident around her eyes as she bit her lower lip. "Maybe I can come by this afternoon?"

That shined a bright spot on his day. "That would mean a lot to her." *And to me.* He stared at her, hoping she knew exactly how much it meant. "Thank you."

He looked at his plate as that painful knot brought about by thinking of his future eased a little. "Really, thank you for making that compromise for her."

Maddie touched his arm. "I know my work is demanding in ways you don't get, but I promise I would never intentionally hurt Jo. I'll do whatever I can to avoid disappointing her again. I'll even let Roz know my phone will be off for the afternoon."

There it was. That hope, a distraction, her warmth—everything he'd been needing from Maddie to wipe away the awful news from the bank—blanketed him. He feared that the sensation filling his heart was much more than he'd asked for. He fisted his hand to resist the desire to reach out and twine their fingers together.

She gave him a final squeeze on the arm and

sat up, pulling away from him into picture-perfect posture.

Maddie was going to have to start facing facts. She craved all the time she could steal with Jo. All through her conference call, she'd had this fog over her brain. Maddie couldn't remember the last time she'd had to read directly from her notes instead of using them as bullet points. She hadn't been able to concentrate with invading thoughts of sitting in a kitchen cooking something.

Pancakes? Cupcakes? She didn't know, but she hoped Jo knew how to work something in the kitchen because food was not Maddie's forte. Eating it, sure. Cooking it? Not a required element in Maddie's skill set.

Maddie need not have worried. Jo had everything laid out in the warm, cozy kitchen, the ingredients placed just so. Maddie sat down with her bowl and wooden spoon and began stirring.

"You know, I have never made a fruitcake before," Maddie admitted.

"It's really easy," Jo assured her.

So far Maddie agreed. Little of this, some of that. She added the things Jo had portioned out and studied Jo's bowl to see how hers compared. Jo's was more like pudding. Maddie lifted her spoon. The batter poured off, watery. "I don't know. Mine is looking a little thin."

Jo *hmm'd* and eyed the concoction with a twist of her lips that told Maddie all she needed to know. Jo had no idea how Maddie had managed to mess this up when they'd completed each step together, and Maddie had copied Jo, measurement for measurement. Well, possibly Maddie had missed a scoop or two, because she'd been lost in the dazzle in Jo's eyes while she'd been giving Maddie instructions. Jo didn't comment on Maddie's batter, but instead came to her aid and scooped in more flour.

Oh, one of those natural bakers who cook by feel, not by a book. She'd thought Jo had memorized the recipe, but judging from Jo's studiousness and consideration, it looked more like a pinch-of-this-and-that situation. Memories spun around Maggie along with the cinnamon-sugar scent of the kitchen. She hadn't baked a fruitcake before, but she'd seen one baked. With Aunt Viv. Maddie eyed the little girl bursting with life at her side—fruitcake, of all the potential recipes to bake? And Viv's was the car that brought her here too?

Maddie shook her head and stayed in the moment. Nothing more than coincidence. "Secret recipe?" Maddie asked.

"Correct."

Maddie checked their bowls to see how she was coming along again. She found Jo staring at her. Jo's small smile slowly spread. "Thank you."

"For what?"

"My Christmas present. Hanging out with me."

Maddie could have pretended there was some

flour in her eyes, but the watering was probably an overflow from her melting heart. "The gift is getting to be with you."

Jo blinked and refocused on her bowl, and they put some more elbow grease into stirring. The last of the fruit was added, and Jo set out two pans. Jo poured hers in and Maddie did as well, noticing they still didn't look the same.

Maddie eyed them. "I don't know. I bet yours is great."

Jo's brows were pulled together with puzzlement. "I'm not sure why yours is so different. We did everything at the same time."

Maddie had clearly missed a step in her bowl. She eased the two pans into the oven and plopped down for one of those movies on TV Jo had asked to watch with Maddie on her first day. It was wonderful. She snuggled under blankets, got toasty warm, laughed at the TV, and appreciated a whole new side of Christmas as Jo curled against her. She wouldn't be able to watch a Christmas movie again without thinking of this. The one thing that could make this day better was if Kevin were piled up with them.

That's dangerous thinking. Even telling herself that, she couldn't stop the thought. This morning, when she'd announced that she'd turn her phone off, she'd never been surer that he was about to kiss her. She'd leaned away, not because she didn't want him to, but because of how much she did want it. Right now, there was no missing a chill that raced across her shoulder—one a blanket wouldn't be able to fix. That spot only had one antidote, and it was Kevin's arm, tucking her to his side while she cuddled Jo to hers. Maddie didn't know where he was. Jo had simply said he was tending to trees.

It was foolish and it put her sanity at stake, but Maddie was definitely going to have to make time to come back this summer. She wanted to see Jo's world in every season of the year and experience everything the girl desired to share with her. She wanted to take Jo to the mall and get milkshakes afterwards, spend the day at a pool, and another day riding go-carts, maybe even take a road trip adventure in the Mustang. Maddie wanted to give Jo everything Maddie had missed out on by not having a mom. The times Aunt Viv had given Maddie were Maddie's fondest memories. There could have been no better gifts growing up. Aunt Viv had given to Maddie, and Maddie wanted to do the same for Jo.

And she'd also get to see Kevin again. What exactly did a Christmas tree farmer do in the summertime? The oven timer called them back to the kitchen. After they'd turned the fruitcakes out on wooden boards and let them cool, Maddie compared her darker, harder lump against Jo's fluffy, light-brown cake. Jo's looked good enough to have come from a Manhattan bakery.

Maddie poked her fruitcake, and it was like poking a stone. "I think there may be a problem here."

Jo eyed the lump and shook her head. "I don't know what you did, Maddie. I've never seen one look so awful."

"Hey!" Maddie pinched a bit of flour and tossed it at Jo with laughter.

Jo's giggles were as sweet as her fruitcake smelled. Jo grabbed flour and flicked it back. Maddie returned another pinch of flour so she could hear that laughter again. It was a sound she never wanted to forget.

Jo sent a puff of flour to land on Maddie's nose, and Maddie shrieked at the surprise hit.

A door opened and closed, and Kevin walked in. "Whoa. What's going on here?"

Jo couldn't stop her chuckles as she dusted her hands. "Maddie and me made fruitcakes."

Maddie eyed her lump. "Speak for yourself." She picked up her fruitcake and dropped it the few inches back to the board. It landed with a thud. Not so much as a corner crumbled off. "I made a doorstop with cherries and pecans."

Kevin reached over her and picked up a fork. "It can't be as bad as you're making it sound."

"Oh yeah. It is."

He poked his fork in—or he tried. He wiggled and shoved. Maddie wanted to hide under the table.

Jo touched his arm. "Dad, you can't eat a doorstop."

"Your dad can do almost anything." He pushed the fork until it bent and refused to penetrate the fruitcake. He eyed his warped utensil and then Maddie. "This is your fruitcake?"

Maddie accepted her failure with a nod, and heat bloomed in her cheeks. She couldn't make wreaths. She couldn't cook. The longer she was here, the more things she figured she'd find out she couldn't do. But she looked at Kevin, and amusement lit his face as if it didn't matter. She found that she didn't care either, because even though she was an utter failure at fruitcake, she'd never been happier. The feeling was so backward from her real world that she was starting to question what exactly *was* real anymore. "Yeah."

Jo slid her cake over. "Do you want to try mine?"

Maddie grabbed her fork, and the cake flaked off on the tines. The juicy, rich cake and berries filled her mouth, backed up with the slight crunch of pecans. Maddie moaned. "This is the best fruitcake I've ever had in my life. And the best time I've ever had in a kitchen."

Jo beamed brighter than the star on the Christmas tree. "Everything is more fun when you do it together."

Maddie eyed the flour streaked down Jo's nose. "Way more fun." Maddie brushed the bit of powder away. "And a really great memory."

"Right." Jo's eyes met Maddie's as she reached into the flour. Her gaze shifted between Maddie and Kevin. "Especially with your dad."

Maddie followed Jo's intent, grabbed a pinch,

and together they pelted Kevin with flour. Jo giggled. Maddie laughed.

"You like that?" Kevin reached in the canister and returned a volley of flour at each of them. He grabbed more, sprinkling it over their heads. "Uh-oh. Merry Christmas!"

Maddie squealed and Jo dove in her arms to duck a second dusting. "Dad!"

Chapter Twelve

*M*addie stretched across the bed, in no hurry to do anything. She could turn on her computer, check her email, but eh, it could wait. She had a pretty big craving for a thick slice of fruitcake for breakfast. At the moment, finding some snow boots and a warm coat to trek the blocks to Kevin and Jo's was the most appealing idea she could craft together.

There was one problem with that. The more time she spent with Kevin and Jo, the more time she wanted with them. This place was turning everything she knew inside out. She grabbed the covers, ready to throw them back and roll with it, to track down Jo for another fun day, when a moment of sense came to her, and she dropped back on the bed.

This had to stop. This wasn't the real world. This was an impromptu vacation that was ending soon—possibly even today.

A bark sounded from the other side of her bedroom door, swiftly followed by whining and the sound of tiny claws clicking against the floor. She tossed her covers back and headed across the room. She opened the door, and Rowdy ran in, tail wagging behind him as he darted past and jumped on her bed.

She laughed, and now there was a reason worth lying around in bed for. She climbed in with him and rubbed his head. "You certainly have me well trained."

He licked her hand and she curled up with him, not wanting to admit how much she was going to miss this when she left, how much she would miss everyone. Maybe she never should have left her room, never gotten attached. Or maybe she never should have come here at all. A bit of nostalgia, the urge to take a drive in Aunt Viv's car, had been a feeling too strong to resist. That car had brought her here, and now what was she supposed to do on this journey? How could she go back to work after this? What did work really give her besides the occasional congratulatory-but-perfunctory *nice job* from her dad? It didn't even come directly to her from him, but was filtered through Roz. Was Maddie solely working to appease a man who'd left her behind for a new family?

Rowdy's brown eyes searched hers as if he could read her thoughts. He whined, and now she felt guilty. She gave him extra love for even thinking she'd have rather not met him. She accepted a lick up the side of her cheek. "If I could stow you away in my bag, I think I would." She stroked Rowdy's head. "But you would be so miserable without Jo." She sank into the covers. Maddie would be too. She was going to miss that kid.

Her phone rang and she halfheartedly reached back for it, not wanting to lose the attention of Rowdy. "Who's a good boy?"

She picked up the phone and brought it around, expecting Roz.

It was worse. She braced herself when she saw who was calling, and answered. "Hello?"

"Hey, Maddie. It's Cory. Can you come by this morning? I've got good news for you."

Her heart seemed to sink into the mattress. "Okay, I'm on my way."

She set the phone aside and left the bed. She wasn't sure, but she possibly left a part of her still nestled warmly in the covers. She dressed quickly. On her way out, she noticed the package that had come yesterday with Jo's gift. She touched the box. Maddie couldn't even begin to figure out how to say goodbye. Tears pricked at her eyes, and Maddie headed for the garage.

There was a bite in the wind that clawed at her cheeks. It was as though it pushed her to go back to Pam's—but she marched on. It was ridiculous, pretty much all of it. She couldn't stay here. She didn't belong here. She told herself that all the way to the garage. Even as she pulled open the door and the scent of motor oil hit her, she still looped the thought in her head. Problem was, it wouldn't stick. She'd fallen for Christmas Valley, and no amount of self-lecturing was going to undo that.

Cory looked up and grinned. "Hey, there."

"Hi."

"This way." Cory headed through the side door. "Your alternator came, I got it installed, and you're ready to go."

She hadn't realized how much she'd been hoping for news of another wrong part until that moment. She followed him through, and there the car sat with the hood down, confirming his words. "Thanks."

"What's the matter? I thought you'd be happy."

So had she. "Who knew Christmas Valley would be so hard to leave?"

He nodded as if he understood, as if he'd known this all long. Probably he had. He lived here after all. He pivoted and faced her Mustang. "Sure is a nice car. It's older than me and still tearing up the road."

Unfortunately, the road hadn't torn it up enough to give her more time.

She gave Cory a hug, squeezing the young man tight. "I hope you pursue your music."

"That's the dream," he said wistfully.

"Then make it happen."

He smiled at her. "Too bad you have to leave. I go caroling every year and put a rock 'n' roll spin on Christmas."

"Put it on YouTube and send me the link." She

Love You Like Christmas

no longer suggested the videos in order to have something to show to a customer. She wanted them for herself, to watch over and over again, to help her remember. And—a depressing thought—to see what she missed.

"You got it," Cory said.

"Merry Christmas." She got in her car.

"Merry Christmas to you too." He closed her door and then opened the garage bay. The route she'd taken so many times, harboring a fierce determination to blow out of this town flew past, and in an instant, she was back at Pam's and dreading that it was time to pack.

Her heart lay heavy as she pulled her things together. Gosh, could she be any more of a sad sack? She was going home, back to work, back to comfort and city life and everything she craved. She had taken her time, eaten lunch, puttered around until she couldn't delay further, and finally zipped her last case. Bob carried it down for her. Maddie crossed her fingers, hoping the zipper would give way and all her things would tumble down the stairs, putting off the inevitable a little bit longer.

Bob hefted her trusty suitcase as he carried it out the door. "What have you got in here?"

"Encyclopedias." She'd have to buy a volume A when she got home. "And too many shoes."

Bob chuckled. "No one around here would come up with a line like that."

Pam walked with her. "No one has that many shoes."

"It's true. I have a lot of shoes." She looked at Pam as Bob loaded her things in the trunk. "Thanks again for letting me stay."

"My pleasure."

"I had such a great time." And now it was over. The bag over her shoulder seemed to weigh twice as much as it should. The package inside wasn't heavy, but it was the source of added emotional pounds. She pulled out the wrapped box and handed it to Pam. "Can you give this to Jo? It's a dress to wear to Holly's and I—" She waved her arms to try to dismiss the sudden emotional swell. "I hate goodbyes. It's better this way."

Besides, this wasn't goodbye, not really. This was *see ya later*. And the beginning of many more dresses and clothes heading Jo's way. Pam met Maddie's gaze before her attention shifted to Bob. She accepted the gift.

Right. Loud and clear. Pam thought leaving without saying goodbye was a mistake. What else could Maddie do, have some tearful, drawn-out departure? Her heart cracked and she swayed, catching her balance on the car. That scenario seemed so much worse.

She straightened and got her emotions together. "I should get going before it gets too late."

"Drive safe," Pam said.

Bob pulled her in for a hug. "I really thought Kevin was going to get you to stay."

She couldn't contain a heavy sigh. Kevin, Jo— they had come close. If there were any way to do her job from here, she would be going to New York to pack her bags. That was ridiculous thinking, though. People didn't move their entire lives and change everything based on the events of a few days. "It was tempting."

Pam cocked her brow at Bob. "He probably needed to be more direct."

"You think?" Bob eyed Pam with an empty, confused expression. This was no longer about Maddie and Kevin, and Maddie held her tongue. She couldn't go digging into someone else's personal business.

Pam's eyes narrowed a touch as her gaze sharpened on him. She looked at him from the corner of her eye. "I know."

Ooh! Now that was an obvious nudge if Maddie had ever heard one. Bob merely looked confused. Maddie waved it off with a laugh. "I'll miss you both."

She gave them both one last hug. If these two weren't together by the time she came back this summer, uncouth or not, she was getting in their business. It seemed to be the town mission anyway.

Maddie climbed in her car and drove off. Bob and Pam stood at the end of the driveway of the home Maddie had come to love so much over the last few days. She blinked and turned on the radio until she found a station with Christmas songs. The music didn't exactly pick up her spirits, but the song reminded her of her time here, and that put a smile on her face as she headed through

Keri F. Sweet

town. It was a bit of a sad smile. Had Bob actually thought Maddie would move to town and stay? Had Kevin? She toyed with her lip, knowing the worst offender of them all was her. Because she'd been honest when she said she was tempted. This place was unexpected in every way. It wasn't at all possible to move here and keep her current life. She drove through the quiet streets, and people on the sidewalk waved. She was going to miss this place more than she'd like to admit.

She drove past the road that would take her to Kevin's and kept her focus straight ahead. It was hard not to turn, but she feared that if she did, she'd never be able to leave.

She turned down Main Street for a final look at Stan's and found a surprise. Holly and Luke were outside, and there was a crane hefting up a sign. She eased over and parked.

Luke smoothed a hand across the front of her Mustang. "My lord, look at this car."

Maddie was too busy looking up at the work being done. The sign was bright Christmas red with a wreath in the center. *Holly's* was scripted across it. "Look at this sign!"

Holly turned to her. Her hands were fisted with barely contained excitement, and a big grin covered her face. She looked completely unstoppable. "You think it's big enough?"

"I can see it from New York."

"I'll send you pictures when it's all done," Holly assured her.

Maddie hugged her and held on a bit longer than necessary. "Send me the menu, and I'll have my guys add some graphics."

"Thank you!"

She would have the whole nine yards fixed up and send Holly back an amazing spread. Maybe she'd bring back some extra things from this year's decorations to put up around town. Most of the stores trashed their end-of-the-season holiday spreads anyway. They wouldn't be reused in New York, but she could think of a few things that would look beautiful in town.

Now she had to go back to New York for the good of Christmas Valley, so she could bring things back. Maddie felt a smile come to her, and she was happy. Her mom would have loved this place. Maddie didn't remember much about her before the accident, but her mom had loved the holidays and everything winter. It had been her favorite season.

Maddie said a final goodbye and relaxed in her car as she drove toward her old life with its old demands. In a few days she'd be back in a steady routine. The sun dipped in the sky, and snow began to flake across the road. Maddie shivered, fumbling with the Mustang's ancient heater controls to try to get warm. The snow picked up, and she glanced down to figure out the windshield wipers. She looked back up a second later.

A reindeer stood in the road.

She grabbed the wheel, slammed the brakes, and slid. Her heart climbed in her throat, and she snuffed a scream as she veered off to the side. The car lurched, bounced, and plowed into a fence. The momentum rocked her against her seat, and she came to a hard stop, fingers still clutched, breath trapped.

Hair was tumbled in her eyes, and Maddie breathed out as the world steadied around her. Oh goodness. She just—a reindeer? Really? Hands shaking, she managed to get her belt undone as she climbed out. The cold air slapped her cheeks and snapped her out of it. The reindeer still stood in the middle of the road.

She shook a fist at it. "Thanks a lot!"

It snorted and huffed, starting a step her way.

"Yikes!" Fear coursed through her limbs, and she froze. "Stay, stay."

It stopped and she eased toward the front of the car. The bumper was all smashed into the front tire. A headlight was broken. She couldn't drive like this. She faced the reindeer. "I hope you're happy, Rudolph."

She took another step—*ow*. Pain radiated from her ankle. How had she even done that? She limped back to her door and faced the reindeer again. "Tell Santa I'm suing."

Kevin took what time he had left with the farm and walked through his trees. He savored the crunch of the snow, the wind circling through, and the light flurries that danced in the air. He reached out and touched a snowflake. Jo had accepted the news of their losing the farm with the sadness he'd expected. News that Maddie had left town had hit her harder than he'd anticipated and served as a double whammy.

Maddie hadn't even said goodbye, to either of them. Kevin didn't even know she'd been gone until Jo delivered the news—after Kevin told her about the farm. On the one hand, he was grateful to have not experienced that teary goodbye. On the other, he thought, Jo had needed the closure. He would have liked the opportunity to ask Maddie to stay in contact with Jo, at least for a little while. They could have tried a slow bow out—let Maddie get back home, ask her to talk to Jo every few days, then drop it back to once a week or something.

Instead she'd jumped in her car and driven off without a word to either of them. He'd heard all about the hugs she'd given to Holly and Luke. Pam and Bob had seen her leave. She'd left him and Jo in the dark. He knew not to expect too much of her time, but he'd thought they'd be worth a quick wave at least. So much for his plan to not disappoint Jo again. Maddie had left a gift behind, as if that was supposed to mean something.

He should trim and shape up this row of trees while they were still his to tend, but with the state of his attitude, he'd do more damage than good. Instead he walked. Marching a few hills in the snow should work this out of him in no time.

His phone buzzed and he pulled it out. It should be from Jo. While his daughter had moped around the cabin, Pam had called and asked her to come over in hopes of getting her mind off things. He crossed his fingers that the plan had worked and this was his daughter messaging with something exciting and upbeat to show she was back to herself again.

He looked at the screen and blinked at the name. It was Maddie. Why—how? The phone buzzed in his hand again and he quickly answered before she hung up.

"Maddie." Relief had him rocking back a step, and he nearly sat down in the snow. Maybe everyone had been wrong and she hadn't left yet? "I'm glad you called."

"I just had a wreck."

"What?" His throat closed up, and a cold sweat broke out on the back of his neck. She sounded okay. At least her voice was strong—not the same as JoAnne's when she had called that one last time. He sprinted for his truck. "Where are you?"

"Just outside of town in front of a church. This dumb reindeer was in the road, and I veered off and hit my brakes and slammed into a fence."

"You're okay?"

"I may not have a job after I call my boss—"

"But you're not hurt?" He jammed his keys in the ignition, cranked, and was pulling on his seat belt as he left his driveway.

"No." Her voice softened. "I'm not hurt. My ankle is sore, but that's it."

"I'm going to lose service in a bit. I'm hanging up so I can call Cory to get your car. I'll be there in a minute, okay?"

"Okay." Her exhale came through the phone again. "Kevin?"

"Yeah?"

"I really am okay. Don't get yourself hurt coming out here."

He had an inkling that the sour feeling in his gut would only ease once he could see for himself. "I'm glad you called me."

"I'll see you in a bit."

He crossed through town, headed west, and called Cory along the way. Kevin slowed as he took the old highway turns. They were skinny roads, and there was a chance for a heavy snowfall later. This wasn't looking good. If he'd known exactly when she was leaving, he'd have checked the weather and told her to stay put. He'd been so wrapped up in the farm, Jo being upset, and his own disappointment that he hadn't thought about possible stormy conditions that might occur when Maddie drove out of town.

He rounded a bend, and the glowing taillights of her old Mustang came into view. He pulled off behind her, set his flashers, and was at the front of his truck as she stepped out of her car, a slight give to her ankle.

Her cheeks were red, her eyes were narrowed,

and he'd never seen a more beautiful sight as she got out, waving her arms. "I can't believe this," she huffed.

"It's okay." His fear eased. She was okay.

"I know, but *argh*."

He squatted at the front of her car and checked the damage. Not too bad, maybe. Hopefully there wasn't engine damage, but he wasn't sure how safe it was to drive with the bumper that close to the tire. Had he said hopefully? If there was engine damage, that would keep her in town longer. Now he was officially a horrible person for even hoping for that. "It doesn't look too bad."

"Not drivable though."

"Not safely with that busted headlight. I'm not sure about your bumper either." He rubbed his hands together. "Cory should be here any moment. I'll be moving your bags over to my truck."

She caught him by the elbow as he started by. "Thank you."

"You're welcome." Her hand lingered on his elbow, and he couldn't bring himself to mind at all. "I'm, um... looks like there's a storm. I'm glad you're not driving in it."

She nodded. "True. I caught the weather this afternoon on the news with Pam, and it's supposed to go a bit north of here and my route, but I guess now I don't have to worry about it at all."

The hum of Cory's diesel engine sounded, and the headlights illuminated the curve as he came around and then parked.

She smiled. "Fast service."

"Small town." Kevin shrugged.

"Yeah, I know," she said, amused. She shook her head and waited as Cory climbed out. "Hey, stranger."

Cory shoved a rag in the pocket of his coveralls. "Looks like you're hanging out with us a little bit longer."

"How much longer?"

"Well, let me see." He lowered for a closer look at the front and frowned. He pulled at the bumper. "Based on what I see here, I'll have to order a new bumper and a headlight. They should arrive in a day or two." He winced. "Depending on the weather."

She groaned. "Christmas is only twelve days away."

"You'll be on your way soon enough," Corey assured her.

Kevin put her bags in the backseat of his truck. "Sometimes these storms aren't as bad as they predict. We'll have to wait and see."

She walked toward him and stumbled.

He caught her by the elbow. "You okay?"

She blew out a breath, blowing her hair up. "I can't believe you have reindeer in Ohio."

"We have reindeer farms." He pulled open his truck door and helped her in.

"Great."

"I'll take you to one," he offered.

She looked at him as she clicked on her seat

belt and finally cracked the tiniest of smiles. He closed her door, hurried around, and got in. He paused halfway through, putting on his belt as a thought hit him. "Huh."

"What is it?"

"Nothing. I just remembered it was a reindeer that also caused me to lose all my trees on the highway when I first met you."

Color spotted her cheeks.

"I called the local farms and let them know where I saw him. I'm sure they're wanting him back. I'll call them again for an update."

He put the truck in gear and started for Pam's. It was hard not to take Maddie to his house. He had the extra bedroom. It was smaller, cozier—and completely impractical and inappropriate, and she would have something to say about it, so he turned into town for Pam's instead. "So a few more days with us."

"Yeah. I can't wait to tell my boss so I can hear him freak out."

"You're good at what you do. You're not getting fired."

The lights were bright enough in the truck that as he looked over, he saw her smile at him. "Thank you for that."

He shrugged. "You are. I know I've been less than nice about it, but you really are good at it. Look at Holly's." He pointed at her. "I still don't like your bossy phone, though."

She laughed. "I don't always like my bossy phone either, but it comes with the gig."

He pulled into Pam's driveway and parked. "I know a little girl is going to be happy to see you, if that helps your day."

"It does."

He climbed out and met her at the bumper of his truck. She limped and was stepping carefully, so he waited to grab her bags to make sure she made it up the walk. She winced and he stopped in front of her. "Hold it."

"What?"

He scooped her legs out from under her and carried her against him.

She wound her arms around his neck. "Really?"

"Really."

"I'm not some damsel in distress."

"I understand that." Never, even if she was facing down something terrifying, would he think she would admit to needing help—until she had exhausted every other option. "I've just always wanted to do this."

"Sweep some unsuspecting woman off her feet?"

"Something like that."

She rested her head against his shoulder, and it was so worth it. It was corny and silly, and he held her a little tighter than necessary as he took the small steps up Pam's porch and then placed her down once they were on a dry surface.

"You have no idea how much that reindeer cost me," he joked.

The laughing woman he'd come to know was back as Maddie shook her head at him and faced the door. Emotion softened her face as she reached up and touched the wreath she'd made, which now hung on Pam's door. "Oh, that was a great day."

He shifted closer, standing close enough to her that it was personal, but too far away to be intimate. "This one is turning out pretty well."

"Except for the bumper and the broken headlight."

"You can't have everything." *Even though he wanted it all.*

"I guess you're right. You do that a lot."

He eased in closer. "What's that?"

"Get it right."

Her hands were loose by her side, and he reached for them. He wove her small fingers through his and brought them in closer. "I try."

Her eyes lowered. He sensed none of the hesitation that had existed in the unsure moment in his house. She leaned in. The front door squeaked with its opening.

Pam stepped out on the porch. "Welcome home! Cory got the call while he was at Holly's, and she called me."

Kevin backed up. "Hi," he said to Pam.

Maddie eased away while she tucked hair behind an ear. Her gaze met his for a brief moment, and a secret smile danced across her mouth.

Bob stepped out next. "You're just in time for

dinner." He weaved between them. "I'll get your bags. You stay here."

Pam couldn't stop smiling. "I have a warm supper ready and a little girl who is going to be thrilled to see you. I didn't tell her yet you were staying." She looked at Kevin. "Jo should be getting out of the shower any minute. I didn't know if you were going to be late, so I planned for her to stay in case."

"Thanks, Pam. I always appreciate your help."

Pam pulled her cardigan close across her middle. "How long are you staying?" she asked Maddie.

"I have no idea," Maddie answered, stress weighing on her features. "What am I going to tell my boss?"

Kevin had a lot of things in mind she could say—that she wasn't coming back, that she quit, that her boss could take her nonstop phone and flush it down a toilet. It was as unlikely that she'd say those things as it was that he'd keep the farm. "Tell him you tangled with a reindeer and twisted your ankle. Happens all the time," he suggested.

"Not to New Yorkers," she countered.

"If he doesn't buy that, throw in some weather," Kevin came back.

Pam nodded. "A really big snowstorm."

Bob returned with bags. "Worst one in years!"

Maddie's smile was back. "That could work." She leaned off the porch and looked up. "Some snow might help me sell it."

She eased under the porch roof as flakes suddenly began to drift down and onto the lawn.

Bob reached out and caught some. "Well, will you look at that?"

"Not exactly a miracle, but that is spooky," Maddie said.

"You know how much *that* cost me?" Kevin winked.

Maddie swatted in his direction, looking a little starstruck. "Amazing!"

Pam opened the door. "Now you don't have to lie to your boss."

Jo's squeals sounded from inside along with a thunderous pounding of footsteps so loud that they couldn't belong to one child. Jo practically leapt out onto the porch—wet hair, fuzzy pajamas, and a wide smile on her face. "*Maddie?*"

Maddie turned as Jo crashed against her, and Kevin caught them both before they rolled down to the sidewalk. They were a bundle of hugs and giggles and happiness. Kevin made his Christmas wish a little early, something he typically waited for Christmas Eve to do. It was also the first time he'd changed it in years. Normally he made a request for Jo to have a good year and for health and safety for themselves and their friends.

This time, he wanted life to stay exactly this way—Maddie against him and Jo against her as they stood together.

Chapter Thirteen

*M*addie rubbed her temples and managed to resist stomping her foot as she filled Roz in on the situation. Her ankle was ten times better this morning. It had been nothing more than a tiny little twinge last night, though she wasn't entirely sure she wouldn't fake a graver injury later if Kevin happened to come by. He'd picked her up as if had been no big deal and curled her against his chest. It had been romantic and sweet. He had been her knight, rescuing her from the perils of a slick sidewalk.

Which—*hello*—massive red flag. Things couldn't be romantic with them. They shouldn't even be friendly with each other. And she for sure shouldn't be staying up at night wondering what their kisses would be like or if they would ever get to have one. *Argh!* She could no sooner stop those dreams than she could tame her commitment to her work. How had her nonexistent personal life suddenly jumped into equal competition with her career? Was the competition even equal anymore? It seemed as though desire for Kevin was surpassing her need for email. He certainly was the only one keeping her awake at night lately.

Roz laughed through the line, oblivious to Maddie's suddenly complicated love life. "A reindeer. You've got to be kidding me."

Maddie did her best to shuffle thoughts of Kevin to the side for a moment to get focused on work. It was getting increasingly more difficult to do that. "I know, I know."

"Are you going to be able to get everything done?"

"I'll be back by the end of the week." When she would throw herself across her desk, work through all of the holidays, and keep her earned place at the company. Everyone thought Maddie had been a working rock star before—just wait.

"I'm glad you're okay." Roz paused, and there was a very subtle click of her tongue and a soft inhale. "Mr. Warren wants to talk to you."

Crap. Maddie spun in the room, and Pam sent her a sympathetic look. Maddie went ahead and stomped her foot then. Two conversations with her boss on the phone in a matter of days. A clicking sounded against the phone as it was handed off. Maddie braced for him.

"What's going on?" His judgment was thick and his concern lacking.

Maddie had never been on the receiving end of that tone before, where there was an utter lack of confidence. Heard it given to others before, yes. She was so hammered if she didn't get back to work ASAP. "Well, ah, there was a reindeer in the road."

"An actual reindeer?"

"Yes. And then I ran into a fence." There was a pause on the line. This wasn't good enough. "I need a new bumper."

"Can't you just rent a car?" Warren asked.

Her boss was troubleshooting ideas to solve Maddie's problem. Ten in the morning wasn't too early for a very large glass of wine, was it? "There was a huge snowstorm, and all the roads are closed." She was spitballing it here. She needed more. "I twisted my ankle." She looked down and rolled the joint. Her ankle felt fine in her heels. "It's... it's pretty swollen."

Pam gazed at her with an arch of her brow.

Maddie frantically—and silently—waved her arms back in return. Could something big make national news, like right now? Nothing that caused anyone to get hurt, of course, but something big— a national power grid outage that was defrosting freezers all over the nation. That was what Maddie needed.

He groaned. Oh goodness, her boss was *groaning* at her current incompetence. Maddie pulled at her hair. "You know what? I can work from here, and I'll be back as soon as I can."

"Look, Hadley is getting a little antsy, and I can't blame him."

She breathed. There was her warning shot. Not

all was lost, but that had been official notice that she was walking a tight line. "I understand."

"I certainly hope so," Warren warned. The phone clicked in her ear.

She pulled it away, ensured it had disconnected, and collapsed on the couch near Pam.

"Oh boy."

Pam's lips twisted. "Your ankle looks okay to me."

"I needed to be convincing, and the reindeer wasn't playing very well." She allowed herself to zone out for a moment as Pam made stitches on the blanket she was working on. The soothing re-peating pattern of Pam's working hands calmed the spiral of nerves in Maddie. "That quilt is so pretty."

Pam smiled at her and stilled. She lowered her hands, stopping her progress. "It's not just your car keeping you here."

Well. It was, but—"Okay, I'll admit I've gotten attached to this place." Maddie glanced around at the beautiful decorations, the charming home. She felt the love in the room, in the town—from the people too. Maddie had only been here for a short time, but there was so much home and heart here. She'd lived in New York her whole life, and all she had to show for it was that corner office.

Next to Christmas Valley, Madison Avenue seemed—dare she complete the thought?—*lacking.* Goodness, she knew more people on a personal level in Christmas Valley than she did in New York. That place was all business—her business, where she thrived, and once she got back and returned to her routine, would flourish again. "But I know who I am and where I belong."

"You're here right now," Pam chided.

"Not by choice."

"Okay, but while you're here..." she nudged.

"What?" Maddie asked, knowing the answer already.

"Make every minute count." Pam returned to her stitching.

Maddie rested against the couch, thinking about Pam's advice and watching the steady movements of her hands over her quilt. Maddie had promised her boss she'd work from here, but the reality was, there wasn't a whole lot she could coordinate from this end. She'd worked with the pace she could achieve and was all caught up. She couldn't, for security reasons, access the company's internal files remotely, so she couldn't begin any potential adjustments to Hadley's campaign. Maybe three days ago she could have absorbed all that information from Roz over the phone and been able to snap off decisions on the spot. Not now. Too much hot chocolate, not enough graphs, and her brain was out of shape for such a task.

She pushed off the couch and walked around the living room for a closer look at Pam's decorations. They'd been charming and quaint on her initial arrival, but now, as Maddie caressed the thick white cotton of a stocking trimming the fireplace, she realized that much of this was homemade. She walked down the row, reading the names: Pam, Bob, Rowdy. There were Jo's and Kevin's. She moved to the next one.

Maddie.

She faced Pam and gestured to the stocking, clearing her throat.

Pam didn't even look guilty with her big grin. "Just in case."

Maddie traced the script lettering that made up her name. She had a spot, a place. For the first time in Maddie's life, the idea of boarding an airplane didn't seem so bad. She could get home, take care of Hadley, and be back before Holly's party on Christmas Eve.

Maddie closed her eyes and thought of takeoff, and a whirling dizziness washed over her, flinging her eyes open. She put a steadying hand on the mantle as the room righted itself. Okay, maybe not. There were not enough pills in the world to knock her out to survive a flight. She'd tried that the last—and only—time she'd attempted to fly. She'd still managed to pull the seams apart on the cushions. And she'd be lucky if she could even get a flight back on Christmas Eve anyway. She'd been on Christmas Valley time. She wasn't thinking about the rest of the world. This was the busiest time of the year for airlines too. Hadn't she paid attention during her latest screening of *Home Alone* with Jo? No flights, from anywhere.

Sorrow weighed her limbs, and she hugged her

middle. There had to be some way to make this work. She eased down the mantel.

Pam's decorations weren't random items. A light-up angel waved a candle held by its end, and from the texture and craftsmanship, Maddie knew immediately it was old. Likely a beloved treasure, handed down. Every piece, every garland strand, no doubt, had a story behind it and an attachment to a person, a place, and a memory. They weren't things bought simply to appeal to the eye—they were loved. So different than everything Maddie had grown up knowing about the holidays, and so different from what she did for a living, which was sell the image of Christmas. The feeling of being cherished permeated the living room. It enveloped her as she walked past figurines and put on her coat and scarf.

"I'm going to Holly's."

"Watch out for any slick spots," Pam cautioned.

"Will do." Maddie set out through the streets of Christmas Valley. She intended to take a casual stroll, since she had nowhere overly important to be at that particular moment—no meeting waited for her attention, no reports to review. She just meandered. It was kind of nice, taking a lovely afternoon walk. No marketing plans to puzzle out or work complications to unwind. Just her and the fresh air.

"Good morning." She nodded to Mrs. Crantree, who ran the bookshop downtown. The slightly hunched older woman grinned back and echoed the sentiment.

Doug from the hardware store around the corner gave the same greeting, and Maddie found herself smiling at everyone, curious to know when she'd managed to learn who all these people were. A couple of meandering trips and she was nearly local. Mrs. Crantree had joints that would ache on a blistering cold day, so Doug would leave his shop to be watched by his grandson and help Mrs. Crantree out. That neighborly love was all over town.

Maddie jaywalked across Main Street the same as everyone else did and pushed through the doors of Holly's. She was a bit later than normal after her phone call with her boss, and things were surprisingly somber as she stepped in. Luke wasn't bouncing around in the back. He stood directly behind the counter, filling ketchup bottles. Holly wasn't skipping around the dining area with a pot of coffee either.

Something was off from her normal visits, when there were big smiles and bustling activity. Even Roy's eyes were downcast, his shoulders slumped as Maddie sat down on a stool. No flirty, harmless pickup line?

Holly came from the back, arms aimlessly swinging at her side. On seeing Maddie, Holly said soberly, "I'm really glad you're still here."

Holly rounded the counter and sat next to Maddie with a slump that curved her back. "We need to talk."

This was not the posture of a former Ms. Ohio Runner-Up. Maddie searched her face as concern worked up her throat. Something *was* off. This wasn't simply a slow time in the restaurant when everyone was recharging batteries and preparing for lunch. Maddie glanced around and lost her breath a bit. Why did she feel as though she were at a funeral visitation?

"Is everything okay?"

Holly reached over and covered her hand. "It's not about me."

Luke pushed the bottles aside and braced his hands wide on the counter as he leaned over with a shake of his head. "It's about Kevin."

Maddie didn't like this. She didn't like this at all. They looked a bit too far down in the dumps to be mixing Kevin's name in—while he wasn't here, she noticed. "What about him?"

Roy picked up his coffee and stared into it. "I've got a friend who works at the bank. He says that Kevin is going to lose the farm."

Her heart dropped, and she almost tossed up the coffee she'd had this morning. Oh no. Poor Kevin. *Jo.* "He said this might happen."

"He thought you'd be gone by now." Holly shook her head, her expression one of loss. "Maybe you shouldn't say anything. You know how men are."

Luke nodded. "He has his pride."

"There has to be something we can do," Maddie protested.

Roy shrugged. "The big suppliers are crowding out the smaller farms. Most of us can barely stay afloat."

Maddie stood. That was too bad for the big suppliers because Maddie was coming after their stolen market share. And whatever pride Kevin may have, he could stick it. As far as Maddie was concerned, he wasn't losing this farm. Maddie was going to take care of business and that was all there was to it. He hadn't taken her up on her offer before, but this time she wasn't planning to give him the choice. If she had known it was this serious, she wouldn't have taken no for an answer then.

"I don't accept that. He and Jo belong on that farm."

Roy put his hands up and leaned away. "Hey, I'm on your side."

Holly smiled. "Maybe that reindeer kept you around for a reason."

Maybe so. It was time to find out. "I'm going over there to do something. I'm not just going to sit here and watch them lose it."

Luke pushed his bottles to the side. "I'll give you a ride. I just got off and was going to pick up my tree today."

"Thanks." She appreciated the loving support from the town too. While Kevin seemed to admire her and better grasped her devotion to her work, she knew she was very much an outsider in his world. And she was about to break into his place with all her big-city ideas. He might not be grateful. He was going to have to live with it. Hopefully Luke's presence—and his being in agreement with Maddie—would grease the wheels a bit while she grabbed control.

Luke and Maddie were there in no time and parked outside the barn. Lights were on inside, and she headed for the side door.

Luke caught up and jogged alongside her. "Go a little easy. Remember that pride thing."

Pride, schmide. Take. A. Seat. Maddie gestured at the epic, quiet beauty before them. "They can't lose this place."

Maddie pushed through the barn door. Kevin stood with a tree and leaned it against a wall. Jo was in the opposite corner with a long face that broke Maddie's heart.

"Maddie." Kevin blinked at her. "What are you doing here?"

"Saving this place."

He winced. "I know you mean well, but there's nothing to be done."

"There has to be something," she insisted.

"Don't you think I've tried?" he asked, sounding exasperated.

Probably, but he wasn't her, and this was her career, her job, her success in life. It was a bit frustrating that he didn't want to accept her help. He'd mentioned the potential for losing the farm, but he'd failed to articulate exactly the level of dire straits he was in. He'd conveyed the *idea* of foreclosure as a possibility, which was something many business owners said, even when a closer look typically revealed they would be okay.

She wasn't accepting his pride as a roadblock. It had stopped her from saving the farm before, as surely as his trees had stopped her trip to Denver. Luke walked past her. His dark eyes pinned her to the spot. Fine. *Stupid pride.* She rolled back the steam that had worked up between her ears and softened her approach. "I can't bear to think of Jo anywhere besides this farm."

Kevin lowered his head. "How do you think it makes me feel? I couldn't hold back the flood, and I can't fight the times. Family farms are a thing of the past."

Jo ran across the room and snuggled against Kevin's side. "We'll be okay, wherever we go."

Luke shook his head. Tears rimmed his eyes. "It doesn't seem right. Tradition ought to count for something."

Kevin rubbed Jo's back. "I don't want to be the end of the story. This farm has been in my family for three generations. Four, if you count Jo."

That was it, the last straw. They were not losing this place, not on Maddie's watch. It was time to roll up her sleeves and pour everything she knew about marketing into selling a Christmas tree. Same theory, different product. Simple.

"All the more reason to keep it going," she countered.

Kevin gave her a gentle smile. "I appreciate your good intentions. I wish they were enough."

Luke shook his head. "The Tyler farm grows the prettiest, most fragrant Christmas trees in the state. I wouldn't get mine anywhere else."

Exactly. They were special trees and clearly not enough people knew that. "That's really good. I can work with that," Maddie said.

"Work with what?" Kevin looked between her and Luke.

Maddie crossed the room to the row of trees waiting for homes and gestured at them. Currently they were a row of trees. They could be anything, but Maddie was about to change all of that. The ideas sparked in her mind. Little flickers at first, but they burst and a plan took shape. Her pulse quickened with a familiar excitement. She loved her work, but this surge of energy as she formulated their strategy was like the high off a double-espresso shot.

"These trees need to be branded," she explained.

Luke frowned. "They're not cattle."

She smiled. Not with an iron. "They need an identity."

Luke looked at her as if she were crazy. "For a tree?"

"These aren't just trees." She touched the lush needles and the movement of the branches stirred the pine scent. It permeated the air. "They are Tyler Christmas trees. The best in the state. The prettiest, the most fragrant—"

"The hardiest." Kevin had moved to stand next her, and he eyed the row. "The freshest. They last the longest."

She nodded. There he was, starting to get it. "I can sell clothes, shoes, accessories. Why not trees?"

That spark of light dimmed in Kevin's eye. "Most of the tree lots are already filled. How do we get around that?"

The same way every other brand moved past that hurdle when they heard the holiday shelves were too full. If there was one thing to be certain of with selling, it was that retailers *always* had room for a little bit more. "By making the Tyler Christmas tree the most popular brand."

Dots of pink happiness spread on Jo's sweet cheeks. "The Tyler Christmas Tree."

Maddie's mind brightened. "Yes. Perfect."

Kevin eyed Jo, Luke, and then Maddie, and he gave a nod. "I guess it's worth a shot."

Maddie had earned many clients over the years. None had filled her with this cheer, with hope and warmth the way Kevin's acceptance did. "The Tyler Christmas Tree just became my number-one client," she insisted.

"Okay." Kevin shrugged. "Tell me what to do."

Music to her ears! He was entrusting his farm to her care. Maybe some of her ravings about loving her job had made an impression after all. Maddie stared at him a moment longer. She mulled over her feelings for him, for this place. Maybe he *had* been listening to her before. He had the right to be skeptical that she was being honest about her work. Surrounded by this place, ready with this idea to save the Tyler farm, Maddie got the concept of *labor of love*. Selling shoes had certainly never elicited this breathless anticipation to get started.

"Get Luke his tree, give me fifteen minutes to call in reinforcements, and let's meet back up in your living room."

It was hard for Kevin not to get his hopes up. Maddie had such passion and drive when it came to her work. The brief display of fervor he'd seen her demonstrate in Holly's diner was nothing compared to the path she was now wearing in his living room rug with her pacing. Bob had arrived at some point, and Jo wrestled on the couch with Rowdy.

The worst part of all this was Jo's confidence in Maddie. If Maddie failed, Jo would have to suffer the loss of the farm again, when she had just begun accepting it.

Maddie rounded an ottoman in his living room and aimed toward him. She looked up and met his gaze. Her mind was running a mile a minute, judging by the way her eyes shifted. "We're targeting the customer, not just the tree lots."

Kevin perched on the arm of the couch. That theory was a bit backward from everything he knew. Farmer took to the market, conveyed how exceptional his trees were, and in a forest of Christ-mas trees, the retailer steered the customer to their needs. Maddie was talking about skipping the middleman. On a busy highway, okay, that could work—when the farmer was also the market and retailer. But out here? Same as most of the farm-ers, there wasn't enough traffic out in these parts for a roadside stand to be a profitable option.

"How do we do that?" he asked.

Maddie opened her mouth several times and then closed it as she seemed to be discarding one thing after another. "We can put a big bow on top of each tree and make it seem like a gift."

Jo sat up. "A big red bow!"

"Perfect." Maddie pointed at her.

His daughter beamed and Kevin's heart melted. They *needed* this to work.

Maddie continued, rubbing her hands together. "But the packaging doesn't matter as much as the *story*."

"Yes." Bob crossed his arms. "The tree needs a story."

"When you're pitching to tree lots, make it personal. Save the Tyler Christmas Tree and the small farmer." She wrung her hands. "It's not just a product—it becomes a cause."

Bob nodded. "A cause we actually care about."

This was starting to sound cold—that same old calculated take on Christmas again. It came across as gimmick ads from the big guys, the ones who were pushing him out of business, all marketing plans and how to hook people. Kevin's life's work and family legacy had been delighting homes for years, and that had been enough. But what if Maddie's calculated take worked? So far everything Kevin had tried hadn't panned out.

Maddie studied his tree in the corner. "We need a label to hang on every tree. Not just the name, something that creates a mood." She fiddled with the top button of her shirt and closed in on his tree as she studied it.

"Okay. What?" he asked.

She ran her fingers over an ornament Jo had made with Pam, then a strip of popcorn Maddie and Jo had strung together. "It's the people, and the things you do together. That's what really resonates. I never knew that until I came here. Pinecones, making a wreath—that's what I'll think of when I think of Christmas."

There was the heart of Christmas he knew, the one he wanted his trees associated with—but it was a lot to evoke. "So let me get this straight. You think you can fit all that on one little label?"

Maddie nodded. "It should be a picture of the traditional Christmas that all of us always wanted—stockings on the mantle, Jo decorating the tree."

At the sound of her name, Jo was back in the conversation. "I love doing that!"

Maddie smiled her way, then her gaze fell to Rowdy. "Maybe a dog."

Jo tapped Rowdy's nose. "Do you want to take a picture?"

Realizing the attention in the room had zeroed in on him, Rowdy barked and jumped off the couch. Kevin laughed. "If he can hold still long enough."

Maddie stepped back from the tree and framed it with her hands. "I'll shoot it right here. I want it to feel very authentic."

He liked the authentic part—and the traditions. He was also a fan of not losing the farm. He eyed Jo. "What do you think, kiddo. We in?"

"In." She held her hand up for a high five.

He high-fived her. "She's the boss, so we're in." But—timeline? "We're eleven days from Christmas. People are buying trees for the next few days and that's it. This is a lot to do in a very short amount of time."

Maddie's grin broadened. "This is what I do for my clients. I'm going to get my camera, we'll set up, and we'll have our label and brand established by this afternoon. Then we'll start calling those lots." She eyed him a little longer. "Trust me."

It was becoming increasingly harder not to.

Chapter Fourteen

Kevin gripped the ends of the spruce he'd clipped and breathed in the earthy scent for a calming moment. The morning had been a whirlwind. The crushing blow of losing the farm, the knowledge that it could be the last time he walked in his barn, and then Maddie sweeping in. A matter of hours that had bowled him over. Kevin had needed a moment to gather his thoughts, so he'd walked out to check his trees. After Maddie had stepped into his barn with all these ideas, it was as though everything he wanted was right there, almost in his grasp. It was possible that he was going to be able to hold on to his farm. Fate had been sketchy lately, so he was braced for failure as well.

Maddie was so upbeat that Jo had completely turned around. Jo's enthusiasm matched Maddie's confidence. It seemed they *knew* all this was going to work. He couldn't sit still, because if it fell apart, he'd be picking up pieces. He'd finally come around to accepting their loss, but now that Maddie had built up hope again? She was driving back to New York, no harm no foul, regardless of their results. If this failed, he'd have to survive the disappointment once more.

In less than half an hour, Maddie, Bob, and Jo had turned his living room into a photo shoot. Jo's outfit had been changed, Maddie was fussing with her camera and testing lights, and Kevin couldn't sit still while they undecorated his tree and prepared to redecorate it again. It was all light checks, thoughts discussed, and scenery ideas passed around. Kevin was left with a headache. He grabbed his boots and got out.

He clipped another tip off the spruce, took a final calming breath, and headed back to a room thriving with positivity. Maybe they were about done. He eased in the back door, and the comfortable laughter of them together pulled him in. If nothing else, at least he had this for now, something to put a smile on his face. Fate might have been cruel lately in regards to the farm and business, but it had sure gotten something right by bringing Maddie here. *If only she would stay.*

"Wow," Maddie's voice drew him closer. "The lighting is perfect."

Kevin held back, not wanting to be in the way, not wanting to bring his concerns into their festive room and turn the atmosphere into a downer.

Bob sat on a chair with a steaming mug and watched them work. "It looks great."

Jo hung ornaments while Maddie held her camera, pointed, and gave Jo directions. "Hang that one over there, a little bit higher?"

Jo reached and looked Maddie's way. "Like this?"

Maddie bent forward with the camera. "Don't look at me, honey."

"I keep forgetting this is pretend. It feels so real. I do this every Christmas."

Maddie stepped back and eyed the scenery. Kevin waited at just the right angle so he could catch the action. Maddie set her camera down and walked to the tree. "We need some more ornaments on the other side to balance it out," she suggested.

Jo typically trimmed the tree while Kevin sat on a couch, unwrapped ornaments, and passed them up. This time, Jo bent over their selections, picked a large silver one, and passed it to Maddie. That moment, right there—it resonated in Kevin, and it wasn't pretend for him. He could see this happening next year and the year after. Instead of Bob sitting up front, it would be Kevin.

Jo handed Maddie another. "This one is pretty."

Maddie accepted. "Okay. Maybe it should go here in the front?"

So much love filled Kevin's heart. It wasn't about the desire to keep the farm. It was the two of them, working together with thought and care as they placed ornaments, the close consideration Maddie gave to each of Jo's suggestions so that Jo's ideas were included.

The ornament slipped, and Jo darted in, caught it, and helped Maddie secure it on a branch. Maddie eyed their work. "This is harder than it looks."

Jo gave her an amused glance. "Haven't you ever trimmed a tree before?"

"Not since I was a kid younger than you."

Right. Her dad, the man who'd named his daughter after a street, wasn't likely to be passing ornaments around a fire with a plate of cookies and mugs of hot chocolate. That thought had never crossed Kevin's mind. What kind of parent let their child grow up not knowing how to trim a tree? After they'd lost JoAnne, Jo had become his number one thought. He would willingly give up the farm before he tossed Jo aside.

Jo added another ornament, and Maddie's grin grew warmer. "That's really pretty. I usually let a set decorator do all this."

Bob moved, picking up Maddie's camera as he did. What was he up to?

Jo stuck on another ornament. "But this is the best part of Christmas."

Maddie nodded. "Do you think we need more candy canes?"

Jo gave the tree a careful perusal and handed a red-and-white-striped cane over. "I think on the top."

Bob suddenly straightened. "I think I got it."

Maddie gave him a quick glance and turned her focus back to the tree. "Got what?"

"I got a shot you're never going to top." Bob

practically skipped closer to the tree with Maddie's camera and held it out. "That's got to be the label."

Kevin knew, without even seeing the picture, that it was the one. Maddie's eyes softened. Jo's mouth dropped open. They hugged each other at the same time. Kevin didn't care whatever other photographs they came up with or pulled together, their reaction while looking at the picture Bob had taken was exactly what Maddie had described.

Maddie toyed with her shirt button. "I've never been a model before."

Bob patted her back. "That's not modeling. I just took a picture of you being you."

"You're right," Maddie conceded.

Kevin couldn't stand it and eased closer. He wanted to be part of it. Their dreamy looks and loving affection reeled him in. Seeing them lessened the pain swirling in his soul.

Bob looked up and spotted him. "Come here, you gotta see this."

Kevin leaned over, and the photo was everything he'd expected it to be and so much more. "That's the prettiest picture I've ever seen."

In the photograph, Maddie and Jo leaned toward one another as they passed candy canes. Their grins were authentic, but the sentiment and affection in their gazes was what made the picture. It was perfect, and it was frustrating that it would only be around forever in a picture, a fraud of what they really were. The moment had been captured, but it wasn't meant to be real for them. Jo leaned against his side, and Maddie eased over. He could smell the vanilla in Maddie's hair. She was close enough that he could lean over and kiss the top of her head. The moment felt right, but it wasn't. They were—he didn't know what they were, but intimate touching, kissing, they were not those things, as much as he may want them to be.

Maddie stepped back first. "Give me a little bit of time to work up some graphics. Bob has started some pitch ideas for us to consider. I think in less than an hour we'll be calling lots."

From ready to pack his bags to fingers crossed in a few short hours. Kevin had been unable to do anything helpful, and that in itself was frustrating. This was *his* business, *his* farm. He should be the one in the middle with the ideas and creative drive to think up all this stuff. "Anything I can do to help?" he asked.

"Coffee?" Maddie pleaded.

Jo straightened. "What about me?"

Maddie pointed at her. "Snacks?"

Jo gave a firm nod. "On it."

It took Kevin no time to set out a pot of coffee. It wasn't what he'd had in mind when he'd asked if he could help, but it was something to keep his hands busy. After coffee, he worked with Jo to make a batch of cranberry oatmeal muffins. According to Maddie, Jo said, oatmeal was healthy, and so was fruit. So here they were, mixing this batch that had both and pouring them into the pan. He'd cook whatever Jo wanted, so long as it kept him from more stillness.

Maddie and Bob ran through ideas, bounced thoughts off of one another, ran lines. Sometimes they talked at the same time, and it left him with a headache. After the muffins, they baked a fruitcake and followed it up with soup for dinner.

When the noodles had softened in the soup, he forced himself into the living room to face their chaos. Maddie and Bob were both pacing. It must be a salesman thing. They were both on their phones, both turning through pages of notes, and he smiled at their teamwork. Maddie was so determined to believe she didn't belong here, but every time Kevin turned around, it appeared she fit right in.

Bob explained into the phone how the Tyler Christmas Tree was in a class of its own, while at the same time Maddie told her caller it was the best in the state. Both of them hung up with looks that Kevin was all too familiar with. He knew exactly what the buyers on the other end had said in response to their efforts—*no*.

He didn't want to be the depressing one in the room, so he shoved his hands into his pockets and stayed silent. Maybe there was some good news he had missed while cooking with Jo. "How's it going?"

Bob sank down on the couch. "Don't ask. We have tried every tree lot in the county and no takers."

Maddie began her pacing circuit again. "They'll

come around. We have to build momentum, get the customer requesting the brand."

Where did she get these buckets of optimism? Didn't she see it was hopeless? When big suppliers got in the business, Christmas trees were viewed as a dime a dozen.

Maddie caught Kevin's gaze and held it. "This is my specialty. Have a little faith."

Jo leaned against him. "I have faith."

"Thank you, Jo." Maddie gave her a nod.

Well, if his daughter was hanging in there and Maddie obviously wasn't the least bit deterred, he could swallow back further concerns. Also, Kevin suspected that if he tried to get them to give it up and accept the future, they would refuse anyway.

"So, what's the plan?"

Maddie tapped a pen against her palm. "I'll start an online campaign. I'll reach out to some contacts who will help me spread news, but what we really need is a grass-roots movement."

Bob rubbed a hand down his face. "But where do we sell the trees? All the tree lots turned us down."

Maddie shrugged. "We'll have to get more creative."

Suddenly, a look dawned on Maddie's face, and that renewed hope Kevin was trying to be wary of rose within him again.

Now they were talking. Maddie fluffed a green limb. This was getting them somewhere. She'd been walking the streets of Christmas Valley for days and knew the people—but look at them all on the sidewalks this morning! She hadn't ever seen so many out at one time.

The Tyler Christmas Trees leaned against the businesses, the big red bows atop, adding a shine to their local decorations. The trees were lined up all over town, readily available as everyone shopped the Main Street stores.

Maddie fastened a bow to another tree and turned as Holly walked out. Holly, their saving grace. Maddie had gone to her first and asked if they could sell trees in front of her diner. This town continually took Maddie back to her roots, her beginnings. There was no reason the marketing for Tyler trees should be any different. This was Marketing 101 stuff, and it was working brilliantly in this beautiful little town, a town that seemed to love its citizens as much as they loved it.

Holly had not only said yes to a makeshift tree lot outside her door, she'd taken her charm to every business down the street and rallied up the rest of the locals to help too.

"This is so nice of you," Maddie gushed.

"Are you kidding? It's the least I can do."

Yet another vehicle pulled up in front of Holly's diner. A family got out and their teen daughter snapped their picture with a backdrop of Tyler

Christmas Trees and typed away on her phone. *Yes! That's what they needed.* Even better, the family headed toward Holly's diner too.

"I better get back to work. A lot of these folks are going inside to grab a bite."

Maddie cocked a brow at Holly. "Maybe you should do this every Christmas."

"I was thinking the same thing."

Building the brand, creating that buzz, and all in the spirit of Christmas Valley—that was what Tyler Christmas Trees should be about. Maddie walked down the street, checking the layout and making sure there were plenty of trees on display. She ensured all their labels were turned out and fixed to a branch along with a candy cane. Kevin had more trees loaded into the back of his truck, and they had decided to sort them by sizes—from cute little ones no taller than Maddie's waist all the way up to giant ones that stood proudly on the street like soldiers.

She gave her thanks to the owners as she walked. She greeted customers and sold tree after tree. It wasn't enough yet to save Kevin's farm, but it was a healthy start to get them rolling.

That was all she needed. Just for *something* to work, to give Kevin some hope. She'd perused Kevin's reports last night to really see what they were facing, and it was a steep incline. They were at less than halfway to where they should be, and with only ten days until Christmas, it was making him doubt that she could do this. After today, maybe that would begin to turn around. Not that she expected them to be in the black right away, but tonight she'd be up with a pot of coffee to crunch numbers and set their minimal sales barriers for tomorrow for each lot she and Bob were traveling to for their in-person pitches.

She stopped on a corner and spotted Kevin with Luke as they unloaded trees. Longing stirred through her veins, and she would be wise to ignore it. For that, she turned away and continued on her path. She could save his home, and that satisfaction would have to be good enough when she left town with a breaking, torn-in-two heart.

She turned the other way and headed for the garage. That little spot should be their best-selling location. With Cory being right off the highway and a gas station, there should be the potential for tons of people passing through. She'd left a selection of each size with Cory, so customers could plainly see what they had to offer. And if they wanted a certain size in a fir or a certain fullness in a pine? Then Cory directed them into town where they could get the perfect tree for their home.

She skipped across the road to his garage. "Jingle Bells" rocked out through the speakers. Not the traditional tinkling version, but one full of guitars and drums, and she recognized the voice in an instant as Cory's.

Cory stepped out the front and met her outside. "Hey, it's going great."

"Awesome." She eyed the lot, which was covered

in Tyler Christmas Trees. "Are you sure your boss is okay with this?"

Cory shrugged and laughed. "Why wouldn't he be? We're selling way more gas than we usually do."

Perfect. The Tyler Christmas Tree effect was spilling over into the town in ways Maddie hadn't expected. The drums kicked up on the speaker, and Cory's voice belted out the tune. She nodded toward the source of the music. "Sounds really good."

"I'm building buzz, just like you said."

"For a mechanic, you're some kind of singer."

He chuckled and blushed. "Thanks."

She headed back through town to return to Pam's. She did have to check on the Hadley account, too, and discuss with Bob their plans for tree selling tomorrow. She jumped a puddle of mushy snow and waved at the hardware-store owner, Doug.

"I can't thank you enough!" she shouted merrily.

He waved in return. "I'm going to need more trees!"

"That's really good news." Yes, that—*this*—was perfect. She sent Kevin a text to let him know to add more trees to the inventory at the hardware store and continued to Pam's, where she found Kevin eating lunch. That giddiness that always occurred in the first few moments she saw him hit her, and then the rest of the room came into focus. Pam stood there, offering her a plate of sandwiches. Maddie accepted them. Maybe Maddie's blush could be blamed on the cold outside. "Thank you."

After walking the streets all morning, Maddie was famished. There had been no time for an egg white special. She quickly ate two cold ham-and-cheese sandwiches. So simple, plain light bread and a little mayo, no flair—but they were filling and tasted like home. Nothing could have hit the spot better.

Pam refilled the tray. "I bought three trees to give as gifts. This thing that you're doing is spreading Christmas all over town."

An impressive feat for a place called Christmas Valley. "Thank you, Pam."

Kevin rested against the counter and nodded Maddie's way. "And thank you, Maddie."

There. That was what she wanted to see. The sincerity in his eyes was wonderful, but the hope that was bringing the color and happiness back to his face was the best part. All was not lost, and he was finally seeing that. Maddie rubbed her hands together. "We have real momentum in the local market. It's time to approach the lots in person."

Bob turned over a page in the middle of the kitchen table and pointed at a map. "If we start here and head north, we can hit every tree lot in the county."

Maddie followed his suggested path and grinned as he returned to the dot marked Christmas Valley. It was no more than a speck, but seeing the name warmed her. "Christmas Valley looks so small on the map."

Pam rubbed her arms. "It's a wonder you found us."

A gamble of a chance, really, all thanks to her instincts telling her to turn right. Her head said that the snow was over, and she should be figuring out a place to hop a train to get back to New York by the end of the week, but her gut was telling her to stay right there. She couldn't possibly leave. Hadley was in good hands with her team. There were things that needed her attention in New York, but none of them were more important than Kevin and Jo.

She found her gaze pulled to his, and he was staring at her with another one of those looks she didn't know what to do with. There was heat in his gaze, and it stoked an answering desire in her—to walk into his arms for a kiss. She put her finger on the map instead. Romance, no. Just business. That was the most she could wisely give him. "There's the fork in the road. If I hadn't turned to the right, I might not be here."

"Maybe it was meant to be," Kevin suggested.

Maddie shrugged. "I'm not a big believer in fate."

Kevin leaned over her and grabbed another sandwich. The spicy scent of trees and outdoors that clung to him sent chills along her skin. He hesitated there, a little close. "Fate is what you make of it."

She wasn't sure she agreed with him, but if fate

was a thing, it was giving Maddie a run for her money on this little side trip of a lifetime. "Maybe so."

Chapter Fifteen

*M*addie kept her giddiness confined to her wiggling toes. She straightened a label until it lay perfectly against the branches. The label was a cutout of a tree, of course. *A tree you can trust!* had been written across the bottom and the picture of her and Jo peeked from the center. A candy cane was affixed. So far, they were three for three on their lots this morning.

Was it going to be four for four? Bob was a great salesman teammate, and he and Maddie pinged off each other like a couple of long-standing partners. After the first lot, they'd made it to the car, looked at each other, and laughed in joy and surprise at how unbelievably well they'd functioned as a team. Other lots had fallen for Bob's tender description of their trees. When it came to an emotional sell, gosh, Bob shined. Some lots had needed the final push, and Maddie showed off the social media movement and pointed out the people walking around with their phones in their hands.

The big thing Maddie had noticed on their trip so far was that the Tyler Christmas Tree was a bona fide knockout. Every lot commented on how beautiful they were, and how much they wished they could take them—before ultimately being convinced to do just that. There was nothing better for a marketing plan than having a killer product to push.

They needed to add QR codes to next year's label that would link to pictures of the farm. Maddie had spun a hundred ideas for sales tactics to implement for next year, and they'd only been on the road for the morning.

Bob lightly bumped her with his shoulder. "Here he comes."

Maddie nodded and forced herself to move away from their tree. The pine was a seven-footer, robust and perfectly shaped. The branches were thick, the needles full. There were no skimpy bare spots on this sucker. She could picture how the lights would twinkle from the center like lightning bugs.

The lot owner, a jolly guy with a lovely smile and a Santa hat keeping his ears warm walked a circle around their tree. He nodded as he moved, brows raised as he touched. "I gotta say, it's a really pretty tree."

Maddie eased back, already sensing this guy's style. Bob picked up on her subtle adjustment and immediately reacted to her cue and took the lead.

She would let him make that first heart-to-heart connection.

"Fragrant, hardy, admirable needle retention, and they last longer than most. Means lots more memories."

Maddie added some facts. "It took three generations of farmers to grow a tree as perfect as this one."

Bob rounded out their elevator pitch with a circle back to the emotional way he naturally spoke. "And it's for a good cause—the smaller farms really need our support."

The lot owner was smiling. He was beginning to nod.

A woman walked by, excusing herself as she eased between them. She stopped. "Oh, this is lovely."

Bob reached around and tapped their label. "It's a Tyler Christmas Tree, the best you can buy."

The woman's gaze fell on the photograph and there was that spark, that moment Maddie hoped to inspire in all the customers. Sure, people were out here making traditions, but it was stressful. It was shopping. It was nine days until Christmas, people had a hundred things to do and think about—but *that* look, the overall expression as the woman's head tipped to the side, embodied the essence of why she was out in the middle of this crowd trying to find a perfect tree. The family, the magic, the reminder of Christmas morning.

The woman smiled at the label. "Oh, *oh*, that's very sweet."

A boy appeared next to her and leaned in to touch a branch. "Can we get this one?"

A man was right behind them. He pulled the boy under one arm, the woman under the other. "I guess we found our tree."

The lot salesman nodded and looked at Maddie and Bob. "Okay. You got me."

Four for four! She shared a sly fist bump with Bob, wrapped up the details of how many trees they'd deliver in the morning, and headed on to the next stop.

Maddie adjusted the car vents and breathed in the lovely pine scent that filled the back seat of their SUV. All the seats had been laid flat, and they'd pushed and pulled as carefully as possible to pack as many trees in as they could. They scouted each lot before even meeting with the lot dealer to find out what varieties they were overflowing with and selected something unique to make them stand out against the high supply.

It was the most bizarre thing Maddie had ever marketed, and she loved it. "I feel like a traveling salesman. I kinda like it."

"I like selling something I believe in. I go out and peddle vacuum cleaners, encyclopedias, and all that in the warmer months, but it's not the same as this. Having my faith in something is 'awesome' with a capital *A*."

That was the clincher. She was proud of her

work—clothes and shoes, *omigod*—but selling these trees, saving the farm, it was so heartfelt. It was something else. She was afraid she wouldn't be able to duplicate this depth of meaning with her work back home.

She turned toward Bob. "You need to keep this up after I'm gone. Start ramping up for next year. Write some copy and send out a catalogue, get a website going."

"Sounds like a plan," Bob said.

"There are a lot of small farmers who could use a good rep. You can earn a steady living and do some good." In Maddie's research, she'd discovered seasonal farms in every county. It would be simple for Bob to manage them. He could pitch the success with the Tyler farm, tie each new farm's product into the current branding, and always be back home for supper with Pam. Where they would go their separate ways at night, which was a shame.

Maddie had a good eye, and there was a spark there. It was in every subtle look, every hand on Pam's back, even in the way Pam fixed his plate. But yet, nothing! No kissing. No hand holding. Not so much as a lingering look—only the ones tossed at each other behind their backs. Maddie cleared her throat. She had said she'd meddle on her return to Christmas Valley if they weren't together, and technically she had left and returned.

"You know, what you do about Pam is up to you. *But* I think it's time you made a move. I'm just saying."

Bob cast her a sly glance. "*Just saying?*"

She gave him an innocent shrug and felt as if she'd earned her Christmas Valley resident badge. If such a thing existed, she would wear it with pride.

"What about you and Kevin?" he countered.

Oh darn. She'd walked right into that. She suddenly took a keen interest in her lap, and thankfully she was quickly rescued by her phone. She turned the screen over, and it wasn't Jo or Kevin. It was Roz. Maddie should have been expecting her, since Roz had messaged earlier about this call. "Hey, Roz."

"I've got updates for you," her assistant chirped.

Maddie looked out the windows at the passing Ohio landscape. "Send them to me and go ahead and schedule the presentation. I'll be home in a few days."

Kevin had never seen his barn so busy and happy. It was all due to that beautiful blonde standing ten feet away, wearing the same pink scarf she'd had on the first time they'd met. She might as well be in New York now for all the chance he had of holding onto her. If only he could convince her to take a chance on him, like the chance she'd taken on his trees.

Maddie and Bob had returned from their county-wide sales trip, and Kevin found his knees weak as they updated him on the news. He'd hoped for success, but as he'd numbly sat while they'd given him numbers, he realized he'd been expecting disappointment. Which had been a grand mistake.

After he'd dazedly absorbed their success, the realization that he was not ready to ship out that many trees the following morning hit him quick. Some lots had asked for five trees as a trial for this year. Others wanted twenty. Most of Kevin's ready inventory had been moved into downtown Christmas Valley and already found homes.

While he mentally crunched numbers to figure out how late he'd be up tonight readying and loading trees, Pam got on the phone and started making calls for help. Jo got her coat. Maddie and Bob got theirs, and they all stood at the door, waiting on him.

He wasn't sure what had happened. Kevin knew he lived in an amazing community. He knew the people were here for him. What he hadn't counted on was how they'd show up and lend a hand. How the farm wasn't only important to him and his family, but to all of Christmas Valley.

That was never clearer until now as his friends stood in his barn, helping him ready trees to deliver tomorrow. His farm was saved. They were going to be okay. Kevin couldn't quite get the impossible thought to stick in his mind. As he looked around at the cheerful workers in his barn while Cory's music played from the stereo, he also couldn't quite get that lump in his throat to go down either. It was a ball of emotion, one he'd been choking on all afternoon. It lingered now into the evening as they worked but for entirely different reasons. Maddie and Jo were tying big red bows. Pam and Holly were stringing labels with candy canes. They all danced with the music. Even Roy did a little side-to-side dance step while he built tree stands. Bob painted them in their new signature color, red. Cory wrapped trees for loading. The bay loading doors were opened, and Christmas lights had been draped from the ceiling to add more light for everyone. The barn was filled with people and bursting with love.

Maddie had talked about making her clients happy, and he'd disregarded her job as some big-city gimmick stuff. Now that he was on the receiving end of her work, of *her*, he realized how foolish he'd been. She'd thrown herself all in to help him, and he'd never be able to repay her for that, though he wished she'd give him a lifetime to try.

Luke helped Kevin load trees. Kevin smiled at the happiness of the occasion. His family. A hodge-podge of townspeople, all working together to save him.

Holly tied off another bow and danced to Cory's music. "You guys sound so good."

Maddie swung around. "You should have them play at your reopening."

Holly inhaled and looked thoughtful for a split second. "You're hired."

Kevin didn't think he'd ever seen Cory blush that hard before. "Cool."

Kevin grabbed another tree and walked with Luke to strap it down. "I just want to say I appreciate you being here," he said to the younger man.

Luke laughed and looked at the party taking place. "It's a Christmas hoedown. You got your place looking like *Hee-Haw*."

Kevin returned for another tree to load, but he veered toward Maddie, who was leaning against a table while she fiddled with a bow. There was a distant look in her eyes, and he'd love to know where her thoughts had taken her. A cozy fire in a cabin on a tree farm where she wasn't alone, maybe? That was what Kevin tended to see more and more.

He stood next to her, and her gaze flicked to his. A stray hair was stuck in her scarf, and he freed the strand. "This is all your doing."

A wistful sigh eased past her lips. "You know, I enjoy my job and the corner office and all that, but this makes me feel like I'm doing something that really matters."

"You look as happy right now as you do on those labels."

She chuckled. "Who knew getting lost could feel so good?"

He wanted her to stay lost out here. The desire to lean in and complete one of those kisses they'd nearly had washed over him. Instead, he played it safe and lightly touched her arm and walked away.

There was no footing with her. No sense of certainty to guide him or tell him what to do. When he'd met JoAnne, it had been comfortable and simple. They'd liked each other. They'd gone out. They'd spent every moment together. Touches and cuddling had naturally happened.

With Maddie, it was a mess.

He liked her. He was fairly certain she liked him. He wanted more. He was fairly certain she did too. He wanted to touch her and kiss her. He was fairly certain she wanted those things as well. And yet there was this awkward gap between them—better known as the highway and about five states.

It plagued him the rest of the evening, and after everyone left and as he climbed in bed, the frustration grew. Dawn broke, and the percolation of the coffee brought no answer to his troubles. Since Jo had gone home with Pam, the silence in the house was no doubt a contributor to his thoughts.

Not even Maddie's appearance that morning to see him off gave him answers. He put the final tree stand in his truck and rested against the bed. He didn't know what to do with her, but he knew he wanted to do something. Something more than watch her stare at her phone before walking away. "Come with me. You've got to see this," he cajoled.

She kept keying. "I have so much work to do."

"Come on. Trust me."

She met his gaze and relented. She climbed in the truck with him, pocketed her phone, and chitchatted. He pointed out places he'd gone with his parents—a road that would lead to a reindeer farm, alternate paths that would steer them back into town. It was only some of the area when he wanted to show her all of it: where he'd gone to school, Jo's favorite things at the playground. There was this burning intensity that clamored for him to wrap her up further into his life, to reach across the console and hold her hand. Still, that gap he didn't know how to cross existed, and it seemed larger than ever.

"So what is this must-see thing?"

"The fruits of your labor."

She cocked a brow.

He laughed. "You'll see." He gestured at the road. "You know, this is the same stretch of highway where I dropped my trees."

She gave him one of those looks. If things had been simpler, he would've called it encouraging. With a soft grin, relaxed, and comfortable sitting next to him, she said, "I'm so glad you did that."

Him too—but to what end? She'd walked in, blown him away, and was about to walk out. "Talk about a lucky accident," he agreed.

He took the next turnoff and drove into the nearby town to the large lot that had requested a stunning twenty trees on their first order. Three days ago, Kevin hadn't been able to sell one tree. He pulled into the unloading zone, helped get the lot's order of trees out, parked, and then took Maddie's hand. "This is the best part. Come on."

He led her back into the lot. All his trees had been stood in rows and put on display. The red bows on top were vibrant showstoppers against the other trees. She was right: the Tyler Christmas

Trees looked like presents. Customers touched the branches, laughed, and leaned into each other as they moved through and looked at the varieties.

A faraway smile worked at Maddie's mouth and warred with a crestfallen expression that continued to appear as she focused on the activity around them. She looked almost sad, which had not been his goal here. There was some thought spinning through her mind. He'd love to know what it was, only he wanted to discover that answer in the privacy of his truck where there was less risk of interruption.

He put his hand to her lower back. "I guess we better get back on the road."

"Just one more minute," she replied.

He pushed his hands in his pockets, trying and failing at figuring this woman out. He followed her gaze to a grouping of trees. A family walked together around them. Mom and dad held hands with a little girl between them.

Maddie smiled, but it didn't reach her eyes. "When I was a little kid, I wanted to be just like that family. A mom and a dad, the little girl picking out the tree. I wanted that Christmas fantasy." She shrugged. "The truth is, Christmas was pretty lonely." She blinked and tears filled her eyes. "Until now. This is the best Christmas I can remember."

"Then maybe you shouldn't let it end." He put his arm around her and pulled her to his side. Her gaze returned to the people she'd been studying, and he stood there with her for a long time, watching family after family live out what she had never been able to think of as anything other than an impossible fantasy.

Chapter Sixteen

*H*is suggestion had haunted Maddie since he'd uttered the advice. *Then maybe you shouldn't let it end.* As if it were that easy. She had to be back in New York—in two days, as a matter of fact. She had a presentation to give, and if she didn't make it back by that appointment, Maddie was no doubt going to lose her job. Hadley trusted her with his business. Warren trusted her to represent his company. She had a career. This time in Christmas Valley had been a fairy tale she'd never seen coming, but it was time for it to be over. She had to go back to her real home.

Any hope of a mechanic-type mishap delaying her trip again died that afternoon as she sat in a metal folding chair in Cory's garage. Cory crouched in front of her car with her brand-new headlight. It just needed to be installed, then the bumper put on after that.

"I'll have it done and back to you by tomorrow. Then you'll be on your way."

"Sounds great."

Cory gently jostled the headlight between his palms. Maybe he would drop it, and it would shatter to provide that much-desired delay, but he confidently caught it, and then his soft blue eyes landed on her.

"I'm going caroling tomorrow tonight with the band. Everybody joins in and sings along." He was all but pleading like a puppy. "It's too bad you can't stay. I think you'd have a really good time."

An unexpected pain knifed through her. Caroling? She had forgotten he'd mentioned that before. It had always seemed to her like another one of those things people talked about, but didn't actually do. Now Maddie knew it was probably the event of the season where the whole community came together. "I'm sure I would."

Heels ticking across the concrete pulled both of their attentions to the doorway as a woman leaned in.

"I'd like to buy a Christmas tree," she said brightly.

Cory set the headlight aside and stood. "Yes, ma'am. I'll be right there." He started off but then paused and looked back. "I'll call you when the car is done."

Maddie stayed seated a bit longer after he left and admired her Mustang, the adventurous, trail-seeking ride that had brought her here. She finally pushed off her seat and walked alongside, stroking over the fender as she moved. The grandest trip it'd ever taken her on ended in her being broken down—twice. She never expected that it would also lead her to feeling built back up.

"It's been a sweet ride." She patted the car.

She headed back to Pam's to make the most of her time left. Rowdy immediately clamored for her attention, so she didn't even bother going upstairs for her computer. She fetched a cup of coffee and squeezed into a chair that was already occupied by Rowdy across from Pam.

Pam was working tirelessly on her quilt, her hands making neat rows of stitches. It seemed unreal that a few days ago Pam had nothing more than squares. Now almost a full blanket covered her lap. Maddie eyed her accomplishment with a little bit of jealousy. She would love the opportunity to learn a skill like that. She wouldn't even know where to go in New York to find someone to teach her. Surely there was someone there who knew, but the disappointing part was she wanted to learn from Pam. She wanted to learn how to cook green eggs from Jo, be a traveling salesman with Bob, take breaks with Holly and Luke, and flirt with the rascally Roy at the same time. She wanted a bundled-up-warm wardrobe so she could walk the farm with Kevin to watch her trees grow.

Pam must have noticed her staring off into space. Maddie blinked away the unexpected dream that she'd soon leave behind. "That gets prettier every day," Maddie said, pointing to the quilt.

"It's nearly done," Pam said, shaking out the length that covered her legs.

Maddie glanced around the room and rubbed the back of her neck. At Rowdy's whimpering, she returned her attention to his ears. Oh, Rowdy. She also wanted walks and cuddles with him. "I'm really going to miss this place."

Pam paused in her stitching at that. "And we'll miss you. You've made quite a difference in your short stay."

Had she? Maybe. She supposed her influence had flipped Stan's down-and-out new owner into a proud business owner. Of course, she'd also saved the farm. But that was just her being herself. How could simply being herself have such a major influence on the town? And how could the town be having such an influence on her life? The things she'd found important about her life before Christmas Valley were hard work, striving, and achieving. Her career had been a series of higher and higher rungs up a slippery ladder, and she'd painstakingly climbed, careful of every move. Here in Christmas Valley, she simply went with what felt right, and her time here had seemed more successful than anything else in her career.

This town had changed her opinion about everything, about what was possible. Those childhood dreams she'd looked back on with fond nostalgia actually happened here. Maddie had moved past denying that she was afraid of missing this place after her departure, and she was now wondering how she was going to function outside of it. It wasn't a good thing when she looked at her upcoming client list and her first thought was *What's the point*. A fantastic sale to make the balance sheet happy didn't seem to be what she wanted anymore.

Her phone rang and ended further thoughts as Roz's name appeared on the screen.

Right. Work, home—where her mind should be focused. She answered the phone with a hopefully confident-sounding hello.

"Mr. Warren would like to know when you will be here." The strain in Roz's voice told Maddie that Roz wasn't alone.

Maddie pushed out of her chair so she could focus on the phone call and not Rowdy trying to lick her face. Before she even got a step away, her suspicions were confirmed as Warren's voice echoed in the back ground. "Let me talk to her."

Crud.

His harsh breath came through the phone line first. "You have to deliver that presentation so Hadley can approve it," he clipped.

"Yes. I've done all the research and prep." Clothes were clothes. They went into a store, had great position, people bought them. It wasn't a complicated process. It didn't even seem that challenging anymore. Really, now that she thought of it, the most challenging aspect of her job was catering to the nervous owners.

The majority of her time was taken up with the nonstop phone calls, constant texts, and urgent messages from clients, not from the actual marketing aspect of her job.

"Exactly when are you coming back?" Warren asked.

Question of the hour, it seemed like. Cory had said most likely tomorrow, but what if he was wrong? What if another snowstorm happened? What if a tree came down, crashing across the road? What if a reindeer broke into his garage and trampled her car in the morning? Then there was Cory's invitation to the caroling to consider too. Plus, gosh, she still remembered the crushing hug Jo gave her when she'd come back after hitting the reindeer. Tomorrow was too soon.

"In a couple of days," Maddie said, bracing for the reaction.

"The weather has cleared up. What's the delay?" His voice was even more exasperated.

Darn it. He was seeing through her excuses. They weren't good enough. Caroling wasn't going to fly with her boss any more than admitting she wasn't ready to say goodbye. She spun around, desperately searching for a legitimate excuse when she tripped on the carpet and came up with an idea.

"It's my ankle. It's still a little swollen."

Pam glanced up and Maddie shrugged. They stared at each other while Warren was silent on the other end of the line. Maddie grasped for anything. "I'd rather leave on Sunday and avoid traffic."

"I need you at your desk first thing next week." His tone seemed to be more relaxed, if only a little.

There. *Whew*. "Absolutely. I'll be there. I promise."

The phone clicked, sounding the disconnect. Maddie dropped her head. She had lied to her boss, again.

Pam glanced her way as she continued stitching. "You've been traipsing all over Ohio with that very same ankle."

Maddie sat on a chair with a defeated groan. "I want to go caroling with Cory so I can hear him sing. And have a little more time with Jo. It's one more day."

Pam arched an eyebrow that was a bit on the saucy side. "And then there's Kevin."

Yes, Kevin too was another complication. "I like him. A lot. But I'm going home."

Why did this have to be so frustrating? It was as if everything was telling her to stay here, in Christmas Valley. She couldn't stay here, but how could she have both Kevin and New York? Did she want Kevin that much? A resounding yes.

If she didn't have obligations pulling her away, she'd be on her way to him right now. She would put her arms around his neck and take one of those missed kisses. She'd tell him how she was feeling, that she was falling for him, maybe had *already* fallen hard for him.

So that meant what, leave New York? No, that was—*ha ha*, no, no. She couldn't leave New York. That was her home and the place she'd carved in the world for herself. Kevin was wonderful, but he wasn't part of her home. He was a happy accident and couldn't be more. She needed that to be true, but she rubbed a cold chill off her arms and lied to herself some more.

"He and I are friends. I need to accept that," Maddie said.

And to do that, she should probably quit thinking about kissing him. And how she liked the way her heart did flips when he walked in the room. Also how she'd like to hold his hand and take long walks through his trees, maybe even let him show her the farm during spring and be there to hear him explain his duties through the fall too. She should forget wanting to watch Jo skip in front of them as she grew from a bright pretty girl to a very competent young lady. Maddie was going to miss all that, and she collapsed in a chair with a heavy hurt. As much as she *should forget*, she never would.

She looked around the room. She'd accidently carved a place in Christmas Valley too. Not only had she made a place here, but she'd let a piece of the place into her heart.

"You can't control how you feel," Pam said gently.

"I can try, for his sake and mine." As much as Maddie had come to love this place and all the people in it, she couldn't walk out on a lifetime of work, of achievement back in New York—could she?

Pam looked thoughtful. "The older I get, the more I regret all the things I didn't do. Don't end up with any regrets."

Maddie could no sooner control potential regrets than she could her feelings. Which meant she was speeding headfirst toward a broken heart. What else could she do? There was no satisfactory option when it came to her relationship with Kevin. The choice was give up her home to have him, or give him up and return to her home. Which one was right?

The night air was clear and calm. Maddie held tight to her candle as the group walked to the next house with Cory and his band leading the way. This had been worth sticking around for. Not that she would ever be able to explain that to her boss. Maddie was taking Pam's advice here: no regrets. This was the best Christmas she'd ever had, and while she couldn't be here for Christmas day, she intended to absorb as much of the holiday feeling as possible. Now when she woke in her apartment Christmas morning, she'd have these memories to keep her company. It was better than nothing.

Jo held Maddie's hand, and they swung their clasped fingers to the rhythm Cory stroked on his guitar. Kevin was at her side, seemingly more handsome. She wasn't sure how he'd managed that feat, but every time she stole a glance his way, it was as though he'd gained something extra. His dark hair seemed more disheveled. An added sparkle twinkled in his eye. Each sneak peek left her aching a little bit more. It wasn't simply a physical thing either.

When they'd begun the night, he'd been handing out candles. Then he'd helped light them. Jo, following her dad's lead, had passed out hot chocolate to warm everyone before they started out. He was such an amazing dad, one who set an inspiring example. The appeal of his actions exceeded the appeal of his physical appearance, and that was impressive.

She breathed, tried to control her feelings, and got lost in the music of the carolers surrounding them in Cory's upbeat rendition of "Sleigh Bells." It wasn't too hard to become swept away in the joyful music and the occasion. Everyone was singing, Jo was giggling, and Maddie avoided looking at Kevin, even though one of his hands often kept her lower back warm. Through her sweater and jacket, she was still able to absorb every movement of his fingertips.

They moved on to the next house. With each step, each song, her control weakened. Lost in the crowd, surrounded by the love of the community, she allowed herself to be moved in nearer to Kevin until they stood so close that her arm was against his side. Bob glanced back at her and made a face that suggested he was letting her in on something. She eyed him, waiting to see what he was about. He reached down and grabbed Pam's hand. Bob brought their clasped hands to his chest, and Pam stepped in close to him.

Oh, my goodness. Maddie could melt on the spot.

Pam leaned into him. "It's about time," she groused good-naturedly.

They were killing her. They were taking a risk, and the stark reminder had her swallowing thickly and reaching for her thin control. She wasn't going to get her hopes up for what couldn't be. She didn't want to wake up Christmas morning with regrets. She wanted to wake, power on her computer for work, and fondly remember the caroling, the laughter, and the smiles.

At the same time, the thought of being alone in her apartment made her cringe. "I never want this night to end," she whispered to Kevin.

Kevin's hand on her back eased a little farther around her waist. "You have given us a very Merry Christmas."

Jo bounced on her toes. "Our troubles are all gone because we get to keep the farm!"

Maddie couldn't resist bouncing with Jo to celebrate. Maddie had been so wrong before. To think, her satisfaction at Christmas used to hinge on making clients happy. Her clients had never been giddy in this way. Maddie didn't know how she'd ever go back to the way she used to think. She couldn't.

Maybe she'd get to know her neighbors and see what they were like on New Year's. Maybe she and Roz could hit Times Square and watch the ball drop? That seemed fun and adventurous. It lacked every bit of the appeal Maddie was looking for, but she should try a new way of doing things when she returned home.

The caroling went on until the crowd slowly thinned out. Jo went off with Bob and Pam to warm up at Holly's, and Maddie found herself strolling the neighborhood with Kevin. He was quiet, and she wasn't much chattier. It seemed awkward to be back to this uncertainty. In recent days, they had easily shared conversation. Her impending departure was having an effect.

When Pam had suggested that she and Bob take Jo for hot chocolate and Kevin had offered to walk Maddie home, Maddie had taken the chance. No regrets, right? As they walked up Pam's driveway, Maddie's mood was heavy with fear and disappointment and a whole baggage cart full of emotions she didn't—couldn't—unpack. They should have stayed with the group. Curious gazes had a way of minimizing intimacy.

She leaned her head back, desperate for anything to distract her, and lost her breath at the sight. "Look at all those Ohio stars."

"A little lightshow we put on every Christmas."

She hadn't seen a sky this pretty in years. Probably since her last trip with her aunt. Viv had also probably been her last real connection to anyone like the people she'd met in Christmas Valley. Real people with full hearts and love and community. It wasn't that the people she knew in New York didn't have those things, but they didn't share those things with Maddie. They didn't invite her into their homes, feed her, treat her as one of their own the way the people of Christmas Valley had.

"I'm so glad I stayed," Maddie said.

"So am I," Kevin said softly.

She felt his gaze on her before she looked over from the corner of her eye and saw it. She looked away from the stars and was pulled into him. His eyes lowered toward her mouth. His gloves cupped her cheeks, and there was nowhere else she could imagine herself being in the world other than right there on this porch. His gloved touch was cool but soft on her face. She wasn't cold now. Not with the heat radiating from him—or maybe that was from within her? He leaned in. She met him part way.

This was it. Her heart pounded, and desire pushed her closer to finally accepting his kiss. This was the moment she'd tossed and turned over, the moment she wanted to selfishly take with her, but then what? They would kiss and she would leave, and that was supposed to be enough to last a lifetime?

He stepped in until his chest was against hers. His head angled and she had never wanted anything more than to kiss him once, now, again later, again tomorrow, and then stay here and kiss him every day.

Holy—*what?* She jumped back. "I can't."

He frowned as he searched her face. "Why not?"

"Leaving is going to be hard enough." She gasped for breath and tried to hold back the tide of tears. Pam had said no regrets, but what would be worse—kissing him and never having more or not kissing him and always wondering?

"I just... I..." She couldn't see past the tears in her eyes. This was *goodbye*, not *hello, forever.* She reached for something to say to break the tension. "Make sure you don't drop your trees on the highway again."

Her attempt at flippancy failed. This was not how things were supposed to go. She wasn't supposed to be here. She couldn't stay. They couldn't do this, and she wished more than anything she could wipe away the disappointment crossing his face. He dropped his gaze. She'd hurt him. She'd caused that stricken look, and there was nothing she could do to fix it because facts remained—this wasn't supposed to happen this way.

"This doesn't end in a kiss. We part as friends and that's it," she said, hoping that her business-like tone would help her detach.

Gosh, she might as well have kicked him. He gave one solemn nod. "All right." He took a deep breath that shuddered on the inhale. "If you could say goodbye to Jo before you leave. Please."

"Okay."

"Maybe... do you think you could call her some? I think it would help her."

What about calling Kevin? Maddie wouldn't dare. She didn't deserve to hear from him, not after this. "I would like that. I want her to know that she can call me anytime."

"Thank you." He eased away a step.

"Well, goodnight." She turned away for the door before she did anything else stupid to make this worse.

"Goodnight." He accepted her measly parting words.

Each step felt as if shards of glass were being driven up into the soles of her feet. It was honestly painful to walk away. She faced the door, knowing he still stood behind her since his booted footsteps hadn't echoed in the night.

A hard breath from him made her feel hollow. That breath was a sound she would hear over and over in her nightmares. This was it? This was how she was to leave Christmas Valley, after dealing this crushing blow and feeling the final rip in her heart? She couldn't even walk, and she was supposed to drive away?

She heard the first thump of his footsteps as he left. She squeezed her eyes shut and tried to block out the sounds. Her racing thoughts weren't loud enough to silence them. A tear slipped out and silently tracked down her cheek. The dry thickening of her throat, the ache beginning in her head—and suddenly, she was ice cold.

She spun around. "Wait."

He stopped. Her heart propelled her across the porch and down the steps, her own thudding footfalls keeping pace with her thundering pulse. His brows were pulled together, but loosened as he stepped toward her. But he needn't go anywhere. She reached him and threw her arms around his shoulders. He wrapped her up tight, not a bit of space between them from chest to legs. She wasn't even sure her feet were on the ground anymore. Maybe Maddie and Kevin weren't either. She didn't dare risk hesitation—she pressed her lips to his. The close calls, the almost-kisses they'd shared, the anticipation that had climbed until her complete breaking point?

Worth it.

His hand eased around the back of her head, and his fingers curled at her back, holding her close in a way that convinced her she'd never been more secure, more safe, more *loved*. He held her with a possessive grasp but kissed her with tenderness that was a treasure.

Sparkling flashes of their time together flitted through her mind, a reminder of everything they had shared, a hint of what more they could be together. This kiss had begun as a need and would end as a promise of more—a promise that was going to be broken. That thought finally pulled her away.

She remained in his arms and caressed down his cheek. One last touch, one last moment to absorb and imprint on her mind. One last chance to be warm in his arms. A final reminder of what almost was but could never be. There was a saying that should have eased the pain that she felt splitting her down the middle—*better to have loved and lost than to have never loved at all*—a concept she'd never quite comprehended, since she'd only had vague memories of her mom to apply it to.

Now Maddie got it, and she didn't agree at all. Ignorance was freaking bliss. This *hurt*. "I still have to leave tomorrow."

The light in his eyes dimmed. "Who says?" There was no hesitation or uncertainty in his voice.

Oh no. Just when she thought the pain couldn't get worse. This was added agony, knowing he expected her to stay. She couldn't stay, no matter what her heart said. "Please, Kevin. Try and understand."

His expression said that he refused. "I think you're running away from what you feel."

No—Yes? Maybe, but not really? It was complicated. She was wrestling with emotions that she couldn't do anything with. This wasn't her place in the world.

"I'm not running away. I'm going home."

"To what?" He gripped her tighter. The pinch of his fingers on her arms didn't hurt, but the tremble in them sure did. "You matter to me and to my daughter."

"My life is in New York. My job, my apartment.

This has been a wonderful uncharted detour. But it isn't real."

His hold loosened, and he backed away, his arms slack. The open warmth that was often in his eyes was gone. There was nothing but cold reflection, and all she saw was how cold she would be without him.

"This is as real as it gets. Maybe that's what scares you," he rasped.

She wrapped her arms across her fracturing middle. "I don't want this to end badly. I think we should say good night."

He stared a beat longer and shook his head. His jaw tightened, and he walked away. The footsteps she had waited to hear a moment ago came again, and this time they kept on until they faded out of earshot. The sound hurt her worse than she could bear, and she collapsed to sit on the porch.

The quiet she always craved so she could think enveloped her, and it was crushing. This was supposed to be all about no regrets. These regrets were sure going to hurt the rest of her life. Maybe it would have been better not knowing, not experiencing the intense spark between them? She could have walked away. She could have convinced herself that they would have been awful together. The cold inside of her that had nothing to do with the weather lingered, and she knew that it was not a possibility anymore.

Chapter Seventeen

*K*evin stood on the sidewalk downtown as Cory
pulled Maddie's car around and parked at the
curb. They'd all had breakfast at the diner. While
Maddie had been busy telling him it wasn't going to
happen between them, that she wasn't interested
in even *trying*, Pam and Holly had been planning a
breakfast send-off. Unable to resist one more time
with her, Kevin had taken his seat at the counter
again. Come tomorrow, he'd be back to his corner
booth, alone. By himself. Staring at the stools and
recalling the glow in Maddie's cheeks as she'd given
Holly ideas to remake the diner.

Luke gave Maddie a one-of-a-kind bear hug.
"I'm going to miss my favorite customer."

Cory took his turn next for his goodbye. "I sure
am glad your car broke down."

"Me too." Maddie's grin was a contrast to the
heaviness in her eyes. She clearly didn't want to
leave, but she also didn't want to stay.

Holly took her turn next. She was all smiles, but her smile was strained as she gestured at the made-over diner. "You see that sign? You see this happy face of mine? How do I ever thank you?"

Maddie seemed to crumple a little. "Your friendship is thanks enough."

Bob stepped up. "What'll I do without you?"

It was subtle, but Kevin didn't miss the hard swallow passing down her throat or the quiet inhale. "Take Tyler Christmas Trees statewide. You're the traveling VP of Marketing."

Bob offered her a fist, and another bit of Maddie seemed to chip off. Kevin didn't know what special bond the two of them had forged, but she fist-bumped Bob and looked a little sadder for it. It infuriated Kevin that much more. How could she not see that her place was here in Christmas Valley? She didn't have this family and love in New York. She had her job, but it didn't love her back.

Pam pulled a blanket off her arm and walked up. "This is for you."

Maddie's lips parted as she carefully took the green, red, and white quilt. Pam hand-stitched one every year. One and only one lucky person received it.

Maddie clutched the quilt to her heart. "All this time, I had no idea you were making this for me."

"Something to remember us by. To keep you warm." Pam rubbed Maddie's arm and walked away.

That was everyone, except Kevin and Jo. Maddie squatted, her eyes on Jo, who had glued herself to Kevin's side. He rubbed his baby's back, hurting because he couldn't help her. For this, he had no answers, no help, no suggestions. He'd tried.

"Go tell Maddie bye."

Jo crossed the bit of space and ran into Maddie. Maddie held on tight, and good grief, Kevin had to look up for a moment. He hadn't looked away fast enough. The pain around Maddie's eyes, the tears that leaked from the corners, Jo's grip on Maddie's coat—Kevin had seen it all. Maddie pulled away and combed her fingers through Jo's hair.

"I'll write to you, call you." Maddie took a breath, but that only seemed to leave her shaken. "And I'll miss you every single day."

For that, Kevin was eternally grateful. He didn't know how he'd manage if Maddie disappeared one day, but knowing Maddie would be checking in with Jo, at least in the near future, gave him some measure of hope that they could work past this—past Jo's disappointment that Maddie was leaving. *Not* work past his and Maddie's missed chance at becoming something. She'd already said they couldn't happen.

"Goodbye, Maddie." Jo took a step back, and Pam caught her hand.

Free, and not wanting to be, Kevin stared at her. He didn't have anything else to say. He had put his cards on the table last night. She had folded.

She pushed her hands into her pockets and shrugged one shoulder. "If you're ever in New York."

"If you're ever in Ohio." He nodded.

Then that was it. She returned the nod and climbed into her car. The engine cranked, turned over, and hummed on the quiet streets of their little town. She slowly rolled forward and started off.

He was angry and frustrated and mostly put out with himself. He'd known from the beginning she wasn't staying. He was a fool. Jo pressed in against him, and her tears seeped through his shirt. He looked up to try to find somewhere else to stare besides Jo's face as she cried or Maddie's disappearing taillights. He looked around and realized he wasn't the only fool who'd fallen for Maddie.

Holly stood between Cory and Luke, and the three of them gripped each other. Pam leaned against Bob. All of them turned into emotional saps as Rowdy whined.

Somehow it was possible to feel like a stranger in her own home. Maddie wasn't quite sure how she'd managed that, and any hope that things had changed overnight died. The apartment that she'd once loved now seemed so... so... *sterile*. The sleek stainless steel countertops were cold after leaning against Pam's golden granite ones. Pam had cute towels and canisters, and there were always containers of cookies or brownies around. Maddie had a fancy coffee pot. *Whoop-de-do.*

Her neatly put-together living room seemed

more like a random place to stay. No pictures of ancestors adorned the walls. There were no Cheerio-coated picture frames, no snowmen made from footprints. Maddie didn't have a single Christmas decoration, never mind anything personal. The designer she'd hired after buying the place had come through and made it beautiful. The results had been everything Maddie had always wanted— clean, slick. Every last design touch was as tailored to the space as her black suits were to her body. Functional, well fit, no-nonsense, with the appearance of professionalism. Not much love echoed in the space.

She returned to her closet, determined to find something of value in this place. She'd lived here for years. This was home, and surely there was something here to snap her mind back together. The overhead lights in her closet cast a sheen over the crisp, ironed sleeves of her suits, and she turned away from the rows to her fun clothes. Date clothes. Because she went out, once a year or so. Her date clothes reflected her lack of a social life. She had more pajamas than she had casual attire. Not a lot of Christmas Valley clothes here. Her shoulders slumped, and she started for the closet door when the polished wood of her jewelry box caught her attention. She touched her tasteful diamond-stud earrings and then lowered a hand to her sensible solitary necklace. Surely she could spice things up with some Christmas red. She pulled the little doors open to pick through her options. With a July birthday, she had plenty of rubies.

She reached through the dangling necklaces, but a solid silver one caught her attention. She caressed down the simple thin chain to the charm hanging from the bottom. Warmth stirred in her as she removed it from the hook and dropped the old thing over her head. The car-shaped charm hung cold against her skin but quickly warmed as the memories attached to the old necklace Aunt Viv had given her stirred. This was more of what she needed. She rubbed a familiar circular pattern over the car. Jo would love this. All the joy she'd managed to create fizzled at the thought of Jo being so many miles away.

Maddie left her cold apartment with an ache in her chest and found herself facing the jubilant, over-the-top door decorations of her neighbor. The quiet halls of the apartment building grated on her. She turned away from the thought, putting one foot in front of the other toward work. Where was the smell of green eggs and the sprinkles on star-shaped pancakes? No cheerful laughter or challenging *A* words to think up. It was dull. Like leaving a run-of-the-mill hotel instead of her home.

She shook off the cobwebs. She needed to get back to her desk and things should be fine. Once she got going, she could hit up the after-Christmas sales in a few days and make some changes to her home. She could buy ornaments and stuff. They wouldn't mean anything to her the way the ones in Pam's home did, but in time they could.

The streets were drab and cold, and everything was yucky gray on her walk to work. People were lost in their own worlds. No one told her good morning. No one asked if she had any fir trees. The bakery on the corner had a line out to the door, and Maddie passed it. There was no chef getting creative with her eggs, no owner with a bubbling personality. Definitely no handsome man she was interested in seeing sitting at the counter, either.

She stopped for the light at the crosswalk nearest her building and looked at her corner office. A row of glass stared back down. Where was her enthusiasm? Her excitement to rule the day? Last time she'd stood in this spot, there had been butterflies in her stomach, and she had been anxious to get upstairs to her desk. She'd rather go home and curl up under the quilt Pam had given her. Maddie shook her head and marched into the building, meeting Roz straight away.

Roz handed over a stack of papers. "It's good to have you back."

"Thanks." She didn't bother looking at the sheets and stuck them against her side.

"You have a really full day. A meeting with Warren to discuss the presentation, then lunch with the client. Irene's people sent thanks for the flowers and were sad to hear about your car trouble. They said to tell you that they hope you're okay."

Gosh, this list. Roz had gotten through very few

items, and it was stressful listening to it. This was her normal day, her routine, and it sounded awful and busy and *structured*. Maddie really didn't care about any of it. Not about her to-do list. Not about her plans to wow Irene over with extra work. She wanted to go home. *But to which one?*

Roz bumped her. "You okay?"

Maddie blinked her thoughts away. "It's just a big transition. I'm still running on Ohio time."

"You want me to cancel anything?"

Tempting. Maddie could leave and go sit at home. "I can't. Only five more days until Christmas. And I have all those sales to promote." *Ugh, so many sales.* "Then the after-Christmas sales. And so it goes, the same seasonal push every year. It takes all the joy out of the holidays."

Roz leaned away as her eyes widened. "Listen to you."

Maddie sounded like Kevin. She should call Jo this afternoon and bundle her up a care package that would arrive before Christmas morning. Maybe she'd stuff a box full of Christmas movies and some of Maddie's favorite things from the city. Maybe she would tuck something in for Kevin too. Roz continued to stare, and Maddie didn't even try to pretend she wasn't distracted.

"Christmas Valley packs quite a punch," Maddie offered.

"You miss it?" Roz asked, her face sympathetic.

"I miss who I was there."

The phone on her desk rang and Roz picked

it up. "Maddie Duncan's office. Yes, sir, I'll let her know." Roz returned the phone. "The meeting with Warren has been bumped to ten."

Maddie nodded. *Blah.* A meeting. Who wanted to do that when she could be making wreaths right now and hugging the sweetest little girl? They had managed to squeeze so much into a few days, but there was surely still so much left to do. She should call Jo later and ask her what else she did during the day. *Ooh.* Jo probably made beautiful garlands. They could Skype and do it together, if Maddie knew what to buy ahead of time. Wire and wire cutters. Probably a glue gun. Ornaments and lights to string around. Of course the green part too—but she would never find a comparable bough to the ones from the Tyler Christmas Trees.

Roz's brows pulled together and her expression was concerned.

"Still lost in Ohio?"

"Yeah, I guess," Maddie said. She took a deep breath of that bustling New York office air, and it didn't do anything for her. It smelled of coffee, with none of the added scents from Holly's.

"You know I don't believe in fate, but getting that wedding invitation, the trees on the highway, the fork in the road. What if I had gone the other way?" Maddie bit her lip and mulled it all over again for about the thousandth time since she had driven out of Christmas Valley. Never had she felt like she was making a bigger mistake than when she left. "It makes you think it was meant to be."

Roz nodded at Maddie, a knowing look on her face. "Yes, it does."

Maddie managed to make it through the rest of the day. She must have said sensible things through her meetings, because she didn't get fired. It was a blur of a day, and as soon as she got home, she crawled in her bed. The only thing she had unpacked was Pam's quilt, and she dove under the warmth of it—warmth that still smelled of sugar and carbs.

Her apartment was silent. Work was piled on her nightstand, and her bed was empty with no Rowdy to cuddle with. She looked at the picture of her with her mom. Maddie's heart hurt. She had almost had everything that was represented in that photograph. The family, the acceptance, the love. She'd thrown it all away for a job. Maddie tightly closed her eyes as the truth settled on her shoulders.

She'd turned her back on everything real, just the same as her father.

Chapter Eighteen

*K*evin leaned over the now-empty worktable in the barn. All the trees that needed to be taken to lots were delivered. There were no more big red bows or pictures of Maddie and Jo to fix to a branch. The Tyler Christmas Trees were all sold for the year. From this point on, it was planning, planting, tending—and taxes. He'd rather climb on top of this table and nap through to next October. Sleeping through the year would certainly make missing Maddie easier.

How would he even cope next year? She'd saved his farm, and he was eternally grateful. He didn't want to think about her not being here or how he'd be packing trees without her boundless enthusiasm and optimism to give him energy. He already had visions of going through the motions, and he flicked a stray pine needle off his worktable. Christmas shouldn't be a time to go on autopilot, and he had about eleven months to get it through his head that Christmas had been wonderful before Maddie and it would be wonderful again without her.

The side door opened, and Jo pushed through. Her pinecone pail dangled from her fingertips. Her face was sad, and her shoulders slouched. She'd been out hunting for pinecones for the last hour, but she stuck an empty bucket on the table.

He kneeled to be closer, already knowing the answer to his question. "What's wrong?"

"I miss Maddie."

He had no reply, no solution. Just sadness of his own and a crushed daughter. "I know you do. I miss her too."

Jo's pleading gaze turned to his. "Did you tell her that?"

"I tried to."

Once again, her face fell. "I want to send her a Christmas present."

"Okay."

"But I don't know what. She has enough clothes and stuff." Jo's lips parted and closed. Tears filled her eyes until one spilled over. "I don't want her to forget us."

There were not many things as a parent worse than being unable to give your child something they desperately needed. "Me either. Let's remind her," Kevin said.

It was another day, and Maddie had to get her head

in the game. It was as simple as that. She managed to comb through her emails, review reports, approve materials. She even got out her notes for the presentation with Hadley, and she looked at each page.

She didn't read anything from them or absorb information, but she looked at the pages, and that had to count for something.

Roz walked in. Her lipstick today was as red as Holly's sign, and there Maddie went again, her memories spiraling her back to Christmas Valley. She was powerless to stop her daydreams. It didn't help that she didn't want to stop them either. She refocused on her papers. She *had* to focus. "I'm about to give my presentation. I'm thinking less graphs and more motivational?"

Roz didn't say anything but continued to stand there. Maddie looked up again and noticed Roz holding a present wrapped in reindeer paper. Roz's grin widened until she beamed and a sparkle lit her eyes. The sparkle reminded Maddie of Pam.

No. *Focus.* Maddie glanced at the box. "Roz? What is it?"

Roz's smile was as big as Luke's had been when Maddie had told him to do what he wanted with her breakfast. "Somebody sent you a present. It's from Christmas Valley." She slid it onto Maddie's desk. "I was told to deliver it personally."

The feathery warmth that touched Maddie somehow managed to be both joyful and painful. She stroked the red bow on top of the present. It was the same ribbon that tied off the Tyler Christmas Trees. "Told by who?"

"I believe she said her name was Jo."

"You spoke with her?" Maddie looked at her phone, but none of the lights were lit up signaling someone was on hold. "When?"

Roz grinned. "When the package was delivered. I guess she had a notification set for delivery confirmation, because I was on the phone with her as someone from downstairs brought it up."

Maddie sank back in her chair and stared at the gift. Her beautiful little girl. Maddie had tried blocking out the memory of Jo's tear-filled eyes as she'd driven away to no avail. The grip of that one last hug. If this was hard on Maddie—

She shook her head. She couldn't think about that. She'd just sit at her desk, crying all day—her beloved desk that she was growing a good bit of animosity toward.

Roz leaned over. "You haven't even opened it yet."

"The thought is enough," Maddie said, trying to sound convincing.

"She sounds like a good kid."

"She is. With a really wonderful father."

"Kevin?"

"Yes." Maddie couldn't get any other word out when Roz said Kevin's name.

"Jo mentioned him. Apparently, he misses you, and she thought I should know that in case I had any sway."

Maddie's gaze dropped, and she couldn't look up. She missed them all too. She lifted the wrapped lid off the box and laughed at the item on top. She pulled the pinecone out and held it against her chest. The prickly ends snagged at her shirt and poked holes in what little resolve she'd managed to scrape together.

Roz chuckled. "As pinecones go, it's very nice, but I'm not sure it merits all the emotion."

Maddie carefully set it aside, peeked in, and found herself laughing again. Her disaster of a fruitcake. Oh my goodness. They'd kept this?

"What is that?" Roz leaned away, looking disgusted.

Maddie held up her fruitcake. It had a ribbon tied around it. Maddie laughed and a tear leaked out. The cake was completely black on all the edges. "A doorstop."

"I guess you had to be there," Roz said, looking at Maddie as if she had gone crazy.

Maddie set the fruitcake aside, dropping it. The satisfying thump of it smacking her desk made her smile, but as she looked in the box at the rest of the gifts, Maddie's laughter turned into a frown, and she fought tears. Real tears, not a sting at a sudden swing of emotion or the result of a punch of laughter—heartbreaking, sad tears that left her hurting. She took out a framed picture of her and Jo decorating the tree.

Roz leaned around and looked at the photograph. "No wonder you miss Ohio."

Maddie touched the glass over them. *Miss* wasn't even the right word to describe what Maddie was feeling.

"Maddie. It's time for your meeting," Roz reminded gently.

Maddie nodded and propped up the photograph on her desk. She gave it a lingering stare for as long as possible before she left her desk and headed down the hall to the conference room. Warren and Hadley waited along with other people. She should know their names, titles, and value to the company. Maddie could barely remember her own name.

She didn't waste time. She didn't have the charm today to set a mood. They wanted facts and figures. She walked to the empty end of the table and pulled out her things.

"Let's get to it. Christmas is only four days away, but retailers should keep their ad campaigns in high gear until the end"—she quickly referred to her notes and read straight off of her opening statement—"end of the year. Buying doesn't fall off a cliff after Christmas. Shoppers are waiting, credit cards poised."

Hadley was checking his watch. Warren's stare hit her like a cold lump of coal.

Maddie scrambled with what little functioning brain cells she had. "Fourth-quarter numbers are breaking records this year, both online and in the brick-and-mortar malls."

Ugh. People were out with their credit cards? Record sales? What kind of gimmick nonsense was this? Where was the heart in all of this—the traditions, family, friends, the gathering of people together? There was no community, no spirit.

She had a sudden realization. "This shouldn't be what Christmas is about."

Warren shifted in his chair. "Maddie, are you okay?"

Maddie closed her book. "No, sir. I'm not."

The room full of strangers looked at her. What was she doing here with strangers? Where was her partner in sales, Bob? That was how she sold things best, with a lunch packed full of love from Pam to power her through a day and an anxious pair of blue eyes waiting at home, full of hope that she'd have saved their livelihood on her return. Maddie toyed with her necklace, and her fingers drifted down the length of the chain to the car charm at the bottom.

Warren cleared his throat. "What's the problem?"

She closed her book of cold, calculated notes. "I'm so sorry. But I don't belong here."

Warren blinked. "What do you mean?"

"I belong in Christmas Valley, Ohio." As she said it, she *knew* it was the absolute truth, and a slow warmth started up inside her.

Hadley glanced around the room. "Is this part of the presentation?"

Warren's frown was deep. "Apparently not."

Maddie scrambled and tried to come up with the words, but then she realized she didn't *need* to come up with anything. It had all been right there, all along, in her heart. She clutched a fist to her chest.

"A home is not about *where* you are and what you can get done there. It's about the people you love. That's what makes a place home." She gestured at the room as a lightness she hadn't felt since Christmas Valley lifted her spirits. "This isn't my home."

She headed for the door and stopped by her boss's side. "I'm sorry, Mr. Warren. I hope you can understand why I'm leaving."

Warren's jaw dropped. "You're going back to Ohio?"

"Yeah. And if I hurry, I can get there before Christmas."

She looked at the spread of meaningless stuff, the room of people, and she backed away. "Sorry." She wasn't sure why she said it—she wasn't sorry at all. She was going home.

Maddie couldn't believe she was doing this, but here she was, driving through the winding streets of Ohio, closing the final stretch to find Kevin and Jo. Her car had purred like a dream through the entire trip as though it knew they were going home.

She'd quit her job. *Hadn't even given notice, just walked out.* She laughed all over again. Goodness, she had surely lost it, but here she idled in her car at the fork in the road. She could take a right toward what fate had planned, into the heart of Christmas Valley where she'd found herself. She eased down the road with confidence, when before she'd hesitantly clicked on her turn signal and taken a guess. Snow glistened along the highways. The surrounding trees called to her.

The Welcome to Christmas Valley sign stood vibrant on the side of the road. She was getting warmer, and it increased as the familiarity of the town brought her nearer and nearer to her goal. Maddie had never been happier.

She was also kind of a mess after packing, loading her car, and then driving straight through from New York. Look at her—Ms. Fashionista running around half the country in fleece leggings. She carefully selected her route, avoiding Cory's garage, downtown, and the streets nearest Kevin's place. Her Mustang wasn't exactly something that could be hidden, and Maddie wanted to look her best on Christmas Eve. It was a big night for Holly, and hopefully for Maddie too. It was hard not to drive straight for Kevin's house. She could picture their reunion—running across the snowcapped front yard, jumping the porch steps, and throwing her arms around him. If she did that, they might never make it to Holly's big celebration.

She turned on Pam's street and eased into her driveway—into home—and Maddie had never been more certain of that. The house was dark at the windows, which was a bit odd for Pam's. Christmas lights shone, but that was it. Maddie flipped her watch around. One hour until Holly's party.

Maddie grabbed the small bag she'd packed. She wanted to run in, be able to dress, and get to Holly's grand reopening without having to unload her luggage. Except no one came to the door when she knocked. Rowdy barked up a storm, but that was it.

Come on, small town, let the rumors be true. She twisted the knob and it gave a soft click and opened. Maddie stepped inside and squatted to catch Rowdy's enthusiastic, tail-wagging love.

"Hey, boy." She scrubbed up his ears and down his body. "I missed you too."

The house was quiet, and nobody answered when she called out. She headed upstairs to her room. The tree remained in the corner, and the bowl of pinecones was still on the little coffee table in the sitting area. Maddie shook her head as she recalled pushing them aside to make room for her computer.

She leaned down now and inhaled their pine scent. It would be all too easy to get lost in every detail here. The twinkle of the lights, the snowmen scattered around. Every familiar sight made her heart fuller. She turned and managed to find things she hadn't seen before—a small tablecloth with Santa stitched on it, no doubt Pam's work. An ornament with a paw print she'd be willing to bet was from Rowdy. Each item had a history, a purpose, a tradition.

This was Maddie's future. Fate had decided for her when she'd arrived in town by accident. She quickly showered, and this time she left her designer soaps in her bag and reached for Pam's peppermint washes. Maddie came out smelling like a candy cane, and she couldn't believe this was her life now. She slipped on a red dress, a zing racing up her spine with the zipper.

Jo had the white version of the same dress. Maddie had grabbed the matching red one on her way out of the office that one last time. She checked the time to see an hour had already raced by, and she hurried downtown.

Music from inside Holly's poured through the downtown of Christmas Valley. Cory's voice led the tune. Garland lined all the windows and spray snow outlined their edges. She wasn't even nervous. She was too happy—the world felt too right. There was a shake in her fingertips, but that was all adrenaline, and okay, maybe a few nerves. What if Kevin didn't want her back?

Maddie pushed in through the door. The diner's tables had been moved to one side to create a buffet line, and couples danced in the emptied middle. The bell rang overhead, giving her away to the few close enough to hear the sound over Cory's live band.

Holly spun around. Her jaw dropped open, and she immediately wrapped Maddie in a hug. Maddie held tight, swearing she'd never have to do this again because she was here to stay.

Maddie leaned back, putting a finger to her lips—the universal sign for hush. She'd come this far. She wanted to see the look on Kevin's and Jo's faces when they saw her. Maddie scanned the room in search of her family and found the whole town packed inside. Grins were toothy and wide, and everyone waved, thankfully honoring her request to not give the surprise away. She had found her family, all of them, in all of Christmas Valley.

She looked the room over, seeking two particular members. His truck was on the street, so he had to be here somewhere. Finally she spotted his tall, lean frame. He cleaned up well. He was wearing a nice jacket and snug jeans.

Jo stood at his side and was focused on the selection of food in front of them—until she looked up. Her unsuspecting gaze caught the big-eyed stares of the town. Her brow furrowed as she followed their nods toward Maddie. Jo turned the rest of the way, and there was that moment—the recognition, the widening of her eyes. Maddie's heart bloomed. Jo ran across the diner and right into her.

Maddie held tight to her, her squeeze even more fierce than when Maddie left before. This was the hug of a girl who wasn't letting go. Jo turned her chin up to Maddie. "Are you here for good?"

Maddie gave her a reassuring squeeze. "Forever and ever."

"Does my dad know?" Jo whispered.

"It's a surprise," Maddie whispered back. She

hugged Jo again and looked up, waiting to see if Kevin was going to turn around. The whole town waited too, but he continued to look over the food, oblivious to everyone staring at him.

Luke leaned over to him. "I can't take the suspense."

Kevin's face lifted toward Luke, but his back was to Maddie, and she couldn't see anything that had transpired. Jo's arms tightened around Maddie's waist, and she hopped on her toes. Maddie found herself bouncing too. Silence descended over the room as Cory's band abruptly ended mid-song. Maddie and Jo were both about to explode as Kevin slowly, ever so slowly, turned around. He spun all the way, and his eyes met hers.

He looked shocked, and then a slow smile lifted his lips. "Welcome home."

Maddie rubbed Jo's arm and let her go to meet Kevin across the room. "Merry Christmas."

He smiled, looking as dumbstruck as Maddie felt. "Best one ever." He stepped forward. His warm hands flanked her cheeks, and that final missing piece of Maddie knit together as he kissed her in front of everyone.

He pushed hair from her face. His eyes were serious but full of joy. "I love you."

"I love you." She glanced back for her favorite girl, and Jo ran to them. "And I love you too."

Epilogue

*N*ow *this* was Christmas and how it should be spent together. The morning around his— their—tree. Kevin flipped pancakes. Maddie poured juice. Jo set the table. A breakfast to leave them stuffed before sitting together for presents. The fire crackled and the air was filled with Jo's pink-cheeked laughter. He could scarcely remember his daughter being happier. It was hard to believe that less than twenty-four hours ago, they'd been moping around the house. Now Maddie was walking back into their lives and changing everything. For good this time.

Maddie had arrived first thing in fuzzy pajamas, and she'd donned Santa slippers the moment she'd walked in. They'd laughed and that awkwardness—gone. It was as if she had always been there. Everything about her presence on Christmas morning was natural. He touched her arm, and she touched his back as they ate. It all worked. None of the worries or fears that had been stressing him for days on end invaded. He looked at Maddie, everything within him stopped spinning, and the world righted.

He followed Jo's lead to the living room and sat on the floor at the base of the tree with Maddie at his side. Jo collected their stockings and handed one to each of them. Maddie's gaze went to Kevin as she touched her name. He knew that it had been added to her stocking sometime overnight. He shrugged, feigning ignorance, but from the absolutely beaming smile on his daughter, he knew where it had come from.

"Pam taught me!" Jo exclaimed as Maddie touched the stitching.

Maddie rubbed the carpet between them as she looked at Jo. "Sit here. I slipped a little something extra in your stocking this morning."

Funny, he had slipped a little something extra in Maddie's stocking too. He sipped his coffee and kept that to himself.

Jo nestled between them and pulled out a long gold wrapped box. Jo looked at them both and he nodded for her to continue, anxious to see what Maddie had given her. Jo carefully unwrapped the package and cracked open the navy box. A necklace was inside with a charm dangling off the end.

Jo gasped. "Maddie. I love it."

Maddie lifted the necklace out of the box and fastened it around Jo. "This has been mine since I was your age."

Jo lifted the charm on the end and Kevin leaned around to see it was a little car. If he didn't know any better, he'd say it was a Mustang. Jo squinted at the gold inscription. "Adventure Together."

Maddie rubbed her arms. "My aunt gave me that. We used to go on these rides, these adventures, and have fun together. We always took her car, the one that brought me here. She gave me that necklace on one of our trips. My times with my aunt are some of my fondest memories, and I hope to share some like them with you. This necklace is one of my favorite things, and I wanted you to have it."

Jo clasped it in her hands. "I promise to always wear it."

"I'm glad you like it."

Kevin could hardly stand it, and he pointed at the red stocking across Maddie's lap. "Open yours now."

A brow cocked in his direction as she reached inside. Since she'd come in last night, he hadn't had a lot of time to get her anything, but there was one item he'd tucked inside that would mean more than anything else he could have possibly found.

She reached in and came out with a small red jewelry box. She looked curious, but no hesitation existed on her face, just a wide smile and bright eyes. She flipped the lid back. The gasp that escaped her lips imprinted in his mind.

A gold band with round rubies set around emerald leaves shined at her. It was designed to look like holly. After looking through rows of rings, Jo had spotted this one at the same time he had. It was meant to be the one.

"Kevin." Maddie put a hand over her heart. "How did you even know I was coming back?"

Small towns. She'd learn. He had stopped Mrs. Grace last night at the party and asked if she'd entertain an after-hours customer at the jewelry store. She'd been more than happy to oblige him. He moved his stocking aside, adjusted to be on one knee and took her hand. "Maddie. You've given us the best Christmas we could hope for. And I—"

"We," Jo interrupted.

He leaned over and kissed his daughter's head. "*We* couldn't be happier you came home. Will you marry me?" He nodded at Jo. "Us?"

Maddie looked at him, at Jo, then back to him. Tears filled her eyes as she nodded and launched into his arms. "Yes!"

Jo jumped up and threw a fist into the air. "I vote for a Christmas wedding!"

Kevin rubbed Maddie's back. "I love the sound of that."

"No." Maddie shook her head and looked concerned.

No? That unsettled feeling welled up in him.

"Christmas is a whole year away! I'm not waiting that long."

Jo's grin started out kind of small, then spread as she shrugged. "Well, the farm is already decorated."

Kevin was following her logic. "The barn is cleaned up, and those lights we put up are still in there. We could open the end up I normally use for a loading bay. There's plenty of room for chairs for an outdoor wedding."

"Today?" Maddie looked at them. "You're going to pull off a wedding today?"

Jo jumped up. "Not just us. Give me ten minutes to make some phone calls."

Kevin pulled Maddie into his lap and wrapped his arms around her. "Well, this is going faster than I expected. Are you ready?"

"Yeah." She leaned her head against his shoulder. "I am."

"We need to get you a warmer coat. And shoes."

She caressed his arms and leaned into him. "I'm plenty warm now."

The End

Christmas Biscuits with Sugar Plum Jam

A Hallmark Original Recipe

In *Love You Like Christmas*, Maddie stays at a small-town boarding house where the owner, Pam, makes green eggs in honor of the holiday. Maddie isn't tempted by those, but Pam's homemade biscuits and jam look and smell delicious. This recipe is a perfect Christmas treat.

Yield: 12
Prep Time: 10 minutes
Cook Time: 20 minutes
Total Time: 1½ hours

INGREDIENTS

Christmas Biscuits:

- 1 cup lukewarm milk
- 2 tablespoons melted butter
- 3½ cups all-purpose flour
- 2¼ teaspoon (1 ¼-ounce packet) instant yeast
- 1¼ teaspoons kosher salt
- 1 teaspoon baking powder
- ½ teaspoon sugar
- 1½ cups lukewarm water
- as needed, cooking spray or vegetable oil

Sugarplum Jam:

- ¾ cup plum jam
- ¼ cup orange marmalade
- As needed, white sparkling sanding sugar
- As needed, butter

DIRECTIONS

1. To prepare Christmas biscuits: combine milk, butter, flour, yeast, salt, baking powder and sugar in the bowl of a stand mixer. Slowly add water and beat on high speed until batter is thick and smooth. Cover and let rest in a warm draft-free location for 1 hour, or until frothy bubbles form on surface.

2. Heat oiled griddle (or cast iron skillet) over medium-low heat. Arrange oiled crumpet rings on griddle; portion ¼ to 1/3 cup batter (based on size of rings) into each crumpet ring. Cook for 8 to 10 minutes or until tops are dry and covered with bubbles. Remove rings and flip each with a spatula. Cook an additional 5 minutes; remove from pan. Repeat with remaining batter.

3. To prepare jam: combine plum jam and orange marmalade in small bowl and gently stir to blend. Transfer to serving bowl; sprinkle sparkling sanding sugar over the top just before serving.

4. Serve Christmas biscuits warm or toasted with butter and sugarplum jam.

Thanks so much for reading
Love You Like Christmas. We hope you enjoyed it!

You might also like these other books
from Hallmark Publishing:

Christmas in Homestead
Journey Back to Christmas
A Heavenly Christmas
A Dash of Love
Moonlight in Vermont
Love Locks

For information about our new releases
and exclusive offers, sign up for our free
newsletter at hallmarkchannel.com/
hallmark-publishing-newsletter

You can also connect with us here:

Facebook.com/HallmarkPublishing

Twitter.com/HallmarkPublish

Turn the page for a sneak peek of

A Heavenly Christmas

**Based on the Hallmark Hall of Fame Movie
Written By Gregg McBride**

Rhonda Merwarth

Chapter One

E ve Morgan sighed as the Christmas song blaring through her alarm clock pulled her out of a deep sleep. "Wasn't it just Thanksgiving?" she murmured to herself. The days were passing faster than she'd realized. She changed the station to a financial report program and slid out of bed.

Though it was clearly cold out with a thick layer of snow covering the trees and ground outside her apartment complex, Eve was cozy in her silky gray pajamas. She padded her way across her smooth tile floor and started her day. Shower, dress, make-up, hair: all finished right on time. She had her schedule down to a science, and she prided herself on it.

Her brain was already running down the massive list of things she needed to accomplish that day. New client cold calls, stocks review for existing clients, meetings... It would all get done, and she'd stay as late as it took to ensure that.

When she got into her kitchen, she saw her cat perched on the countertop and shook her head. That doggone cat was so stubborn, refusing to stay on the ground where she kept trying to move him, but oh well. She could indulge him. "Good morning, Forbes," she said lightly, putting down her cell phone on the granite counter and shifting to the drawer where she stored the cat's food. "We need to look at your portfolio," she teased the animal. "I think it's time to diversify."

The cat meowed its opinion on the topic. At least her clients showed more enthusiasm for her suggestions. She'd helped them make a lot of money, and they appreciated that—and her.

She slid the bowl across the counter to the cat. "There ya go." With a smile, she grabbed her phone, taking a peek at the stock app she'd pulled up. "Catnip is trading up, ooh!" Eve grabbed a bottle of water from her stainless steel fridge, then added to the cat, "All right, text me if you need me."

Forbes ignored her teasing comments, focusing on his meal.

Eve stepped out her front door, locking it behind her, then headed to the elevator. Before the doors could shut, her neighbor Ruth slipped in, dressed in what could only be described as a garish green Christmas sweater. Her Yorkie was curled up in her arm, as cozy as a bug. The dog was rather yippy and not that friendly to anyone but Ruth.

"Hello, Eve," Ruth said with a smile as she moved to the back of the elevator. Her dark skin was glowing with her happy mood, and she hummed under her breath—probably a Christmas song. The woman had been singing them since early November.

"Hey, Ruth." She could see the red and green lights on the sweater blinking in the elevator door reflection. "Wow, that is some sweater," she said as tactfully as possible.

"Well, thanks!" She could hear the perkiness in Ruth's voice. Her neighbor loved the holidays and was always inviting Eve to participate in this or that Christmas celebration in her apartment next door. Eve always declined, not really one for parties—or holidays, to be truthful. Thankfully, the walls were thick enough that she barely heard the ruckus. "I could pick you up one. There are quite a few left."

Oh, heavens no, Eve thought with a mental shudder. Totally not her style. She replied to a client's text, confirming their upcoming meeting time later today. "That's okay," she said to Ruth in what she hoped was a non-horrified tone. "I think that is a one-sweater-per-building sweater."

She stepped out onto the sidewalk and made her way to her office, scrolling through her phone at her emails. Her heels clacked solidly on the concrete. The morning air was crisp. It felt like winter even though it was technically still a few days away. Christmas decorations covered all of downtown Chicago in preparation for the holiday festivities. People were bundled up in their warmest gear as she strolled past them, barely glancing up from her phone.

Her brain was already whirring with the day's tasks and the potential clients she wanted to reach out to. One in particular would be a sweet success to acquire. She dug up his office number and dialed him, mentally prepping herself and getting into saleswoman mode.

But it didn't matter. The client was already on vacation for the holidays, diving in the Caymans. Fighting back her surprise and disappointment, she left a message asking him to call her back when he returned to work.

A Santa ringing a bell caught her attention for a moment, and she grabbed a few bucks from her pocket, dropping them into the Santa's cup. There, her good deed for the day. She dialed the next call in line.

As she entered her building and walked back to her office, she continued chatting on the phone with her current client, briefly noting that the office was decorated for the holidays, too. Bright lights were strung across cubicles, along with sparkling garland and wreaths filling every visible surface. Well, not in *her* office—she didn't have time for such things. Her apartment wasn't decorated, either.

Why bother when you were just going to take it down a couple of weeks later? It seemed like a waste of time.

Eve ended the call, tucked her phone into her pocket, and went to the coffee station, greeting her coworker Carter as he prepared a fresh, steaming cup of java for himself. The thick smell filled her nose, and she could almost taste the concoction.

"Coming to the party tomorrow?" he asked, pouring a dollop of creamer into his holiday mug.

She chose a plain one for herself and grabbed the coffee decanter. "What party?"

He looked over at her in disbelief. "The... office Christmas party."

"Oh. Right." Yet again, she realized how fast December was flying by—and how much work she still had to get done before the end of the year to meet her personal goals. These Christmas events took up important business hours when she could be doing more for the company. Who had time for those kinds of distractions? She poured her coffee mug to almost full.

"Tell me you're not working," he said.

This was their typical conversation every holiday season—okay, not just Christmas time. The company liked to throw parties for everything, and she never went to any of them. "Well, while you're drinking eggnog, I'm going to be improving our bottom line," she tossed over her shoulder as she headed toward her office, clutching her mug.

"I remember being like you once," he said lightly.

"Mm-hmm," she said with a smile. Carter teased her, but he knew her dedication was to Crestlane Financial, to getting things done and making the company prosper. And she was a success at that.

The morning passed in a fury of calls. As a

financial consultant, Eve excelled at her job. She kept detailed notes of personal information about her existing clients, and potential clients, to make them feel important. Small things like that could make a difference. She kicked up her heels on her desk and rang up a potential client she'd been wooing, chatting with him for a few minutes. She asked about his daughter and her dressage lessons.

"Yes, of course I remember," she said, chuckling at his disbelief over her recalling something so minute. Okay, enough chitchat. Time to get down to brass tacks and make this happen. She plopped her feet down on the ground and straightened her spine. "Look, I am just gonna say it and let the chips fall where they may." A hooky line she'd perfected over the years that worked wonders on clients she was pursuing. "Apex East is a solid firm. But what are they doing for you, three percent?" She paused then dropped her bombshell. "I can double it."

There was a moment of silence, then he said in his rumbling voice, "Okay, I'm interested in hearing your spiel. Let's get together soon."

A warmth filled her chest. She had him! "Drinks tonight?" she said with a smile, then her grin got bigger when he agreed. "Yes, of course, *très bien*! I'll have my assistant set it up."

"Fantastic," he replied.

"Okay. Bye!" She couldn't hold back her giddiness now. This was going to be a good catch for them. Fontaine Fowler was a reputable pharmaceuticals company, and taking them from Apex East would be a solid victory.

Her assistant, Liz, came through the glass door and paused. "You bought a tree?" she asked in shock, staring with large brown eyes at the scrawny, plastic green tree sitting against Eve's far wall.

"A client gift," Eve corrected.

"What color is that?" she asked, wrinkling her nose.

"Celery?" Anyway, enough of that nonsense. Eve couldn't keep the pride out of her voice as she said, "We need to set up and print a new client signature pack because I'm going to sign Fontaine Fowler."

"That's fantastic!" her assistant declared, beaming. "I thought they were with Apex East?"

"Yeah, but not for long," she said in a singsong voice, getting out of her chair.

Liz clutched a pack of folders to her chest. "That's why you're my idol."

She knew the woman admired her, but hearing words of affirmation along that vein gave her a flush of pleasure. Eve had fought hard to get where she was, and it made her feel good to have her successes recognized by those around her.

"I'm going to sign one new client before the new year, and I'm going to beat out Carter for that partnership." This was finally hers, the goal she'd worked long hours day after day for. Victory was on the horizon, and her dreams were about to come true.

Not that she would be content to sit back and rest. No, after she became partner, she had big ideas to help the company be even more aggressive in finding new clients and maintaining their existing ones. Eve lived and breathed her job.

Leaning over to check something on her computer, she instructed her assistant to book a table for the City Club at six and to note that she had a conference call at twelve-thirty with Gibson so she'd get him on the line.

"Conflict," the assistant said plainly. "You have lunch with your brother today."

Eve closed her eyes and groaned. *Crud.* "That's today?" Apparently, the refrain for the day was going to be about how fast time was flying and how she couldn't squeeze in non-work distractions—not when there was so much to do before the end of the year. Every second counted. The pressure of looming deadlines made her chest tighten.

Seeming to predict her next thought, Liz added, "And you told me to not let you cancel again since you have three times already."

Eve shook her head, scrambling to figure out a plan to squeeze it in and still make her meeting. "You know what? We'll book the conference room for noon. That way, I can have half an hour and catch up with him."

"Okay," Liz said briskly.

"Thank you!" she hollered as her assistant left.

A half hour would suffice. Her brother would understand. This really was a crazy time of year for them. He knew how it went—she'd explained it to him enough, anyway. Eve pushed the thoughts from her mind and focused on the rest of her morning tasks. Emails had to be answered, and they'd wait for no one.

"Hey!" Eve said cheerily as she walked into the glass-walled conference room. Her brother, Tyler, and his two sons were there waiting on her. "I didn't know you were bringing the boys!" She waved them toward her and gave them big hugs. "What a great surprise!"

"We wanted to make sure you're real," Caleb, the oldest boy, said.

Her brother laughed at the flippant comment.

"Where were you hiding?" Bobby, the younger, asked, peering up at her.

"Hey," Tyler said in a sterner tone, clenching the boy's shoulders. "Manners."

All right, the comments from the boys stung her a bit; her smile wavered. She fought off the flare of negative emotion and said lightly, in an effort to change the subject, "Hmm. Okay, so big question. What do you want for Christmas?"

"You already gave us something," Bobby said.

"What?" She frowned. She hadn't done any holiday shopping yet; she never had the time.

Not that *she* did it—Liz helped out with those

things. But she liked to give Liz the ideas for gifts, and that had to count for something.

"A company fruit basket." Bobby's voice was flat.

She winced. Big, big fail. She loved her nephews and couldn't believe she'd done something so bone-headed. How had that happened? Lines must have gotten crossed somehow. She'd have to pull Liz aside and see where things went wrong. "Oh. Okay, so uh, what do you think about... bikes?"

The boys gasped and yelled in unison, "Bikes? That's awesome!"

At their pleased expressions, some of her guilt faded. She'd make it up to them. This year's present would blow it out of the water.

"That's... that's too much," her brother protested.

"No, it's fine!" she said, patting his arm to try to convince him. The more she thought about it, the better the idea seemed. Bikes were the perfect gifts for the boys—they loved being outside whenever the weather was good. At least, that was what her brother had told her, anyway. "It's for Christmas. It only comes once a year. Thank goodness," she added under her breath. "Come on," she said to her nephews, guiding them toward the table. "Look what I got for you. Let's have some cookies. Yum-yum."

As she poured them drinks, she apologized to Tyler about the change in lunch plans, explaining she had a conference call she couldn't move.

"Please tell me you're still coming for Christmas," Tyler said instead, not addressing her apology.

Eve froze for a moment.

"Sherry's making your favorite. It's the, uh, special green beans," he continued.

Eve grimaced and purposely didn't look at her brother. That familiar guilt came back, hot and heavy and sitting in a lump in her stomach. Every year, he nagged her about coming to the house, and she often did. Why, she was just there last... no wait, was it two years ago? Maybe three? Anyway, it was pretty recently.

Her brother thrust his hands into his pockets, disbelief ringing in his voice as he scoffed. He always could read her. "It's Oak Park. It's a half-hour cab ride."

She finally turned to him, shaking her head with regret. She had to make him understand. "But I'm just so busy."

Tyler sighed. "Eve..."

"I'm about to make partner," she emphasized as she poured herself some coffee. The boys were chatting at the table about what cookies they wanted to try. "I mean, I'm this close. You know, Chris Lane hasn't even nominated someone for partner in ten years." She was going to be the one nominated. Then Tyler would support her in this.

Tyler sipped his own coffee and gave her a cursory glance. "That's great, sis." His voice was chilly.

She hated letting him down, having their old, familiar argument crop back up again. The one where he called her a workaholic and she protested that she wasn't, that she was just as passionate about her work as he was about his family. "But?"

He sighed again. "Look. I know we didn't have a lot when we were kids, but we had each other."

She rolled her eyes. *Here it comes.* So predictable. Tyler didn't understand her drive, never had. And to bring their past into it? Okay, yeah, their family had always been tight on money. So?

"Now you're working all the time," he continued. "I mean, what about the rest of your life?" He waved in the direction of her nephews, the gesture saying more than words could.

She didn't have a family of her own. Not like he did.

"I'll get to it," she protested. And she would. On *her* schedule, not because people were pressuring her. She wasn't like Tyler, who lived for his kids and wife and didn't have bigger aspirations for himself. She wanted more. At least, for right now. There would be time later for all of that stuff—the house and kids and white picket fence.

"When?" His voice warmed up with the strength of his convictions. "You never see your family. You put all your relationships on the back burner."

"No, that's not true," she lobbed back. Irritation at his words festered in her. And she did see her family, when she could. Truth be told, maybe it wasn't as much as they wanted her to, but she made the effort.

"Really? When was the last time you let anyone in?" Tyler took a sip of his coffee.

Ugh, and here we go, she thought with a wry smile. Moving on to the fact that she didn't have a significant other. The argument pattern was as familiar as it was tiring.

"Well... actually, I have a relationship," she declared, putting her mug on the table. Time to end this argument. She wanted to enjoy their remaining minutes together, not bicker. "My relationship is a long-distance relationship, because... my boyfriend is in the future." She slugged his upper arm, and he groaned, but a peek of a smile warmed his face.

Tension leaked from her shoulders, and she relaxed. Crisis averted. She knew the topic wasn't dropped, and he'd be back to poking at her about it soon enough. But for now, she could just enjoy their company.

"Eve," Liz said, entering the room. "Can I talk to you for a second?"

"Yes," she said, spinning to face her assistant. "Definitely. But first, go get my nephews some bikes."

Liz just eyed her, and Tyler gave a heavy sigh.

"Eve," he started, but she waved Liz away to go on her errand.

"They're going to love them," Eve assured her brother when the woman left. See? She could do this—have family time *and* do some personal shopping. She'd picked out the gift idea on her own. What did it matter who bought it?

Wasn't he always telling her it was the thought that counted?

The rest of the day flew by in a flurry of meetings, and before Eve knew it, it was time to meet the doctor for drinks. She shut down her computer and exited her office. The whole building was dark. When had everyone left? She'd been too busy to notice.

"Taxi!" Eve hollered with a frantic wave as she stepped out of the building into the bitter-cold night, striding across the snow-sloshed sidewalk toward the street. One cab slowed down, so she rushed across the asphalt to catch it.

Only to have a man reach for the door handle at the same time.

"Oh, sorry," she said to him on reflex, pulling back.

"Sorry," he echoed and did the same.

Taking his apology as affirmation that the cab was hers, she reached for the handle again—at the same time he did.

She eyed him. Snow coated his thick black hair and dotted his eyelashes. He was striking with a strong jaw and piercing, dark eyes. Still, she didn't have time for this. "I was here first."

"Well, I'm pretty sure we were here at the same time," he answered smoothly. His voice was warm and rumbling. After a moment, he said, "Uh, are you going north?"

She nodded. "Yeah, north side."

He smiled, and the gesture made her stomach flip for some odd reason. "Me, too. Wanna share?"

She glanced down for a moment, pondering it, then shrugged. "Okay." Why not? She could be magnanimous. So long as she made her meeting on time.

They got in and rode down the street, him tucking a guitar case between his legs, resting the bottom on the floor. She flipped through her email notifications on her phone and made brief, idle chitchat with the stranger. But the Christmas music playing was irritating and distracting. She asked the driver to change the station.

"You don't like Christmas music?" the guy beside her said.

She snorted. "Oh, it goes on and on and on." And every Christmas season, all the stations were inundated with it. Nonstop. How was no one else but her burned out on hearing it so much? *Ugh.*

He started to sing a Christmas song, and she side-eyed him. He stopped.

"Partridges in trees," she said, leaning toward him and waving a hand. "What do those words even mean?"

"I'm pretty sure they're called 'lyrics,'" he said evenly. Funny guy.

"But... they're non-migratory birds. If they did make a nest, it wouldn't even be in a pear tree." The stranger didn't say anything, just stared at her. Whatever. She knew she had a rational point.

When she realized they were close to Madison, she directed the taxi driver to turn onto it.

Funny Guy quickly protested that they should stay on this road because of traffic.

"Yeah, but my stop is first," she retorted.

He tightened his arms around his chest, eyeing her. "Well, you're going to make me late."

"You're going to make me late for a *very* important meeting." She tried to maintain her patience even though frustration was welling in her at his presumption. First, he'd tried to take her cab, and now he was going to possibly ruin her drinks with her prospective client.

No way. So much was riding on this.

"Life-or-death important?" he asked her, brows raised, clearly not believing it was.

"Actually, yes." Her words were firm. She knew this was more important than whatever he was doing. Some kind of open-mic night thing? It could wait.

"Okay," he murmured, giving in.

Thank heavens. She returned her attention back to the driver and instructed him to turn right.

Into a thick batch of traffic.

"Aaaand jingle all the way," her ride partner said flatly.

She sighed. No way could she wait in this traffic. She'd never make it in time. "Well, I'm going to walk." She grabbed a handful of cash and handed it to the driver. "Here. Thank you. Um, good luck with your... guitar thing," she said to the passenger.

"Happy holidays," he told her with a slight wave of one hand.

When the woman exited the cab, Max Wingford told the driver, "Um, you can turn the music back on."

What an odd encounter. Yes, it had left him a touch bristly over being left in terrible traffic... but he was also curious about who the mysterious woman was. Who argued logistics about Christmas songs? Strange, cab-commanding women, he supposed. Ah, well. Time to focus and get his head in the game. His audition needed all of his attention. And he knew Lauren would be grilling him about it tomorrow when she returned from her sleepover at her grandparents'. He didn't want to let her down.

Max finally arrived at the auditorium and stared at the marquee declaring auditions tonight for the Christmas Eve concert being held there. No one seemed to be entering or exiting the building, but he was pretty sure that, even though he was late, he could probably slip in. His guitar case, as heavy as a rock, rested against his back, his hands shaking as he clenched the strap.

Passersby wandered down the sidewalk in the thickening snow, and he stood there for a moment, willing himself to go in. He could do this. Yeah, it had been a long time, and yeah, he was solo now. And okay, he was pretty out of practice, and his original songs weren't all that great anymore without his sister's help...

He couldn't do this. Couldn't make himself step inside. His feet felt glued down, his heart frozen behind his ribcage.

His throat was tight as he turned and walked down the sidewalk.

Away from the audition.

It was probably better this way.

Read the rest!
A Heavenly Christmas is available now.